N.P. BOYCE is a writer and editor based in London. He's previously published short stories in magazines including *Litro* and *Dark Horizons*, and with Big Finish's *Doctor Who* and *Bernice Summerfield* ranges. He has also provided non-fiction material for *Classic Doctor Who* DVDs.

Veronica Button
Chronic Detective

N.P. BOYCE

CROMER

PUBLISHED BY PROXIMA BOOKS
AN IMPRINT OF SALT PUBLISHING
12 Norwich Road, Cromer, Norfolk NR27 0AX

Salt Publishing 2012

Printed in the UK by TJ International Ltd, Padstow, Cornwall

Typeset in Paperback 9 / 13

ISBN 978 1 907773 38 9 paperback

1 3 5 7 9 8 6 4 2

Dedicated with love to the original Hodge,
whose book this is.

CONTENTS

'I knew I was an Anachronic Man; my age was still to come.'
H. G. Wells, *The Chronic Argonauts*

PART ONE

The Thief
of Time

1

ONE

The shopkeeper looked up from his newspaper to see a woman in a plain black dress tapping on the glass door. There was something *different* about her, something he couldn't quite put his finger on.

The woman smiled and waved. She was certainly good-looking enough. Her black hair was tied back in a pigtail, and this emphasised the strength of her features. Her eyes were dark, her nose aquiline, her jaw firm and defined. She looked, the shopkeeper thought, like a woman in a painting—a pre-Raphaelite daub, perhaps, some Victorian society hostess posing as Cleopatra.

He got up slowly from his chair and hobbled over to open the door, reminding himself for the hundredth time that he really needed to get the entry buzzer fixed.

'Good afternoon,' he wheezed.

'Hello,' said the woman. She smiled again. It was a confident smile: the kind the shopkeeper had come, throughout his long career, to associate with money.

'Come in, come in.' He shuffled back into the shop. The woman followed him and the door swung shut behind her, closing out the racket of the Holborn traffic.

'Now,' he said, positioning himself behind the desk and pulling out the drawer in which he kept the keys, 'what can I interest you in?'

'The necklace in the window,' said the woman. 'I was just passing, and I couldn't help but notice it. Is it new?'

'That depends on what you mean by *new*,' the shopkeeper replied, as his fingers skimmed the key ring and picked out the right one. 'If you mean *is it new to this shop*, then the answer is *yes*. I acquired it around a week ago.'

'And if I don't mean that?'

'Well,' said the shopkeeper, 'then the answer is *no*. Not by a long chalk.'

He lumbered up to the cabinet, unlocked it, and gently lifted the necklace from its stand. It was wrought in silver, and inset with sapphires that shimmered and rippled in the light like drops of clear blue water.

'The Constellation of the East,' he said. He liked the way the words sounded, so he repeated himself. 'The Constellation of the East. Made in India in the 1870s. It was brought back by someone high up in the Raj for his wife.'

'Really? Might I try it on?'

The shopkeeper undid the clasp at the back of the necklace, and draped it around the woman's neck. It rested there perfectly.

'There's a story behind it,' he said as he pressed the catch gently. It snapped into place with a satisfying *snick*. 'Would you like to hear it?'

'Oh yes,' said the woman, but she seemed distracted.

'Would you like a mirror?' he asked.

She nodded, and he led her to the counter. She stood looking at herself in the glass; her fingers, slim and dextrous, ran over the stones, testing their weight.

'It went missing only a couple of weeks after it arrived in the country,' the shopkeeper said. 'One of the maids of the household vanished around the same time, so everyone assumed the two went together. No one ever found out where to. Then, a couple of weeks ago, the Constellation showed up again. In someone's attic, if you can believe it. They reckon the girl hid it there, and was too scared to try to sell it on. It came back on the market, and I managed to get hold of it.'

The woman turned around so that she was facing the man. They were no more than an arm's length away from one another. There was something unusual about her scent: a fresh, clean smell of sandalwood and citrus.

'But what about the original owner?' she asked, frowning.

'The family's long gone,' said the shopkeeper. 'There were the usual legal issues, but the long and short of it is: *finders keepers.*'

The woman smiled, but he saw that there was still a hint of concern in her eyes. *Time to close the deal,* he said to himself. *You talk too much. That's always been your problem.*

The woman turned back to the mirror and inspected the necklace again.

'It doesn't look 150 years old,' she said after a minute.

The shopkeeper sighed with relief.

'I can reassure you on that front, too,' he said. 'I've had it checked over by the experts. It's the real thing, all right. It's barely been touched, is all.'

The woman turned back smartly, as if she had suddenly made her decision. She was smiling now, not worried in the slightest. The shopkeeper thought of the asking price, and added a few thousand to allow for negotiation. She wanted the necklace, that much was clear; she wanted it very badly indeed, and she would walk out of the shop with it, no matter what.

'I'm terribly sorry,' she said.

'What?' The shopkeeper's brain struggled with the mismatch between the woman's manner and her words.

'You seem like a nice man,' she said. 'And I'm fairly sure

you bought this in good faith. *Fairly* sure.'

'Yes?'

'So I'm sorry.'

'Sorry for what?'

When the shopkeeper woke up three minutes later, crumpled up on the threadbare carpet, he was so bewildered it took him a further three minutes to activate the alarm.

So far, thought Veronica Britton, as the second police car pulled up at the end of the alley, blocking her escape route, *I have only made three mistakes*.

One: *I didn't hit the shopkeeper hard enough*.

Two: *I stopped to admire my reflection in a shop window*.

Three: *I turned down this street*.

Veronica ran through the various maps of London she held in her mind. She saw the city in all its ages, felt the weight of past and future straining upon the present moment. Forcing the images out of her head, she reduced the options before her to a single path. No way to go now but forwards. She registered one of the officers struggling to get out of the car, his seatbelt tangled with his jacket radio. His colleague looked younger, fitter, and thoroughly on the ball. He was out already. He shouted at her to stop. She saw him crouch and brace himself.

The policemen at the other end of the alley were close behind. She could hear the clatter of their boots and the squawk of their radios.

Veronica ran straight towards the young policeman. He wasn't expecting this and flinched. She delivered a quick, efficient chop to the side of his neck, and vaulted over the bonnet of the car and into the main street.

She ran as fast as she could towards the green hut that stood on the quiet square just off High Holborn. She twisted the handle and dived through the door.

A man sat inside, comfortable in a worn leather armchair. A tea urn rested on a table by his side: a plate of biscuits stood next to it. He was dressed in jeans and a warm jacket, and filling out a crossword: the typical London cabbie on his break.

'You look like you're in a hurry,' he said, putting his paper down.

Veronica was too out of breath to reply. She waved a hand at the back of the hut.

'Of course,' said the man. He got up and dusted some biscuit crumbs from himself.

'Could you — ?' Veronica managed to choke out. 'Really — quite close — now.'

'Don't worry, Miss Britton,' the man replied. 'I'll handle them.'

He inserted a key into the concealed door at the far end of the hut and swung it open. Although it looked like it was made of wood, it seemed to have the heft of a substance far, far heavier.

'Safe journey,' he said.

Veronica rushed over to the open doorway and ran though.

The man closed the door behind her, and listed for a moment as her footsteps faded into the distance.

The cabbie went over to the urn and poured out a mug of tea. 'I'd offer you one,' he said to the police officer, 'only we're down to one cup now. Someone keeps nicking them. Don't suppose you'd consider investigating that?'

'I'm looking for a woman,' said the police officer. 'Black dress. Black hair. Wearing a very expensive necklace — not hers.'

The man smiled. The effect was disconcerting — his face

had no particularly distinguishing features, but at the same time the police officer had the strangest feeling he had seen this man before. Not just once, but *hundreds* of times.

The man shook his head and settled back into his chair with his newspaper. The police officer walked over and pulled the paper away.

'You don't want to mess with me.'

The cabbie stood up and put his hand on the police officer's shoulder. Something in the gesture — some sense of power and authority — gave the police officer pause.

'Oh no,' said the anonymous little man, his eyes deep and hollow, 'you don't want to mess with *me*.'

The police officer tried to speak, tried to say something in reply, but no words came. He moved to try to break the man's grip, but realised he couldn't move a muscle.

'This one,' said the man, his voice low and hoarse, almost a whisper, 'this one is one of the ones you let go.'

The police officer nodded. The man released his grip, retrieved his newspaper, and sat down. After a moment, he looked up.

'Are you still here?' he asked.

The room was stuffy: a fire roared in the grate, and heavy drapes held in the warmth. The paper on the walls was thick and luxurious, the furniture overstuffed and so soft you sank into it like quicksand. There were several personal touches, of course, mostly mementoes of India. Pride of place was a stuffed tableau, a real testimony to the taxidermist's art: a snake and a mongoose entwined in a battle to the death, the latter rearing back, claws out, teeth bared, poised to strike the killer blow.

Lady Holloway, sitting opposite Veronica, opened the box, took the necklace out, and put it on.

'Divine, isn't it?'

It looked better on me, thought Veronica.

'Quite,' she replied.

'And the culprits?' asked Lady Holloway.

'It's not possible to bring such cases to justice through the criminal courts,' Veronica explained. 'I have, however, given them fair warning that if they do anything of this nature again, I will report them to the Ministry.'

As she said those last words, she saw Lady Holloway shudder slightly.

'Well,' said Lady Holloway brightly, though her voice shook a little. 'I think our business here is concluded.'

'Indeed.' Veronica stood up and offered her hand.

'*Miss* Britton! A word in your shell-like, *if* you please!'

Veronica paused, her hand on the doorknob of her office. She had come in early today, hoping to lurk within for the morning and avoid seeing Carter. Still, no matter how early you were, Carter would have arrived there five minutes earlier. Good timing was his speciality.

'*Miss* Britton!' Again he emphasised the *Miss* — in his better moods, he would simply call her *Britton*. She sighed and turned to face him.

He stood at the end of the corridor, half-in and half-out of his office. He was a tall man, with small round glasses and a long, luxuriant beard: he looked like an illustration in a picture book of Father Time himself.

'Right this way, if you please!' He waved at the open doorway. Veronica walked down the hallway and entered.

Carter's office looked even more disordered than the last time she had been in, if such a thing were possible. Books and papers were stacked randomly around the shelves; the floor was littered with cups, saucers and cigar-ends. There was a newspaper on the desk dating from the week before, half the pages burned away, no doubt as a result of Carter's habitual carelessness with tobacco.

Carter swept his arm across the desk, clearing a sight line between the two sides, and sat down heavily in his chair. He gestured for Veronica to be seated.

'I've had the Ministry around here,' he said.

'Really?'

'They had a report from one of their porters. Said a chronic detective cut it a bit fine recently. In 2012 or thereabouts.'

'Goodness,' said Veronica, feigning surprise, 'did they say which agency the detective worked for?'

'Don't play daft with me, Miss Britton.'

Veronica shrugged and smiled apologetically.

'I'm sorry,' she said. 'I didn't hit the shopkeeper hard enough.'

Carter tutted.

'What do I say every time you come in here?'

'Mind if I smoke?'

'Eh?'

'That's what you always say,' Veronica replied. '*Mind if I smoke?*'

Carter harrumphed.

'You can keep your sense of humour to yourself this morning.'

He rummaged around in the pile of papers on his desk and pulled out a battered wooden cigar box.

'Mind if I —?'

'Go ahead,' said Veronica. 'But you know it causes cancer.'

Carter shrugged, put a cigar in his mouth, and lit it.

'That's in the future,' he said. 'Look, Britton, you're going to have to be more careful. We're an open secret as it is. But we can't have every Tom, Dick, and Harry knowing about the timepools. Things are best the way they are.'

'Okay,' said Veronica. 'I'll be more careful.'

Carter spluttered on his cigar.

'*Okay? Okay?* It's language like that that draws attention. Just watch it.'

Veronica nodded brusquely and stood up.

'If that's all,' she said, pulling a watch out of her pocket and consulting it, 'I have an appointment in a couple of minutes.'

'Sit down, Britton! That's not all.'

Veronica resumed her seat. Carter got up and walked over to the window: in the Strand outside, carriages were fighting for position and pedestrians were scurrying to their offices, the last stragglers late for work.

Carter took off his glasses and rubbed his eyes.

'I've been meaning to talk to you for some time about this,' he said. 'I just never found the right opportunity.'

For one terrible moment, Veronica imagined that he was about to propose to her.

'We're alike in a lot of ways, you and me. My wife died — oh, 40 years ago and more. And you lost — well, you know. But when you think about it, we couldn't have done what we've done if we'd had normal lives.'

'Is this about Gabrielle?'

Carter nodded.

'She was on at me again the other day,' he said.

'You're going to have to let her start sometime.'

'I promised her parents I'd look after her.'

'And you have, Carter, you have. But if you keep putting her off, she'll train with another agency.'

Carter turned around.

'Do you think?'

Veronica nodded.

'The other day,' she said, 'she was talking about going to

Temps Perdu.'

Carter thumped the wall, sending sparks flying from his cigar.

'*Temps Perdu*? *Temps Perdu*? Should've stayed in Paris, that lot. Couldn't run a bath, let alone an agency. Their name's pretentious, too.'

'It's French.'

Carter sat back down in his chair, sucked heavily on his cigar, and glowered.

'Exactly.'

'Look, Carter, you may not want to hear it, but it's the truth. If you don't let Gabrielle train with us, you'll lose her for good. She's 21 now, after all. She can do what she wants.'

Carter shrugged.

'Fine,' he said. 'You can train her.'

'What?'

'I'm getting old, Britton. I'm not as fast as I was. Let's face it, the best man for the job is you.'

'She's *your* niece.'

'Listen, Britton. There's no one I'd trust more — not in this agency, not anywhere else — to get me out of trouble. Having said that, there's no one I'd trust more to get me *into* trouble. But that's not the point. You cut it fine, Britton, but you always cut it.'

There was silence for a minute, punctuated only by the clatter of wheels on the road outside, and the ticking of a clock buried somewhere in the debris on Carter's mantelpiece.

'All right,' said Veronica. 'I'll do it.'

It was only when she was back in her own office — sipping her first cup of tea of the day and reading a letter — that she realised Carter had just played her perfectly.

TWO

Gabrielle Pendleton tapped once, firmly, on the glass of the office door.

'Come in!'

Veronica sat at her desk, looking over a letter on lilac notepaper.

'Gabrielle. Good,' she said, without looking up.

Gabrielle cleared her throat.

'Your client is here,' she said. 'Mrs Mortimer.'

'Ah yes,' said Veronica. She glanced up at Gabrielle. Although they only made eye contact for a moment, the experience was intense; Veronica's eyes were hazel, flecked with green and gold. They seemed to be glowing brightly, to have absorbed some of the energy and life she had seen in one of the greatest cities in the world over thousands of different time periods, past, present, and future.

Veronica smiled and waved for Gabrielle to sit down. Gabrielle realised she was blushing.

'I think it would be good for you to sit in on this one,' Veronica explained, holding out the letter. Gabrielle took it and pored over its contents.

'First thoughts?' asked Veronica.

'A couple of tear stains,' said Gabrielle.

'Hm, yes. Could mean genuine distress, could be that she

wants to *convey* the idea she's upset. We won't know till she's in the room. Anything else?'

'Agatha Mortimer. The name's familiar. Not the wife of Professor David Mortimer?'

'You've heard of him?'

Gabrielle shrugged. 'Not much. I remember seeing his motor-driven vehicles at the Crystal Palace exhibition when I was a little girl.'

'Really?'

'Yes. They frightened me. They looked like giant woodlice.'

'They were his life's work,' said Veronica. 'Ironclad warships, but designed to run on land. The ironclads would do the heavy work, and the infantry would only come out to clean up after the main battle was over. The only problem was that he couldn't work out a decent power source for them. But he made a lot of money from the by-products. Patents and so forth.'

'Land ironclads!' Gabrielle exclaimed. She saw a landscape of mud and stone, dotted with the exposed white flesh of bodies half-embedded in the ground; heard the rumble of machines, ungainly things crawling over the earth; smelled cordite and singed flesh.

'Gabrielle? What's wrong? You're white as a sheet.'

Gabrielle shook her head.

'It's nothing,' she said. 'I just have something of a vivid imagination.'

'Good,' said Veronica, 'you'll need it. Perhaps you can bring Mrs Mortimer in?'

'Mrs Mortimer,' said Veronica, chewing the end of her pencil thoughtfully, 'you have me at something of a loss.'

Mrs Agatha Mortimer, a slender, handsome older woman, began to sob again. Veronica opened a drawer in her desk, took out a freshly laundered handkerchief, and handed it over.

'Why?' gasped Mrs Mortimer. 'What have I said that can possibly leave you in any doubt that my husband's disappearance is the result of foul play?'

'Your husband's disappearance is certainly suspicious,' said Veronica, gently. 'I just don't understand why you decided a chronic detective agency would be best suited to investigate. Why not the police?'

Mrs Mortimer blew her nose noisily and sniffed. Her eyes were bloodshot, the lids red and tender. Veronica noticed she wore a veil attached to the brim of her hat; perhaps she had been crying non-stop for weeks.

'I—I didn't want to go to the police. People talk—I feared a scandal.'

'Do you have any reason to suspect a scandal?'

Mrs Mortimer took a deep breath.

'My husband has been absent before,' she said. 'Sometimes for a week, sometimes longer. He told me he was travelling—conferences, you know.'

'But you had reason to suspect otherwise?'

Mrs Mortimer bit her lip and nodded.

'Still,' said Veronica. 'I'm not sure what we can contribute as a chronic agency. Might not a regular detective agency be more suited to your needs?'

Mrs Mortimer sat, silent and miserable, debating some point with herself for a minute before she spoke again.

'There was something I didn't tell you,' she said at last. 'Something I couldn't put in the letter. I wondered if I should tell anyone at all—oh!'

She began to sob again. Gabrielle, sitting in the chair next to her, laid a hand gently on her arm.

'If you just tell Miss Britton everything you know,' she

said, softly, 'we can begin to unravel your problem.'

'It was around six weeks ago,' said Mrs Mortimer. 'It was late—I'd been having trouble sleeping, and my doctor prescribed a draught. I'd decided to try doing without it—I feared I was becoming too dependent on it—yet it was now past one and I still hadn't enjoyed a moment of rest.

'The draught was kept in the medicine cabinet in my bathroom, which is at the end of the first-floor landing, immediately adjacent to my bedroom. I did consider ringing for the maid, but—well, it seemed so much trouble, just for a little drop from a bottle.

'I had just left my room when I heard someone knocking at the front door. Now, I'm quite used to my husband having callers at all hours of the day and night; they'd normally knock the door rather than ring the bell so as not to wake the house, you see. But this knocking—it sounded *different* somehow. Angry, violent even—oh I don't know if I'm describing it well at all. It's such a muddle.'

She paused, fretfully. 'Go on,' said Gabrielle. 'Every detail you give will help us to find your husband.'

Mrs Mortimer dabbed at her eyes and continued.

'Our man—Strevans—answered the door. I couldn't see who was out there, but I heard a man's voice—and a horrible voice it was, too.

'"Hello," he said, "is the master at home?"

'I knew that very instant that something was wrong. I crouched down behind the banister, and watched to see what would happen next. I am hardly up to the task of defending my property, but I thought that if I kept myself concealed, I might get a good view of what was going on, and be able to summon help if need be or even identify the man at a later date.

'It was then I heard my husband coming out of his study—it's at the back of the house, looking out onto the garden—and talking quite sharply to Strevans.

'"These are the men I told you to expect," he said. "They have come with some data I need to present at a meeting tomorrow. I told you that they were to be sent directly to my study, and that you had no need to enter into conversation with them."

'Strevans made his apologies and left: I remained watching at the top of the stairs, although my tiredness and the shock of the events downstairs made me quite agitated. My teeth chattered in my head; I felt my skin turn to damp goose flesh, and my bones ached terribly.

'I saw the front door open more widely, and a light come on outside. It was a glowing disc no more than a couple of inches in diameter, but its intensity was far greater than any lamp I have ever seen. My husband shielded his eyes and backed away.

'"I told you I needed more time!" he said.

'"Don't worry," said the other, in that insolent voice of his. "I've only come here for a little advance."

'My husband shook his head and glanced over his shoulder. I darted back into the shadows.

'"We can't talk out here," he said. "My wife's nerves—she might hear us."

'"Oh dear, we don't want that," said the man in the doorway, mockingly. "Do you have somewhere quieter?"

'"My study," said my husband, and turned to go. I crept forward and caught a glimpse of the men—there were two of them—who followed him."'

Veronica leaned forward. 'What did they look like?' she asked.

'I didn't see their faces,' said Mrs Mortimer, 'but the

fabrics they were wearing—they were slick, like oilskins, but thin and light. The cut was strange; their hats, too, were an odd sort of design. Then there was the lamp the man was holding.' She paused, summoning up the courage to continue. 'Miss Britton,' she said, 'the more I think about it, the more I believe that these men were *from the future.*'

'Can you sketch these men? And the lamp?' Veronica asked, offering a pencil and a scrap of paper torn from her notebook.

Mrs Mortimer took them, and produced a sketch that she handed over to Veronica.

'What happened next?' she asked Mrs Mortimer. 'Did you overhear any more of the conversation between the men and your husband? Or did you see them coming back out?'

'I'm afraid not,' Mrs Mortimer replied. 'By that point, my nerves were utterly shredded. I made straight for the medicine cabinet and my draught. I was worn out, and the medicine worked quickly. I returned to my room, and slept through the night.'

Veronica looked up.

'Mrs Mortimer,' she said, 'my colleague and I would like to pay a visit, and see your house for ourselves.'

Mrs Mortimer nodded assent.

'Oh,' Veronica added, 'one last thing. Why haven't you told the Ministry? Your husband must have connections there.'

'I couldn't,' Mrs Mortimer said, 'because I was afraid.'

'Afraid of what?'

'Afraid of the Ministry, of course.'

The Mortimer residence was a tall, narrow building on the north side of a square of imposing Georgian townhouses. Veronica and Gabrielle were shown in by a maid, who informed them Mrs Mortimer was resting upstairs and they were free to search any part of the house they chose.

'In that case,' said Veronica, 'we'll start with Professor Mortimer's study.'

The maid took them along a passage off the entrance hall. The corridor was gloomy and there was a pervasive smell like oil and candle wax. She unlocked the furthest door, and showed them in.

It was a small room, but kept in perfect order: not a scrap of space was wasted. Bookcases lined one wall, their contents alphabetically arranged in uniform binding. The other walls were covered in technical drawings and artists' etchings of the land ironclads. There was a large desk at the end of the room, its green baize surface clear except for a single blank sheet of foolscap, and a pen-tidy and ink bottle lined up neatly to one side.

'Thank you,' said Veronica to the maid. The maid stood there awkwardly for a moment; Veronica repeated herself, and she retreated reluctantly.

Gabrielle studied one of the ironclad pictures. It depicted a battlefield; horses and men of some foreign army were fleeing in terror before the machine. Lines of motion indicated projectiles bouncing off its surface, whilst others depicted a hail of bullets tearing from a stubby, pig-nosed muzzle at the front of the vehicle. The underside of the ironclad consisted of a sort of belt threaded around a set of wheels; looking closely, she saw a horse and rider trapped beneath, helplessly trampled under the weight of the monster.

'Gabrielle,' said Veronica from somewhere far away, 'could you help me, please?'

Veronica was kneeling on the floor of the study; she had emptied Mortimer's waste paper basket, and was sifting through its contents carefully. Gabrielle walked over; without looking up, Veronica pulled a crumpled piece of paper from the pile and handed it to her.

Gabrielle opened it up. It consisted of just one line of text, made up of newspaper letters pasted together.

'40 — *I KNOW*

'He's being blackmailed!' she exclaimed.

'Yes, yes, I'd already guessed that,' said Veronica. '1840 — that would make him a young man. Young enough to do something he'd regret, something he could be blackmailed over. It's not a bad scheme, you know: find someone rich and prominent, go back in time and catch them when they're doing something they'd be ashamed of later, then return to the present and blackmail them.

'On the other hand — '

She bent over and resumed searching. Gabrielle knelt down and joined her.

'It doesn't fit,' Veronica muttered, half to Gabrielle and half to herself. 'Those men Mrs Mortimer saw were from the future. They must have made two hops back in time — one to this time period, and one to 1840.'

'So they have access to more than one timepool?'

'That's rare. These must be some very well-connected blackmailers.'

'Or they've never been to 1840 at all,' said Gabrielle. 'Maybe something comes out in the far future about Mortimer. They'd just need to bring the evidence back here, and then they could go ahead and blackmail him.'

Veronica nodded noncommittally and continued to rummage through the papers. Finally she stopped and rubbed her eyes.

'It's no use,' she said. 'I'm looking too hard. I'm not seeing it.'

'What?' asked Gabrielle.

'There's something else in here,' said Veronica. 'Something more. I know it's there, but I can't find it. Carter would get it in ten seconds flat. He's far more time-sensitive than me —'

She stopped and stared at Gabrielle in that same intense, unsettling way she had earlier.

'Maybe it runs in the family,' she said. She distributed the scraps from the wastepaper basket evenly over the floor.

'Look,' she said to Gabrielle. 'No — not too closely. Just out of the corner of your eye.'

Gabrielle became aware of a trembling, shivering sensation somewhere on the floor. She moved her eyes slowly downwards. Yes, there it was: a glow like a guttering candle on the edge of her field of vision. She reached down and felt around. The object was a small, crumpled piece of card, just over an inch across and two inches in height. It glowed brighter still as she held it, though it was cool to the touch.

'Bravo,' said Veronica, snatching it out of her hand and taking it to examine at the desk. 'Got it in one.'

Gabrielle got up and studied the object over Veronica's shoulder. 'What is it?' she asked.

Veronica straightened the card out and held it up to the light. It was a photograph of a man: his hair was slick with pomade, and he had a neatly trimmed moustache. He was smiling — an unusual thing, Gabrielle thought, for a man to do in a portrait of this sort. To smile in a photograph usually indicated some want of seriousness on the part of the subject, but this man was grinning in a shrewd, intelligent manner, as if he knew he was bright, and clever, and charming and didn't care what anyone else thought.

'Clark Gable,' said Veronica.

'Who?'

'That's his name. I knew I recognised him.'

'You know him?'

'I wish,' said Veronica. 'He's a film star.'

'Eh?'

'A sort of actor. An American actor. I'll explain later. This is a cigarette card. Pictures of famous people.' Veronica turned over the card and read the back.

'There you go. Clark Gable. *Boom Town*, 1940.'

'So that's when the blackmailers come from!'

'Yes,' said Veronica. She closed her eyes; Gabrielle could see her eyelids flicker as she went through all the possible options.

'There's a timepool near here, one that goes several decades into the future. That would be about right. It's another of the cabbie huts — you know, the green shelters. But how would the blackmailers get through?'

She reached up and tugged the bell-pull hanging over the desk. A moment later the maid appeared.

'I wonder if you could tell me,' Veronica asked her, 'if anyone's moved into the square lately?'

The maid thought for a moment, and then shook her head.

'Or perhaps someone's moved out? It may not have been recently. It could have been years ago. Something odd about one of the houses, maybe.'

The maid pursed her lips and shifted her weight uncomfortably from foot to foot.

'Come on,' said Veronica, gently. 'You can tell us.'

'There's number 17,' the maid said. 'At the other side of the square. The folks moved out three years ago.'

'Why?' asked Veronica.

'They said —' the maid began, and stopped. 'No, madam, I really shouldn't. Mrs Mortimer doesn't like us to talk to no one about it.'

'I have good reason to believe your employer's life is in danger,' Veronica said. 'If you don't tell me what you know, I won't be able to help him.'

'It was haunted!' the maid blurted out. 'Imps and demons down in the basement—that was what they said!'

Although the house had only been vacant for a few years, nature was already well on the way to reclaiming it. The front steps were cracked and uneven, with weeds forcing their way up between the gaps: the boot-scraper at the front door was rusted through, and the door itself was warped and hanging off its hinges. The thick slabs of wood had been eaten away by rot and woodworm: it gave readily to the touch as Veronica pushed it.

The planks of the hallway stood at crazy angles, scraps of underlay clinging to them. There was a smell of mould; the temperature was unnaturally high, the atmosphere dense and muggy like some tropical swamp. Paper hung off the walls in strips; the glass in the windows had melted down to thick, smooth globules spilling out of the frames.

'Veronica,' said Gabrielle.

'What?'

Gabrielle stumbled and clung to the wall. 'It's just so stuffy in here. I can hardly breathe. And I have the most awful, splitting headache.'

Veronica put out an arm and helped to guide her across the hallway.

'That's your time-sensitivity catching up with you,' she said. 'Time's out of joint here. The edges of the timepool have been torn. It's growing outwards, like a wound.'

They made their way across to the door leading down to the basement. Veronica pulled it open; it turned to sawdust and splinters in her hand. There was a vast, misshapen tree growing out of the stone staircase. They picked their way around it and descended to the kitchen.

'We shouldn't stay too long,' said Veronica. 'It's not safe.'

'Can't we just go back now?' asked Gabrielle, hopefully.

Veronica shook her head. Her image seemed to blur and stutter with the motion.

'No,' she replied. 'We need to be sure.'

They stood at the entrance to the pantry; the door here was made of metal, with a heavy bolt across it. Veronica reached out and tore it like paper.

There was nothing beyond; or at least, that was how it seemed at first. Just a black space, which somehow gave the impression of endless depth. As Gabrielle's eyes adjusted, however, she caught a red, flickering glow in the darkness; she opened her mouth to speak, but Veronica put a hand to her lips. They listened together, in the silence of the dying house, and Gabrielle thought she could hear screams, explosions, the sound of toppling bricks and breaking glass in the distance. And then, above it all, a mechanical howl that was like the lament of something in pain. *The sound of a wounded city*, thought Gabrielle.

Veronica took her arm, and they began the slow process of hauling themselves out of the house. It was like wading through a dense liquid, one that seized up around their limbs if they moved too quickly, forcing them into a painful, slow motion trudge. By the time they were back in the square it was dark, and all the gas-lamps were lit.

THREE

Veronica opened the trunk in the corner of her office and took out a dark navy dress. She held it up against Gabrielle.

'We're about the same size,' she said. 'It'll do. We'll get you fitted for your own when you come back.'

Gabrielle took the garment: its fabric was surprisingly soft against her skin. It was designed to be a neutral item that would fit in with practically any era in London's history, from the distant past to the far future. Then again, there was something slightly exotic about the way it was cut: it had a short collar, and buttoned up like a Chinese *cheongsam*.

'If you seem a little strange,' Veronica said, 'you can always pass yourself off as a tourist. Now get changed.'

She indicated a screen next to the fireplace. Gabrielle slipped behind it.

She heard Veronica opening a drawer, and the chink of money.

'What are you doing?' she asked.

'Stocking up,' Veronica replied. 'It's embarrassing when you're caught with the wrong currency.'

Gabrielle emerged from behind the screen.

'Excuse me.'

'Ah yes,' said Veronica. 'The corset.'

Gabrielle turned away as Veronica came over, untied the

cords, and loosened them.

'Can you take it from here?' she asked.

'Oh yes, thank you,' Gabrielle replied.

'It's nicer without, isn't it?'

'It is.'

'You can breathe. And run.'

When Gabrielle emerged, Veronica was carrying out a final check of the items in her belt. She pulled out a silver cigarette case, flipped it open and examined the contents.

'I didn't know you smoked.'

Veronica turned around distractedly.

'I don't,' she said. 'Filthy habit. Deadly, too. But cigarettes are good to trade.'

'What about protection?'

Veronica smiled as if Gabrielle had just said something amusing.

'I mean a gun,' said Gabrielle.

'Absolutely not,' said Veronica.

'Why not? You said it'll be dangerous.'

'Very few situations are dangerous enough to warrant carrying a firearm,' Veronica replied. 'Do you know how much damage a gun in the wrong place can do to history?'

The porter stood to attention as they entered the hut.

'Good evening,' said Veronica. 'Would you like to see our passes?'

'No need, Miss Britton,' he said, cheerfully. 'And you must be Miss Pendleton. I've been looking forward to meeting you.'

He stepped over to the back of the hut and pressed one of the wooden panels. The wall slid back to reveal a darkened doorway. Gabrielle felt a cold wave of air roll out of it and flow over her.

'Nip in the air tonight,' said the porter, pleasantly. 'What do you think it's like over there?'

'Hot, I imagine,' said Veronica.

She took Gabrielle's hand and led her into the tunnel.

It seemed to Gabrielle that they walked out of the other side of the timepool almost immediately; however, when she thought about the experience later, she seemed to remember spending an incredible length of time — months, or even years — wandering through the darkness towards the future.

They emerged into a flat, harsh light, one that hurt her eyes and sent little ice picks of pain along her skull. Gabrielle heard a murmured conversation in the background. She turned and saw Veronica chatting pleasantly to the porter. At first, she imagined there had been some sort of mistake, that they had turned back on themselves. Then she noticed the porter looked different; his basic features were identical, but his moustache was thin and waxed, his hair short. His outer garments, meanwhile, had changed from a heavy black greatcoat and cape to a brown woollen overcoat and scarf.

The hut, too, had altered. Where previously the wall held framed prints of the various landmarks of London, it was now covered in bright posters with bold lettering. The imagery was simple and direct: injunctions not to waste food, or indulge in gossip. The colours seemed to deepen and bleed into one another as she watched.

'I'm terribly sorry,' she said to Veronica and the porter as she dashed for the door.

The chill of the air hit her hard: not a bracing, refreshing blast, but the sort of fog-bound, bone-aching cold that London could serve up from time to time, the sort that stopped all thought in its tracks. Gabrielle stumbled and sprawled forwards onto her hands and knees. Those first sensations of pain were now fully blown agonies ripping through her skull. She was sick on the pavement. Exhausted, she lay on her side and closed her eyes.

She became aware of someone tugging at her sleeve.

'Gabrielle,' said Veronica, 'are you all right?'

Gabrielle allowed herself to be helped up into a sitting position.

'I'm so sorry,' she mumbled. 'So sorry.'

Veronica's warm hands massaged her temples.

'Here,' she said, 'this sometimes does the trick. It's my fault. I forgot how time-sensitive you are. I should have warned you.'

Gabrielle smiled wanly; Veronica's fingers seemed to instil new warmth and life.

'Does it get better?' she asked.

'Oh yes,' said Veronica as she helped her to her feet. 'You just need to acclimatise.'

They walked in silence along the darkened street. The city seemed to be holding its breath, preparing for the worst.

'Where are we going?' she asked.

'The Wheatsheaf,' Veronica replied. 'Do you know it?'

'No.'

'Shame. It's not too bad, for what it is.'

'What is it?'

'It's a pub,' said Veronica, with the mixture of wistfulness and longing with which Gabrielle had heard priests talk of Heaven.

'A public house? Should we - '

Veronica cut her off. 'We're chronic detectives. We're allowed everywhere. Anyway, pubs are useful. We like pubs. They're one of the few places that don't change their use over hundreds of years. If we ever get separated, leave a message in a pub. Or a church—they're good, too.'

The bar was a little island of light in the centre of the room, its glistening optics like jars of boiled sweets in a shop. The barman was a rotund, dapper man; the few strands of hair he still possessed lay across the top of his scalp, and he wore an immaculately clean white apron.

'Now, now,' he shouted as they walked in. 'We'll have none of that in here. I run a respectable house!'

'That'll be the day,' Veronica replied. The man laughed loudly, and there was an appreciative rumble from the drinkers bent over their pints in the little snugs around the room.

'Miss Britton!' someone exclaimed. A ragged, gangly figure emerged from the shadows. Veronica hastened towards him; he held his arms out, and they embraced.

'Well, well, old girl,' he said. 'You said you'd write. I haven't seen you since—'

Veronica glanced over her shoulder, very briefly but significantly, at Gabrielle.

'Since—' the man faltered. 'Since—well, since I don't know when. Who's your charming friend?'

Gabrielle stood forward and offered her hand.

'Gabrielle Pendleton,' she said. 'I'm Veronica's new apprentice.'

'Well!' the man said again, and raised his eyebrows. He seemed amused by her, but there was something kindly in his expression. Gabrielle realised with a start that he was not as old as she had thought: true, his skin was weathered and wrinkled, he stooped like a man in pain, and he kept a red cotton scarf tied tightly about his throat. But his eyes were those of a much younger man.

'My name's Blair,' he said, softly.

'Blair?'

'Just Blair. Come on, have a seat, you two. You look like you need a pick-me-up. How about gin and tonic? Everyone likes gin and tonic, wherever they come from.'

Veronica and Gabrielle settled into their seats. Blair walked over to the bar, and returned a few minutes later balancing a pint of dark, turbid beer and two glasses of clear liquid.

'No ice,' he said. 'No lemon, no lime, and the tonic water's a little flat. The gin's still good though. London stuff, the best.'

He set the drinks down on the table, and took his seat next to Veronica. He put his hand on her arm and whispered something into her ear: she coloured, and tapped his hand lightly.

'So,' he said to Gabrielle, 'I suppose you'd better tell me why you're here.'

'We're looking for a missing person,' she replied, cautiously.

'Ah!' Blair turned to Veronica. 'Information, information,' he scolded her, 'that's all you ever want. *Almost* all you ever want. But do you ever share what you know with me? Never. Not a word.'

Veronica opened her mouth to protest, but Blair interrupted her.

'I know, I know. The future is unwritten from your perspective; you only know the broad sweep; you don't want to compromise the timelines.' He took another sip of his drink and loosened the scarf around his neck; Gabrielle caught a glimpse of the skin underneath. It was puckered and scarred. 'Never mind. Right now I'm not too sure I want to know what the future holds. Warm, dry, and smoking. That's enough for me right now. Well, smoking and drinking.'

Veronica took a photograph of Mortimer out of her pocket and laid it on the table in front of Blair. He picked it up and examined it.

'Do you know him?' she asked. 'Name of Mortimer.'

Blair held the photograph up to the light.

'When was this taken?' he asked.

'A couple of years ago,' said Gabrielle.

Blair smiled at her. 'Time is relative, Miss Pendleton.'

'Around 1870,' said Veronica.

'Goodness me,' said Blair. 'Then the man is good for his age.'

'What do you mean?' asked Veronica.

'I don't know him as Mortimer,' said Blair. 'He calls himself Morpeth. Been living in the neighbourhood on and off for a good few years now. Working for the government on some top secret project—a special sort of tank, I think.'

'A tank?' asked Gabrielle. 'Like a water tank?'

Veronica shook her head grimly.

'No,' she said. 'Like an ironclad.'

'But if it's a top secret project,' said Gabrielle, 'how do you know about it?'

'Oh dear.' Blair shook his head. 'You haven't been to a pub before, have you?'

The quiet of the pub was suddenly broken by a wailing noise that shook the windows and vibrated up through the floorboards. Gabrielle started, and looked around anxiously. She was the only person who seemed remotely bothered by the sound: all around her, the customers were grumbling, shuffling to their feet, putting their hats, coats, and scarves on, and ambling towards the door.

She looked back over at Blair; he was scribbling an address on the back of the photograph with a pencil.

'That's that,' he said, picked up his drink, and drained the glass. He turned to Gabrielle and prodded her gin and tonic.

'Are you going to finish that?' he asked. 'For that matter, are you going to start it?'

She shook her head. Blair took it and knocked it back in one. He looked expectantly at Veronica, but she had already picked up her glass and swigged down the rest. She coughed and wiped her mouth with the back of her hand.

'Come on Gabrielle,' she said. 'Time to go.'

Veronica, Gabrielle, and Blair hung back as the crowd moved in the direction of the air-raid shelter.

'Time to say goodbye, then,' said Blair.

He leaned forward and kissed Veronica: she patted his arm fondly as they separated.

'Look after yourself,' she said.

Blair smiled and shrugged.

'It would be a lot easier if you were here to show me how,' he replied. Then he turned and joined the crowd. Gabrielle saw him slap someone on the back and crack a joke. Veronica tugged at her sleeve and led her away.

They made their way along the darkened streets in silence. The sirens continued for a while, and then they heard the rumble of engines and the sound of bullets slicing through the air towards their targets. Spotlights began to pierce the blackness. The ground trembled beneath them as the first bombs hit.

'That's not good!' said Veronica. 'We need to get to the timepool!'

They broke into a run. The explosions around them came faster and faster now. Gabrielle saw an orange glow suffuse the sky, outlining the roofs of the buildings around her.

'Oh God!' she shouted. 'They're destroying the city!'

'Not the first time,' Veronica replied, 'and not the last!'

They cut through a courtyard and into a narrow alley. Suddenly, Gabrielle felt strong, thin hands pinning her arms by her sides. She struggled as she was dragged back through the alley and towards the courtyard. She turned to try to break

free and caught a glimpse of her attacker's face. He seemed
to be wearing a mask made of a tight-fitting material. She
got a hand free and grabbed at it. Her fingernails dug into
something warm and rubbery: the man gave out a horrible
cry of pain, and she realised she was looking at his real face.

The creature's grip on her loosened. She ducked to one
side and ran back down the alley. Gabrielle heard a snarl,
and felt his fingers clawing at the back of her dress. Then
she was flung to one side, and heard the crack and scrape of
broken masonry. The walls of the alley lurched and shifted
like a house of cards. As she leapt forward, she heard the
brickwork collapse behind her.

Gabrielle landed facedown in the rubble, tearing her dress
and cutting her hands on the jagged fragments. She looked
up and saw Veronica and another of the creatures locked
together fighting: she was trying to wrestle something from
it. Suddenly, it slipped from both their grasps and spun off
into the shadows. Veronica and the creature separated, and
both leapt for the object. The creature was agile as a cat, and
before Veronica had time to reach him, it had picked up the
gun — it must be a gun — and aimed it at her. Its slender,
death-grey fingers tightened around the handle.

FOUR

From nowhere, Gabrielle saw a blade flash out of the darkness and cleanly sever the creature's hand at the wrist. It screeched with pain: a sound like the cry of a fox. The creature dropped to its knees, picked up the severed hand, and re-attached it to its wrist. It turned to face the newcomer, froze — as if in recognition, Gabrielle thought — and leapt away, scampering off into the ruins of the alley behind her.

She saw a man in a dark cape rush forward to retrieve the creature's gun, but, in an instant, it exploded in a magnesium-white flash. The ball of light expanded and stayed static for a moment. Then it collapsed rapidly to a brilliant, tiny spark, and snuffed out.

The man ran over to Gabrielle. She saw Veronica leap up to intercept him. She rugby-tackled him and the two of them fell to one side and rolled over and over on the ground. Gabrielle scrambled to her feet and ran over to join them. Veronica was sitting astride the man with her hands around his throat. He was young—in his twenties—and quite handsome, if you were prepared to overlook his rather large and prominent nose. He wore a neatly trimmed goatee beard. His eyes, meanwhile, were virtually popping out of their sockets as Veronica tightened her grip.

The man coughed and choked out a few words.

'Ver—onica,' he spluttered, 'it's me—K.'

Without loosening her hold, Veronica leaned forward and examined him more closely. She released him, stood up, and dusted down her dress. The man—K—retrieved his sword, wiped the blade on his cloak, and returned it to a sheath that hung from his belt. He was dressed in black, and his clothes were fastened with an elaborate array of cords and laces.

'Charmed,' he said, testily. 'Is that all the thanks I get for saving your life?'

'Sorry, K,' said Veronica. 'I'm a little on edge at the moment. And anyway, I'm not completely convinced they wanted to kill us. I believe those weapons of theirs have a stun setting. I've heard they carry people away sometimes to communicate with them. That's where half the alien abduction stories come from.'

'You think those two just wanted a chat?'

'Maybe.'

'So why were you fighting with them?'

'It's not a convenient time for a chat. My companion and I are in a hurry.'

K approached Gabrielle and performed an elaborate bow.

'Gabrielle, this is K,' said Veronica, 'K, Gabrielle. K's an agent with the Ministry.'

Gabrielle smiled and held out her hand cautiously. This was the first Ministry agent she had ever met: knowingly, at least. When she had been a child, and under the care of her uncle, he had frightened her into behaving with stories of Ministry agents. They came out of nowhere, he had said; they knew exactly what you had done, and what your next move was going to be. And if they wanted to, they could erase you from history entirely: make it so that you never existed.

K seemed to sense her coolness; he took her hand and shook it formally.

'You're the new girl, eh?' he said. 'Come on!' He turned to go. Veronica and Gabrielle stayed where they were.

'You can't stay here in the middle of a raid,' he said, and as if to underline his point, there was a series of explosions nearby. 'In any case, I have my orders. You're to come with me to see Mailfist.'

'Mailfist?' said Veronica. 'What does he have to do with this?'

The ground shook again, and a row of tiles fell from a nearby roof and shattered at their feet.

'I'll explain. We have to go now. There's going to be a direct hit here in—'

K pulled a small pendant watch from the front of his doublet and looked at it casually. Then his eyes widened.

'Actually,' he said, 'any moment now.'

They heard a whistling noise rising above the general cacophony as they began to run. K led the way, darting here and there over the piles of masonry and through the burning, smoke- and fog-choked streets until they saw the cabbie hut they had arrived through what seemed like a century ago.

'Mailfist heard something was going on with a timepool nearby. Illegal movements back and forth. Asked me to look into it.'

The three of them—K, Gabrielle, and Veronica—were walking along a cobbled street that wound between the warehouses of Shad Thames. It was barely light, but the area was already a hive of activity, with stevedores moving crates of goods back and forth. A steady rumble came from overhead as barrels were rolled across the bridges running between the buildings. The air was fragrant with spices.

'And you just happened to turn up at the exact moment we were there?' said Veronica.

'It was a happy coincidence,' said K, smiling as if he didn't really expect them to believe him.

'Who — what were those things?' asked Gabrielle.

'The ones who attacked you?' said K. 'Why don't you explain, Veronica? You know as much as anyone.'

'We don't know what they are, Gabrielle,' said Veronica. 'We think they used to be human, but we're not sure.'

'No one's ever managed to capture one,' K added. 'No one's ever taken a picture, even. Eye witness accounts are all we have.'

'Carter reckons they're from the distant past, or maybe the deep future,' said Veronica. 'He thinks they're the people who built the timepools. They seem to appear when the timepools are threatened in some way.'

They were approaching a door set into a short passage between the street and the riverfront. It was painted dark grey, to match the stones of the wall around it: it was the sort of door one might pass by every day and never notice. There was a small plaque on the wall next to it.

PHAETON — IMPORT — EXPORT

K knocked sharply on the door and waited. After a moment, it swung open, and they went inside.

They walked down a spiral staircase that descended through several sharp twists like a corkscrew into the earth. Oil lamps burned with dirty orange flames in little alcoves set into the wall. The staircase terminated in an office: a clean and well-lit place with a high ceiling and tall bookshelves filled with row upon row of ledgers. A man sat on a high stool at a narrow desk, bent over a piece of paper and scratching away with a pen.

Gabrielle was the first down. The man looked up at her: he was dressed in a black velvet suit with a stiff white collar. By the time Veronica and K joined her, Gabrielle realised she had seen him before: twice before, in fact, on either side of the timepool.

'Miss Britton,' the man said, putting his pen behind his ear. 'And Miss Pendleton. How good to see you.'

'Have we met?' asked Gabrielle.

'As good as,' the clerk replied. 'You've met my brothers. I am them, and they are me.'

'I don't understand.'

'Good.' The clerk grinned broadly; a grin that dissipated as he turned to K.

'K,' he said. 'You're very early, or very, very late.'

'I think you'll find I'm exactly on time,' K replied, smiling. 'Mailfist is expecting me.'

The clerk walked over to the shelves, got up on a step-ladder and reached for one of the volumes. He descended again, returned to his desk, and began to flick through the pages.

'Ah,' he said, running his finger down a list. 'I see you *are* expected.' He did not sound pleased. 'Well, if you'd like to go on through.'

K walked over to the far wall, grasped one of the books by the spine, and opened a concealed door. He bowed and gestured for Veronica and Gabrielle to go ahead.

They walked through a dark tunnel, with a cold, damp feel to it. Gabrielle could hear the lapping of the water above, and the bump and scrape of boats navigating the river. Then the lapping faded, to be replaced by a steady, deep *tick tock*, like the working of a gigantic clock. The sound was joined in its turn by a variety of other faster, lighter ticks in counterpoint, fine bells chiming, and the whirr of cogs. Then the sound of a babble of voices — or maybe the echoes of a single voice splitting up and resolving again and again.

They emerged into a vast, high chamber filled with row upon row of desks. The first row was staffed by clerks identical in dress and appearance to the man they had just met at the entrance. As they advanced, she saw that the next group wore the fashions of the men in the pictures she had seen of her parents in their youth; then further back, to a group dressed in wigs and jerkins, back again to a group dressed like 16th-century clerics; and further and further back, a steady procession of men sharing the same face, voice, and mannerisms, differing only in the way they dressed.

The walls of the room rippled and glittered. It took Gabrielle a few moments to realise that the light came from the walls themselves, shimmering energy from the cogs, springs, and pendulums of an enormous clockwork mechanism.

K walked ahead, smiling and greeting people; Veronica stayed with Gabrielle.

'What are you thinking?' she asked.

Gabrielle looked from face to face. Some smiled and waved; some simply stared, indifferent to her presence.

'They're all the same person,' she said.

'You get used to it,' Veronica replied.

'No,' said Gabrielle. 'They don't just look the same. I mean they're literally all the same person. Just — I don't know — displaced.'

Veronica looked curiously at Gabrielle.

'Carter said something similar to me once.'

Gabrielle nodded. 'It's hard to put into words,' she said. 'It's as if they're from somewhere *outside* of time.'

Veronica opened her mouth to ask another question, but

they were interrupted by the sound of shouting ahead of them. K was standing in front of a green baize door set into the wall at the end of the office; he was arguing with a man, of the same appearance as all of the others, dressed in the short tunic of a Roman servant. The man's desk was completely clear, with the exception of a small silver bell.

'I have an appointment,' K said. 'Check your books!'

'I don't need to check my books,' the man replied. 'He said he's not to be disturbed.'

K turned on his heel to face Veronica and Gabrielle as they approached.

'The man's impossible,' he said. '*You* talk to him.'

Veronica leaned across the desk, picked up the bell, and rang it vigorously.

The door opened, and a portly man dressed in a brown herringbone suit emerged. He wore rimless glasses; his face was round and chubby, his hair an unnaturally rich shade of chestnut. He had a napkin, covered in crumbs, tucked into his collar, and was holding a half-eaten slice of white toast slathered with marmalade.

'Ah,' he said. 'K. And Miss Britton! How pleasant.' He wiped his fingers on the napkin, and held his hand out. 'Miss Pendleton, too! I really am so glad to meet you. Your uncle and I go back a long way. We go forward a little, too, as it were.'

Gabrielle shook his hand. He placed his fingers on her elbow to guide her into the office. His hold was light and precise, but Gabrielle got the impression of immense power behind it, like a delicate machine that nevertheless had the power to crush whatever it held in its grasp.

Mailfist's room was lined with dark wood panels, on which hung various portraits of the man himself. One, a mosaic, featured Mailfist wearing a laurel wreath; one, with the distinctive brushwork of a Holbein, showed him in a black robe and skullcap. In another, he smoked a pipe, and wore a navy uniform with a peaked sailor's hat.

'Do sit down,' he said, carelessly, waving at three seats that had been placed facing his desk. He settled himself opposite, finished off the rest of his slice of toast with one bite, and began to butter another from the toast rack.

'I suspect,' he said, 'that we've been looking at two ends of the same case. Why don't you tell me your side of things, and then I'll tell you ours.'

Veronica smiled and shook her head.

'It's a long story,' she said. 'Why don't you go first?'

Mailfist smiled and winked at her. 'Miss Britton, your manners are impeccable as ever. Very well—though there really isn't much to tell. Nothing K won't have shared with you already. The Ministry discovered that something was awry with one of the timepools. This sort of thing tends to draw attention, and by the time we become aware of it, there's usually some scheme or other afoot. So I sent K to assess the damage at both sides, and it so happens that he arrived at roughly the same time as you.'

Veronica nodded as if she didn't believe a word of it.

'I arrived,' said K, 'just in time to save them from the Nameless.'

'Nonsense!' Veronica interjected. 'I had everything under control.'

Mailfist frowned, and Gabrielle thought his face had turned a little pale.

'The Nameless?' he said. 'The Nameless were there?'

K nodded. 'Two of them.'

'Anything tangible?' Mailfist asked, eagerly. 'A picture, a fragment of clothing, anything?'

K shook his head. Mailfist shrugged.

'Ah well,' he sighed. 'So, Miss Britton, perhaps you can tell us what you were doing in 1940?'

'Might we have some tea?' Veronica asked.

Mailfist struck his forehead with his hand, leaving a small patch of marmalade and crumbs.

'Goodness me,' he said. 'My manners! What must you think of us, Miss Pendleton? I would hate for you to get the wrong impression of the Ministry.'

He pulled a silver bell — identical to the one on the desk outside — from a drawer, and rang it. The receptionist entered the room, with an expression of cheerful anticipation on his face, as if he expected he was about to receive instructions to show Mailfist's visitors the door.

'Tea, please,' said Mailfist. He turned to Gabrielle. 'English Breakfast tolerable?'

'Perfect,' she replied.

'Good. It's all we have.'

Once the tray had been brought in, and the tea poured, Veronica told the story of Mortimer's disappearance, the double life he appeared to be living between the late 19th and mid-20th centuries, and the blackmailers.

'I assume,' said Veronica, 'that he was planning to take the engineering secrets of the future back in time and make a success of the land ironclads.'

'It wouldn't be the first time,' Mailfist said, thoughtfully. 'Sometimes it's even supposed to happen that way. But not in this man's case. Not at all.' He tugged the napkin from his collar, threw it on the tray, and strolled over to the only window in the room. It was a large porthole, with a gleaming copper frame; golden light spilled from it, the colour of a sunrise. It looked out onto the heart of the great machine that housed the Ministry, a long, gleaming vista of clockwork.

He studied it for a moment before he spoke again.

'It seems to me,' he said, 'that matters have moved ahead of us. Professor—Mortimer, Morpeth, whatever he likes to call himself—has managed to get to 1940. Much good may it do him. If the Nameless are involved, I dare say they'll have sealed the breach in the timepool. So we control the only gateway, and we won't let him back. He can stay in 1940. He can't do much damage there. And that is the end of that.'

'But what about the blackmailers?' asked Gabrielle.

Mailfist shook his head. 'Little people,' he said. 'We don't bother with little people here at the Ministry.'

He returned to his desk and sat down heavily.

'Well,' he said, 'things have resolved themselves very nicely, don't you think?'

'But sir—' said K.

'That will be all, K.' Mailfist barely stirred; he didn't even raise his voice. But there was something about his tone that silenced K instantly. His expression was suddenly blank, his eyes cold. After a moment, he seemed to remember himself, and turned to Gabrielle and Veronica.

'I'm so sorry, ladies,' he said. 'I don't want you to waste any more of your time on this case, and I need to have a few words with my agent here.'

'Professor Mortimer's wife came to us for help. What are we supposed to tell her?' asked Gabrielle indignantly.

Mailfist scratched his head. 'Oh, the man's wife. Well, if she's reluctant to pay for your services in view of the outcome, I'm sure I can arrange for some form of—ah—compensation to be granted by the Ministry. Your agency has been a good friend to us, and we like to look after our friends, hmm?'

Veronica stood up suddenly, the scrape of her chair on the floor discordant against the soothing, regular ticking in the background.

'I'm sure there won't be any need for that,' she said. 'Come on, Gabrielle. We have to file a report for Mr Carter. Good day, K. Good day, Mailfist.'

Gabrielle rose to her feet to join her. Mailfist reached out for the silver bell on his desk.

'No, no,' said Veronica, coldly. 'We can show ourselves out.'

'As you wish,' said Mailfist, smiling placatingly.

Without another word, Veronica turned and walked out of the room. Gabrielle followed her. K reached out for her hand as she did so: he placed a single kiss on it and smiled at her sadly.

'Something's not right, Gabrielle,' said Veronica, as they wound their way back out of the maze of Shad Thames. 'In fact, something is very, very wrong.'

'I can't believe the Ministry would just let things drop like that,' said Gabrielle.

Veronica shook her head. 'I can't believe it either.'

'What are we going to do?'

'For a start, I need some food and an hour or two of sleep. What about you?'

'I'm feeling very well, thank you.'

Veronica put her hand to Gabrielle's cheek. Her skin was warm, glowing almost.

'You are, aren't you? Something to do with the Ministry. Carter always comes back from it in the pink of health. Anyway, let's have breakfast. I can skip sleep for the time being, but breakfast is one meal I can never do without. Then we're heading back to 1940.'

'Shouldn't we talk to Uncle Jim first?'

'We'll tell Carter once we're finished. Never tell anyone what you're going to do until you've done it.'

FIVE

The landscape was a mass of rubble. It made distance impossible to judge: it interfered with one's sense of direction and perspective. After a little while, however, one could distinguish separate colours: a flash of red brick, say, or a jet-black streak of ash. The ground was constantly shifting and unstable, liable to give way at any moment.

To Gabrielle, it looked like nothing less than the end of the world.

The two women picked their way over the ruins towards the street Mortimer lodged in. Of course, there was a possibility that he was now at work—wherever that was—but the fact that it was a Saturday meant there was a good chance he was not. In any case, Blair had only been able to furnish them with the location of his lodgings, and this was as good a place to start as any. A letter left lying around, or an indiscreet landlady, might reveal the location of his laboratory, if that were needed.

None of the Londoners they passed seemed remotely curious about the destruction around them; they strolled past with the same disinterested air with which the drinkers in the pub the previous night had made their way to the air raid shelter. As Gabrielle and Veronica descended a small hillock of debris into Mortimer's street, they saw that one of the houses had been knocked clean away, leaving a gap in the terrace. The interiors of the adjacent properties stood exposed to the air, like the rooms of a doll's house.

'No,' said Veronica, looking again at the back of the photograph on which Blair had written the address. 'No, no, no!'

She rushed into the pile of rubble that had once been a house, and began to pull stone from stone.

'We're too late!' she said, angrily. She looked down at Gabrielle, who had retrieved a small tin box from the rubble and was trying to open it. The lid came off suddenly, and she held the contents up to the light: a large, amorphous mass of glass with little streaks of colour running through it.

'Marbles,' she said. 'A child's toys.'

'Keep looking.'

Gabrielle put the box down carefully, and sat down on the remains of a wall.

'This can't happen,' she said.

'It already has,' said Veronica. 'K wasted our time. We lost Mortimer's trail, and now we need to find him again.'

'I'm not talking about the case,' Gabrielle replied. She gestured around her, at the wreckage of London, at the plumes of smoke still rising into the cold blue sky. 'This. None of this. It can't happen. We can't allow it.'

Veronica took hold of her shoulder gently.

'No, Gabrielle,' she said, softly. 'Don't start. Not now.'

Gabrielle continued as if she hadn't heard her.

'I'd heard Uncle Jim talk about it,' she said. 'But I never really thought — never *imagined*. Veronica, we have to go back. We have to stop this happening to London.'

Veronica shook her head.

'You can't stop it, Gabrielle. Believe me. You try to make things better; you just end up making them much, much worse. I know.'

Gabrielle brushed Veronica's hand away.

'We can change it,' she said. 'Maybe that's why the time-pools are there. To help us. We can go home, write a letter to the Prime Minister — the Prime Minister they have now, I mean. Something he can open when the time is right. We could tell him what's going to happen, tell him it's something he's got to stop whatever it takes —'

'Gabrielle!'

Veronica knelt, and placed both hands firmly on Gabrielle's shoulders.

'Gabrielle, you can't. You just can't.' There was something in her tone that Gabrielle had never heard before: a frightening mixture of hurt and anger.

'How do you know?'

Veronica hesitated for a moment before she gave her answer.

'Because I've tried,' she said.

She took Gabrielle by the hand and helped her to her feet.

'We can talk about this later, as much as you want,' she said. 'But for now, I need you to be strong. I need you to help me.'

Gabrielle let out a sigh.

'What can I do?' she asked.

'I need to know if the Professor was here when the bomb hit. I'm going to have to ask you to concentrate.'

'What?'

'You're very time-sensitive, Gabrielle,' Veronica explained. 'You can pick up things that are there when they shouldn't be. People who don't belong. But more than that, you should be able to pick up the trail they've left through time. Tell me, Gabrielle: what do you see?'

Gabrielle closed her eyes. She saw the house in darkness: then there was a sudden, intense flash of light inside, so bright that she could see the edges of the blackout blinds illuminated. There was silence and stillness for a moment; then the whole structure seemed to inflate like a balloon, breaking up and scattering fragments of glass, wood, and masonry in all directions.

'What do you see?' Veronica asked again; in Gabrielle's mind's eye, her friend stood there in the wreckage of the house, unhurt despite the destruction around her.

'Veronica?' she gasped.

'Don't worry about me,' said Veronica. 'Look around you. Who else is here?'

Gabrielle obeyed; at the far end of the street stood a figure half-hidden in the shadows. As the flames grew fiercer and higher, she could make him out more clearly; he was dressed in a long, dark overcoat, and carried a brown leather brief-case. He was old, with a white beard and thick, round spectacles. He was looking straight at her, his eyes wide, and for a moment she thought he could see her; but he was staring, she realised, at the destruction of the house in front of him, calculating the best course of action.

Then she saw him smile: not humorously, or ruefully, but with an expression of cold calculation. He turned away from the burning building, and ran into the shadows.

Gabrielle opened her eyes. She had no idea how long she had been in the trance-like state. She stumbled and Veronica took her in her arms, helping her to sit down.

'He's alive,' said Gabrielle.

'Where did he go?'

Gabrielle gestured in the direction she had seen the Professor escape.

'Back towards the damaged timepool!' said Veronica. 'So he got away while we ran into the Nameless. He must've got through and gone home. Do you feel able to get up yet?'

Gabrielle nodded and stood up slowly. She took a few unsteady steps. There was a sharp pain behind her eyes; she put her hand across them for a moment.

She saw the house again, intact, in darkness. Then the flash. Then the—

She opened her eyes.

'Veronica,' she said.

'What?'

'The house wasn't hit by a bomb.'

'What do you mean?'

'It wasn't hit. Something went off inside, while he watched. He was making sure it did.'

Veronica put her hand firmly on Gabrielle's shoulder.

'Are you sure of that?' she asked.

Gabrielle nodded.

'You know what this means?' said Veronica.

'Yes.'

'Mortimer. He planted a bomb. He wanted to cover his tracks, so he could disappear back to his own time. His work here is over.'

'We have to stop him! Surely the Ministry will do something now.'

'No,' said Veronica. 'The Ministry can't be relied on. Not to finish this job, at least. We're going to have to do it ourselves.'

Without another word, the two of them hurried away from the ruins and towards the timepool.

'Which way now?'

'Don't ask me, Gabrielle, I'm thinking.'

'I thought you knew London.'

'I know the streets. The trouble is there aren't any left.'

Veronica picked up a crumpled piece of card from the

ground: someone had helpfully scribbled street names on it, and it had presumably acted as a signpost for a few hours before being trampled underfoot.

'Veronica!'

'What?'

'The timepool!'

Veronica looked up and saw the bright green exterior of the cabbie hut standing out against the grey rubble.

'They really are indestructible,' she murmured to herself.

'What?'

'No time,' she said to Gabrielle. 'Let's go!'

They were halfway to the hut when she heard a cry behind her. She looked back to see Gabrielle sitting up in the wreckage.

'Nothing broken?' she shouted.

'No —' Gabrielle said, cautiously. 'But I think you should come over here.'

Veronica picked her way over to where Gabrielle sat, propped up against a slab of concrete.

'What is it?' she asked. Gabrielle pointed at her feet.

There was a hand sticking out of the rubble; it was covered in a fine layer of white dust.

'Oh,' she said. 'Look, Gabrielle, I know it's sad, but there's nothing we can do for him.'

'There's something odd about it,' said Gabrielle, not taking her gaze away from the body. 'Something *wrong*.'

Veronica swept the debris away from the body. It was that of a man in his thirties, quite recently dead.

'Poor man,' she said. 'He must have been killed in the bombing.'

Without a word, Gabrielle put her hand on the man's forehead. There was a small bullet hole just next to his hairline.

'There's someone else,' said Gabrielle. She got up and

heaved away the slab she had been leaning against. The torn fabric of a tan-coloured raincoat was just visible. The two women hauled the body out: he was a younger man than his companion. A dark flower of congealed blood blossomed across his chest.

'You take that one,' said Veronica. 'I'll take this one.'

'What?'

'Search his pockets.'

Gabrielle unbuttoned the man's coat gingerly as Veronica reached in to the first man's inner pocket and retrieved his wallet. She went through it quickly and expertly, then turned back to Gabrielle, holding a slip of paper.

'Here,' she said. 'Let's compare notes.'

She heard a *crack*, and a fragment of brick flew towards her, catching her forehead and drawing blood. Instinctively, she ducked forward, and pushed Gabrielle's head down as a second and a third shot whistled past them. There was silence. Gabrielle shifted uncomfortably beneath her. She rolled away. They lay there, side by side, looking at the London sky already tinged with the deeper blue of twilight.

'Who is it?' Gabrielle whispered.

'I didn't get a good look,' said Veronica.

Gabrielle reached out and clutched her hand.

'Is it the Nameless?' she asked, urgently.

'I don't think so,' Veronica replied. 'Whoever's firing at us is using good old-fashioned bullets.'

Another bullet whizzed overhead and ricocheted off the rubble.

'What are we going to do?'

'We're going to have to run for it.'

She shifted position so that she was crouching, ready to spring. Gabrielle did the same.

'Now,' said Veronica, 'when I give the signal, run towards

the hut as fast as you can. Don't stop for anything. In particular, don't stop for me. If I don't make it, go to Carter and tell him what's happened. I'll join you later. Understood?'

Gabrielle nodded.

'Alright,' said Veronica. '*Now!*'

Veronica leapt to her feet and ran for the hut. The door was slightly ajar. She threw herself inside, tripping and hitting the floor hard. She rolled over, winded, in time to see Gabrielle skidding into the hut.

Veronica put her hand in her front pocket, and pulled out her pass. She turned to the porter, held it up and forced the words out.

'Veronica Britton, Chronic—'

She stopped. The porter was sitting in his armchair, just as he always did. A mug of tea steamed on the small side-table next to him, and a newspaper was spread out on his lap. But he was still, and his head was tilted back at an unnatural angle.

Without a word, Veronica moved across to the end of the hut, and opened the door. The tunnel stretched out in front of them, the dark path that would take them home. She took Gabrielle's hand, and they ran in together.

The porter at the other side of the tunnel was also dead, but he had evidently put up more of a fight. The contents of the hut were in disarray, the fragments of a plate scattered across the floor, the urn on its side with its contents spilled out into a dark pool. It seemed to Veronica as if all of the violence of the future had been unleashed by Professor Mortimer, and was seeping back into her own time.

'Now we know for sure it's not the Nameless,' she said. 'They'd never do something like this. Too messy. And it leaves the timepool unguarded.'

'Then who is it?' asked Gabrielle.

'I'm not sure,' said Veronica. 'But whoever it is must be very well connected, or very foolhardy, or possibly both. Killing the porters is like declaring war on the Ministry.'

She knelt down next to the dead porter, and gently closed his eyes.

'We can't help them now,' she said. 'And we don't have any time to lose. Whoever killed these men is after us now.'

'Where do we go?' asked Gabrielle. 'The agency? The Ministry?'

'Neither,' said Veronica. 'We need to go back to where all this started.'

It was raining heavily and a thick fog had set in when Veronica and Gabrielle left the hut. They ran the short distance to Mortimer's house, the cold rain lashing against their bare heads and soaking their dresses.

Veronica went ahead up the main steps and rang the doorbell. It was the type that pulled out, and sounded as the cord retracted into its housing, setting off a set of chimes deep within the house.

No one answered.

'Are we too late?' asked Gabrielle.

'I hope not,' said Veronica.

She hammered on the door: it opened a fraction to reveal a lined, wary face.

'Who is it?' said a man's voice, harshly. 'What do you want?'

'We need to see Professor Mortimer,' Veronica replied.

'In that case,' said the man, 'I suggest you write to make an appointment. An appointment at a reasonable hour. Good night.'

He began to push the door closed, but Veronica wedged

her foot into the gap. She slipped through, and Gabrielle followed her.

The hallway was dimly lit by a single low gas lamp: the man stood before them, uncertain as to what to do next. Gabrielle realised that, despite his gruff tone, the man was actually *afraid* of them.

The butler backed away from them towards a door at the far end of the entrance hall. 'If you would be so good as to wait,' he said, 'I will see — I will see —'

The door behind him flew open.

'Strevans!' said a high, nasal voice, buzzing like a wasp in a jar. 'Strevans, who is it? This is intolerable!'

Strevans stood aside sheepishly as Mortimer stormed into the entrance hall. He glared at Veronica and Gabrielle imperiously.

'Who are you?' he demanded.

'Professor Mortimer!' Veronica said. 'We think your life may be in danger.'

Mortimer rolled his eyes and made a clicking noise with his tongue.

'Strevans,' he said. 'Leave us alone, would you? I'll ring if I need you.'

Strevans gave the two women one last searching look, and backed out of the hallway.

'Now,' said Mortimer, 'why don't the two of you explain yourselves?'

'Professor Mortimer,' said Gabrielle, 'it may be better if we went through to your study.'

Mortimer grinned coldly and shook his head.

'Better for who? Better for you? I don't have too much to worry about. But what about you, eh?'

He stepped forward and looked them up and down: the gaslight reflected in his glasses, turning them into twin blanks where his eyes should have been.

'You have something of the time traveller about you. Are you Ministry agents?'

'No,' said Veronica. 'We're private detectives.'

'What?' The Professor jerked his head up sharply. 'Who sent you?'

'I did.'

The three of them looked up at the source of the voice. Mrs Mortimer, clad in a black silk dressing gown, was descending the stairs.

'You?' said Mortimer indignantly. 'You went to an agency?'

'I was so worried,' Mrs Mortimer protested. 'I thought—well, I don't know what I thought. When those horrible men came around ... '

'Men?' Mortimer replied. 'What men?' He thought for a moment. 'Oh, *those* men. I thought I saw you at the top of the stairs that night. Well don't worry, my dear. No one of that sort will bother us ever again. I have friends, you see.'

'Friends?' Veronica gasped. 'Friends? Mortimer, I don't know what they told you, but there's more going on than you know.' She pulled one of the dead men's wallets from her pocket. 'We found your address in here. *Both* your addresses. These men were blackmailing you, and your employers killed them for it. And on their way there, they murdered two Ministry porters.'

'Really?' said Mortimer with a bored air. 'How terrible.'

'Whoever these people are, they're not your friends. They're not anyone's friends—'

She was interrupted by a *bang*. The door leading down to the basement opened suddenly and Strevans stood there, his eyes wide and his mouth open as if about to ask a question. His lips trembled, but he seemed to be having some difficulty finding the words he wanted to say, perhaps even having trouble forming the thought behind them.

'Strevans?' said Mortimer irritably. 'Strevans, what is it?'

Strevans took two steps forward. Then he crumpled at the knees, and fell to the floor. He pitched onto his front, revealing a wound on the crown of his head. It was a broad, blunt laceration: dark blood oozed out.

Gabrielle ran over and helped him into his back. He looked at her stupidly, with the expression of an animal ready for slaughter. She pulled a handkerchief from her sleeve and pressed it against his wound, trying to staunch the bleeding.

Mortimer came and stood over him.

'What happened, Strevans?' he demanded. His tone, Gabrielle noticed, was wavering, and even in the dim gaslight she could see he had begun to perspire.

'The kitchen window—' Strevans mumbled hesitantly. 'Breaking glass—I heard—I went to see . . .'

His head lolled back and he closed his eyes. Mrs Mortimer let out a stifled gasp.

'Is he—?'

Gabrielle took the man's pulse. It was rapid and thready.

'No,' she said, 'but we need to fetch a doctor.'

'Out of the question,' Mortimer snapped. 'No one leaves.'

'Quite right.'

None of them had noticed the man appear in the open doorway. He was dressed in a plain black outfit, cut smartly around the waist and shoulders like a military uniform. His hair was cropped short, and he was clean-shaven. He tilted his head to one side, smiled, and pulled a small pistol out of a holster at his side. It was compact and sleek: obviously the product of future technology, but, unlike the weapons carried by the Nameless, still recognisably a gun that fired bullets.

Mortimer started back as if he had received an electric

shock. Then he turned and walked towards the intruder, his arms outstretched.

'So you decided to show up, eh?' he said. 'About time. Frankly, sir, I have no idea how you allowed this situation to spin as far out of control as it has. Strictly speaking, I should report your negligence to your superior officers.'

His words didn't fit with his hysterical pitch. The intruder raised his pistol. Veronica sprang forward and pushed Mortimer to one side at the exact moment that the gun went off. The explosion shook the whole room. The glass covering the gas lamp exploded. Everything went black.

Several more shots rang out and Gabrielle heard the impact of hot metal slicing through flesh and bone.

There was the sound of sliding metal, and the *click* of something being snapped into place. The assassin, she realised, had reloaded. Mortimer had been his priority, but he wouldn't stop until all of them were dead.

SIX

Veronica ran towards the intruder. She saw the glint of the muzzle of his gun pointing at her: heard, as if time were slowing down, the trigger being pulled, catching, the hammer descending, the bullet rushing along the barrel towards her. She winced and ducked.

She felt herself being pulled away to one side, and then picked up as if she weighed nothing. She was lifted gently through the air and propped up carefully against the wall, in the way a child might put down a favourite doll after playing with it. She looked around her; she could make out the outline of Mrs Mortimer, curled up in a ball only a few yards from her, and of Gabrielle, who had thrown herself across the wounded Strevans to protect him from the bullets.

A loud, low bellow sounded from the far side of the room. She saw the assassin lift his gun again, but this time, he seemed to be flailing wildly rather than aiming at anyone. It was only then that she noticed the two thin, dark figures that were wrapping themselves around him. It was like watching a giant spider devouring its prey in slow motion.

Things began to move very quickly after that.

The hallway was suddenly flooded with light, the first rays of dawn, although she and Gabrielle had arrived only a little after midnight. Time was distorting. Veronica stirred to get up at the exact moment that the bullet, fired at her what seemed like several minutes ago, struck the wall just above her head, missing her by inches. She caught a glimpse of the intruder being dragged away through the doorway to the cellar. For a moment, a pale hand grasped the doorframe, resisting to the last; it was pried away, finger-by-finger, and then he was gone.

Veronica rushed over to Gabrielle. She was still pressing hard against Strevans' wound, although she looked desperately pale herself, and her hands were shaking.

'Are you alright?' Veronica asked.

Gabrielle's eyelids fluttered as if she was fighting to stay awake. She looked like she had the first time they had gone through the timepool: only much, much worse.

'Time disturbance?' she asked. Gabrielle nodded.

There was a sob from the main doorway. Veronica looked up, and saw Mrs Mortimer embracing her husband. All of the pride and anger seemed to have drained from his face. What Veronica saw now was intelligence, luminous intelligence; it was perhaps the face of the man his wife had married. He coughed once, and a little blood spattered across his shirt-front.

Mrs Mortimer turned to face him.

'Oh, David,' she said, quietly, 'what was it all for?'

The Professor smiled lopsidedly.

'For the Empire,' he whispered in a wet rasp.

'The Empire?' Veronica asked.

'The Empire.' The Professor forced the words out. 'You have no idea—'

He coughed again, and his head lolled back. His eyes remained open, yet it was perfectly clear the life had gone out of him.

'And that was it? Vanished without a trace?'

Carter leaned back in his chair, tilting it on its hind legs so he could reach the cigar box on his mantelpiece.

'Not quite,' Veronica replied.

'Eh?' Carter swung forward heavily, the front legs of the chair slamming into the floorboards. 'What do you mean *not quite*? No footprints, no weapon, no body, just a broken window, a dead scientist and a half-dead butler.'

'Gabrielle had a look round. She said she could sense residual time currents.'

'And you?'

Veronica shook her head. 'I'm not as sensitive as her.'

Carter lit his cigar. He took a deep pull to get it started, and the tobacco gave a satisfying crackle as it caught.

'Nameless,' he said.

Veronica nodded.

'So why didn't they want you?'

'I'm not sure,' said Veronica. 'It's clear that the Professor wasn't working alone. He was part of a bigger organisation. The fact he was careless enough to allow himself to be blackmailed meant he became more trouble than he was worth. Perhaps he'd outlived his usefulness by then, anyway. His best work might have been behind him. I understand it happens to academics.'

Carter smiled and took another puff before he spoke.

'So they—his employers—sent someone to get rid of the blackmailers *and* him. Then the Nameless went after this agent, whoever he was. But *why*?'

'This goes beyond anything we've dealt with before, Carter. Something big is at stake. And Mailfist is hiding something.'

'I reckon you're right, Britton. Anyway, you've certainly impressed them. You and my niece.'

'Eh?'

'I had K in here an hour or so ago. Asked if I'd be happy to subcontract you to the Ministry for a little job. One that requires discretion.'

'Discretion?'

'Yes. So I've no idea why they asked for you. Anyway, the terms seemed very reasonable. If you're willing, I think we can come to an arrangement.'

Veronica nodded. 'I'll take it. If nothing else, it might mean I get a few more clues as to what's going on. By the way, did K say anything about the Empire?'

'Empire what? The Empire Theatre? The British Empire?'

'That was what he said—the Professor—just before he died. That he had done it for the Empire. What do you think he meant?'

Carter shrugged. 'People say all sorts of strange things before they die. My grandfather couldn't stop talking about meat pies. It might not mean anything.'

'Still—'

'Might mean nothing, might be the key to the whole thing. No way of knowing at the moment.' He took a battered watch from his waistcoat pocket and glanced at it. 'Now get along with you. Just keep your eyes open, Britton, and your ear to the ground. And take care of my niece.'

PART TWO

The Last Londoner

ONE

The chamber was bare, with the exception of a single arm-chair, a plain table, and a hollow at the far end that served as a natural fireplace. The old king set down his bundle, and unpacked the contents: there was a flask of water, a small parcel of salted meat, and a few loaves of bread along with a beaker, a wooden plate, and a sharp knife. A separate compartment held a bundle of wood, some smaller pieces of kindling, and a flint. Finally, at the very bottom of the bag, there was a bronze pot and a small quantity of dried leaves that a merchant had brought all the way from the far side of the world, across continents and great oceans, and finally up the river to the little muddy village.

The old king lit the fire, filled the pot with water from his flask, and set it at the centre. Soon, it began to bubble and steam. He wrapped his hand in his cloak, and took it off the heat; then he dropped a handful of leaves in.

They released their aroma straight away; his mouth began to water, and he had to resist the temptation to drink the whole lot down at once. *No,* he thought, *allow it to steep. You have all the time in the world.*

He sat back in his chair: there was time, indeed, for another of his dreams as the drink infused. He had become so adept at dreaming that he could now slip almost instantaneously from the waking world to sleep, and back again. So he closed his eyes, and let his mind loose. He began to dream of the settlement growing, of the river that flowed deep and mighty through its heart being bridged and re-shaped, of the people from all over the world who would come there and make it their home. A city that would, one day, offer everyone refuge. A city of darkness and light, a city that would hold the very best and the very worst. He dreamed in particular of one woman, one who would turn up time and again in this city of his, in every possible age. He had often talked of her to his citizens, and she had become something of a legend even now, long before she would be born. He had wondered for a long time what her full significance was: only now did he realise it.

She was going to save the city. She was going to save the world. But, most importantly, she was going to save *him*.

TWO

'This is never going to work.'

Gabrielle Pendleton shifted nervously as the police officer turned away from them and dialled a phone number.

'Shh,' Veronica whispered. 'Mailfist said they would be expecting us. Nothing to it.'

'If there's nothing to it,' said Gabrielle, 'why didn't they send one of their own agents?'

Veronica had no good answer to that — didn't want to think about it too much right now, in fact — so she gave Gabrielle a frown and looked back at the desk officer who seemed to be deep in conversation. He glanced up and smiled at them.

'Okay,' they heard him say, his voice muffled behind the thick, scratched plexiglass of the station front desk. 'I'll tell them.' He put the phone down, and swivelled his chair back around so he was facing the grille.

'Okay, Stephanie's on her way up now.'

Stephanie, when she came, turned out to be a young police officer with cropped blonde hair.

'Vera Brecon?' she said.

'Yes,' said Veronica. 'And this is Gill Peterson, my colleague.'

'And you're here about the man they picked up in the tunnel?'

'Yes.'

Stephanie led them along a corridor painted a dirty yellow that may once have been cream, and down the steps to the cells. She keyed in a code and took them through a barred door. When it shut, she keyed in another code and opened the next one.

The cell area had a warm, damp atmosphere; there was a smell of disinfectant, and the noise of someone shouting and banging on one of the doors. The occupants of the other cells, meanwhile, were yelling for the man to shut up and let them get some sleep.

Stephanie grinned. 'You're welcome to this one,' she said. 'He's going to start a riot if he stays here any longer. A bit of an odd bod. Stops and starts, angry one minute, quiet the next. Says he was working in the tunnel, something about an injury. Naturally, we checked with the tube maintenance people. No one unaccounted for, so he's definitely not telling us the truth. The trouble is he seems convinced he *is*. He says his name is Arthur Jacobs, but there's no record of him anywhere, and the address he gave doesn't even exist. Or rather it did, but it was demolished fifty years ago. We were about to call the doctor to have a look at him. But now you're here—'

They reached the cell, and Stephanie opened the viewing slit. It was stiff with layers of chipped grey paint.

She glanced in quickly then turned to Veronica.

'All yours.'

Veronica looked in. The cell was covered in grimy ceramic tiles. The bed consisted of a shelf with a thin mattress covered in a blue plastic material, and there was a small steel toilet without a seat plumbed into the wall at one side.

Arthur Jacobs looked bedraggled and confused. He paced the short distance from one end of the cell to the other, not seeming to notice he was being watched. Veronica thought he looked like an exotic creature captured and anaesthetised in the wild that had just woken up in a zoo.

'That's him,' she said.

Stephanie accompanied Veronica, Gabrielle, and Arthur back up to the station reception area. The workman grumbled to himself and studied the fading posters on the walls. Gabrielle tried to engage him in conversation, but he turned away.

'Where are you taking him?' asked Stephanie, as they stood at the station entrance.

Veronica's hand was already in her pocket, her fingers closing around the car keys. She smiled and shook her head.

'I'm sorry,' she said. 'That's —'

'— Classified information.' Stephanie said. 'That's what they said on the phone. Worth a try, though.' She winked.

Veronica winked back, shook hands, and steered Gabrielle and Arthur towards the door just as the reception phone began to ring.

'I ain't going!' Arthur shouted suddenly. He made to run, but Gabrielle grabbed him tightly around the forearm. 'Don't be a fool,' she hissed. 'You're being rescued!'

'Can you manage?' asked Stephanie. Her tone was suddenly less warm.

In the background, they could hear the desk officer talking on the phone.

'Yes,' he was saying, 'they just came here now — no, two women. What?'

'We're fine,' said Veronica. 'Really, we're fine.'

She pushed Gabrielle and Arthur out into the street, and the glass door slid shut behind them.

'Okay,' Veronica whispered. 'Nice and slowly.' She pointed at a black Volkswagen Beetle parked a short distance away. 'That's your ride home.'

'What,' said Arthur sceptically, 'that?'

'Come on,' Gabrielle said. 'There's been a mistake. We're here to take you back. You just need to get in, and soon this will all seem like a bad dream.'

'If this isn't a bad dream already,' said Arthur grumpily, 'I don't know what is.'

They were halfway across the road when they heard a voice shouting 'Stop!'

Veronica swung round to see Stephanie and the desk officer running towards them.

'Quick!' she shouted. The three of them sped towards the car. She fumbled with the button on the key fob, and the vehicle gave an obedient bleep, a flash of its lights, and unlocked itself. Then she pressed the button again by accident, and it went through the reverse process.

'Open the doors!' Gabrielle was already tugging frantically at a handle.

Veronica pushed the button a third time, and the doors unlocked. She pulled open one of the back doors, and bundled George inside. Then she got into the front seat. She heard something hit the opposite window, looked out, and saw Gabrielle trying to free herself from Stephanie who was holding her from behind in a bear hug.

Veronica leaned across, opened the door, grabbed hold of Gabrielle, and pulled her away from Stephanie and into the car. Stephanie stumbled and fell backwards. Gabrielle scrambled into her seat, slammed the door shut behind her and pushed the lock down.

'Come on!' she shouted at Veronica. 'Drive!'

'Oh dear,' said Veronica.

'What?'

'You're actually in the driver's seat.'

'Oh, bloody hell!' cried Arthur.

The two women turned around to face him.

'Shut up!' they shouted.

'Nothing for it, Gabs,' said Veronica, passing her the keys. 'You drive. It's easy. Like riding a bicycle. Actually, more like firing a gun. Easier than that, even.'

The window next to Veronica shattered as the desk officer drove a baton into it.

'Go!' Veronica shouted, brushing the pebbled glass off her clothes. 'Go, go, go!'

Gabrielle jabbed the key into the ignition and turned it. The engine rattled into life.

'Right,' said Veronica, 'right foot down, left foot across and down a bit.'

Gabrielle found the biting point straight away: Veronica released the handbrake and the car lurched forward. It heaved and groaned its way down the road. Stephanie and the desk officer managed to cling on for the first couple of yards before the car bucked suddenly and threw them off.

'Good!' Veronica exclaimed. 'Now go left at the end of the road. Left foot down, we're taking things up a gear.'

The car careened through the midmorning traffic, swiping vehicles and mounting the kerb several times.

'Where are we going?' Arthur shouted.

'Somerset House timepool,' Veronica replied. The sound of police sirens started up in the distance. 'Or possibly prison, if we don't hurry up. Gabrielle, put your foot down!'

It was night when Veronica, Gabrielle, and Arthur walked out of the timepool doorway and into the silent courtyard. Snow covered the ground and coated the windowpanes. K stood alone in the centre holding a lantern. He smiled and saluted as they approached.

'Thank you Miss Britton; you too, of course, Miss Pendleton. I knew we could rely on you.' He turned to the workman. 'And — Arthur, isn't it? Arthur Jacobs, common labourer? Welcome home.'

Arthur shivered and hugged himself. K took off his cape and draped it around the workman's shoulders.

'Keep it,' he said. He leaned in and whispered confidentially as he straightened it. 'Excellent quality. Made by Raleigh's tailor. Very water-resistant.'

'I don't understand,' said Arthur. 'Where the hell was that? It looked like London but . . . ' he shook his head.

K tutted and nodded sympathetically. 'I know. Hardly the most elegant or appealing era in the history of this great city.'

'You're from the Ministry!' said Arthur. 'That's who you are!'

K raised an eyebrow. 'You've heard of the Ministry of Chronic Affairs?'

'I'd heard the stories,' Arthur shook his head, 'but I never thought . . . '

'You and I need to have a long talk,' said K.

'But what about the man? The one in the tunnel, the one who was hurt. He's still there, you know.'

'Yes, what about that?' Veronica interjected. 'What went on down there in the underground?'

'Nothing to worry about,' said K, sharply. 'Everything's under control.'

'And another thing,' said Arthur. 'It was summer when — well, whatever it was — happened.'

'Ah,' said K. 'Yes, that's something else. You've come back a little earlier than you left. It's 1899.'

'What?'

K put his arm around the man and led him off.

'The best we could do, I'm afraid. We couldn't bring you back at exactly the right point, and if you'd arrived later than you left—well, there would have been an absence to explain. It's quite alright; you'll just have to lie low for a few months in one of our safe houses. Nothing to worry about. They're really very pleasant. Then, on the day you go missing, you just step right back into your life. We can hardly have two of you running around . . .'

The men's voices began to fade as they walked out of the archway and onto the Strand.

'Wait a minute,' said Veronica.

'The cheque's in the post!' K answered over his shoulder.

'That wasn't the question!'

'I can't hear you!' K shouted, as he and the workman vanished into the swirl of snowflakes.

THREE

Veronica split the log with the poker, and pulled the grate out to let a little more air in. The fire flickered back into life. She added a shovelful of coal, and sat back in her armchair.

'Toast?' Gabrielle offered.

'Yes, please. But can you help me get these boots off first? I must have a hole in this one. I think some snow got in.'

Veronica undid the buttons at the sides, and Gabrielle tugged them off. Veronica's left stocking was soaked through; she peeled it off and put it in front of the fire to dry as Gabrielle cut a thick slice of bread and impaled it on a toasting fork.

The women had taken a timepool back to Veronica's flat on Gower Street. The drawing room surfaces were covered with various knickknacks she had picked up during her travels: a bronze pot, an ormolu clock, a set of paperback books with orange and white striped covers. The gas lamps were down low, and the curtains pulled fast against the cold outside.

'So is that it?' asked Gabrielle, holding the slice of bread over the fire.

'Is what it?'

'Is that the end of the job?'

'From the Ministry's point of view, yes.' Veronica replied.

'And from ours?'

'I'll make sure the cheque's there first thing tomorrow.'

'Oh.'

Veronica wiggled her toes, warming them. Steam was beginning to rise from her stocking on the hearth.

'You don't sound happy, dear.'

'I'd like to know what exactly happened to that man. One minute he was working on a new underground line in 1900. The next, he was transported 100 years into the future. It could have been a timepool, I suppose, but if it was —well, why not just send him straight back the way he had come, instead of going through Somerset House?'

'Keep going,' said Veronica. 'And turn over.'

'Eh?' said Gabrielle, before realising that Veronica was referring to the toast. She pulled the fork back and examined it. One side was crisp and golden brown; exactly the way Veronica liked it. She flipped it over and started toasting the other side.

'There must be something else down there,' she said.

'Gabrielle, why do you think the Ministry asked us to retrieve that man for them?'

'I don't know. Because of our reputation?'

'No. Because of theirs.'

'What do you mean?'

Veronica shrugged. 'This is how they operate. They like to play at being the unseen hand. When they're too embarrassed to admit they've made a mess of something, they get a private operator to sort it out. Either that, or —'

'Or,' said Gabrielle, 'they wanted it done, but they didn't want to be seen doing it. Because someone was watching.'

'Or both. Well, whatever it is, there's something under St Paul's that that poor man got caught up in. He said someone was hurt —I don't know, that might mean it's a machine of some sort, one that's malfunctioned. Anyway, the Ministry stepped in quickly enough to stop him telling us anything more.'

'So?'

'Aren't you a little bit curious, Gabs?'

'Curiouser and curiouser. Oh!' Gabrielle pulled the burning piece of toast from the fire; it slipped off and fell to the floor where it set a week-old copy of the *Times* alight. Veronica stood up, lifted the teapot, and calmly emptied its contents over the blaze.

'Feet off the desk, K. You're not in Eastcheap now.'

'Sorry, sir.'

Mailfist took another bite of toast and let the silence hang there for a moment. It was a good thing to assert one's authority every now and again. The *tick tock* of the Ministry seemed especially loud in the background.

'It's a shame Miss Britton and Miss Pendleton had such trouble getting him out. I wonder who it was that tipped off the police.'

'You're not suggesting—?'

Mailfist shook his head. 'An enemy within? I hope not. But their network may have spread deeper and wider than we thought. What did the workman tell you?'

'He was only in there for a moment or two,' said K. 'From his point of view, of course. He said there was a man on the floor. Face down, out cold. No idea if he was alive or dead—the workman just panicked, and ran to get help. He said he felt there was something strange about that place. He's not the type to scare easily, but it unnerved him.'

'As well it might. I don't like this, K. I don't like it at all.'

Mailfist lifted the slice of toast from his plate and nibbled at the edge of it.

'Fine cut,' he said, distastefully, 'and far too sweet. Whatever happened to the Wilkins and Sons' Tawny? I like that. Bittersweet, you see. Bittersweet.' He took hold of the silver bell on his desk.

'Sir?' K interrupted.

'What?'

'Sir, what are we going to do? If he's hurt, if he's dead?'

'I think that for now we should leave it in Miss Britton's capable hands. We can rely on her to investigate further — even if she guesses that is exactly what we want, she still won't be able to help herself. I look forward to learning what she discovers.'

'But what if it goes wrong? What if she spends too long in there? You never know when she might end up. She may never come back!'

Mailfist sighed. 'Miss Britton's no fool, K.'

K made to reply, but saw a look of danger pass across his superior's face.

'Don't forget,' Mailfist added. 'That I know exactly where you are at all times.'

K's fingers went instinctively to the chain around his neck.

Veronica and Gabrielle, both carrying torches, made their way along the tunnel. They had returned to the day in the 21st century after the workman emerged, waited until the trains stopped running in the early hours of the morning, and then broken in to the now empty St Paul's tube station.

The tunnel echoed with creaks and groans, the sounds of metal and cable settling after the day's usage. Gabrielle shone her torch on the tracks; a pair of dust-coloured mice, caught in the beam, scuttled away silently.

'Veronica,' she said. 'I don't think there's anything down here at all.'

'There must be,' Veronica replied.

They walked on a little further in silence. Then Gabrielle felt it. It seemed at first like a tremor in the ground beneath her, and for a moment she thought a train was approaching.

'Gabrielle? Do you feel something?'

Gabrielle put her hand out and ran it along the tunnel wall.

'Don't *you* feel it?' she asked. 'It's as if the stones are melting.'

Gabrielle's hand dipped into what looked like a patch of shadow. Veronica shone her torch along it, but all she could see was a pool of blackness, like a mass of tar, surrounding her companion's arm. She could smell damp earth and coal gas, and beneath it, incongruously, the aroma of English Breakfast Tea.

'This is it,' said Gabrielle.

She stepped into the darkness.

K finished his tankard of ale — one for courage — then slipped away to the back of the King's Head tavern, and down the stairs to the basement. It was late, and most of the drinkers barely registered his presence, drowsing as they were over their cups. The 16th century — home — was somewhere he really should come back to more often. There was much to love about it: the air of intrigue, the fact that everyone seemed to be known by at least three names, to profess several different faiths, to serve many masters.

The cellar was filled with barrels of ale and racks of wine. K picked his way through to the rear wall, and began to run his hand along it. He had managed to strike it lucky; although being lucky was, in K's opinion, a skill much like any other, and one he had perfected during his time working for the Ministry. He had remembered — quite by chance — that there had always been stories about this particular tavern: strange goings-on in the basement. He had known what was in the basement, of course, though he had kept his peace. But he had never put two and two together before, and realised there was more to it: here was a point of weakness, a moment in time when it became possible to access the chamber from the outside. They cropped up irregularly at intervals of anything from fifty to five hundred years. This moment, in particular, seemed to have arranged itself nicely around his plan.

He felt his hand sink into the wall. Steeling himself, he stepped into the quivering texture of time and space, letting the tides bear him onward and into —

A room. A warm, smoky room with a crackling fire. An old man sat in a roughly carved wooden chair, his eyes darting around under closed lids. He was fast asleep, in the middle of a dream, no doubt. He stirred and muttered to himself. There was a pot at his side, from which wafted a pleasant herbal smell.

K stepped forward and shook him.

'Come on,' he said, urgently. 'You've got to wake up! You're in the most terrible danger—'

There was a sharp blow to the back of his head, and the sudden *snap* as the lights went out.

K regained consciousness slowly. There were two figures standing over him, looking down.

'K?' said Veronica, sharply. 'K? Come on, wake up.'

K tried to sit up, but his head suddenly ached terribly and a wave of nausea forced him back down. The room doubled and spun around him, and he grasped at the earth floor to steady himself, his fingers digging into the clay. He felt a hand resting on his forehead; it was cool and smooth.

'He's concussed, I think,' said Gabrielle.

K opened his eyes again cautiously. The room was, at least, still and solid.

'Mmph,' he mumbled.

'Nice to see you, too,' said Veronica.

A wave of fear hit him as the full import of his surroundings sunk in.

'How long was I out for?' he asked urgently.

Gabrielle put her hand back on his forehead, which was suddenly damp.

'He's not well, poor thing,' she said. 'Not well at all.'

'How long?' K repeated, sitting up successfully this time. The room trembled and yawed off at a strange angle for a moment, but then tilted back and held firm.

'Not long,' said Gabrielle.

'Was there someone here with you?' Veronica asked. 'Only there's a rather nice pot of tea on the side here, and it looks about ready to drink.'

K tried to stand, but collapsed onto his knees. He began to crawl towards the door.

'We have to get out of here *now*!' he yelled.

'Steady on,' said Gabrielle, putting a hand on his shoulder.

'No!' K shook her off, and hauled himself through the gap, allowing its dark, thick waters to propel him forwards as he heard Veronica shouting for him to stop.

'Come back, K!' she cried. 'We're all in this —'

Then he was lying face down in a pile of ash. It was fine and white, like chalk dust; he stood up, trying to brush it off, but it clung like paint. He stopped and took stock of his surroundings.

The sky was dull gunmetal, the sun a dab of pale yellow. He was standing outside a cave at one end of a deep crater, whose gently sloping walls were made from rock of the same whitish-grey as the dust.

He stayed there for an hour or so. It simply didn't occur to him to do anything else. Then he heard a voice behind him.

'—together!' it said. 'Now where are you?'

Veronica stood outside the humped, barrow-like chamber. K glanced at her, but didn't answer. Veronica turned to look expectantly at the entrance. After a few minutes, she turned back to K.

'What's happening?'

K shrugged listlessly. He sat on the ground and put his head in his hands. Veronica tried talking to him again, but he simply turned his face away, and eventually she gave up. The watery sun had already begun its descent by the time Gabrielle emerged.

'What took you so long?' he heard Veronica demand.

'Eh?' said Gabrielle. 'I was right behind you. You left just a second before me.'

The women turned to K. He looked up.

'Where are we, K?' asked Veronica.

'We're exactly where we were,' he replied, his voice shaking. 'Just—'

'What year is it?'

'I have no idea. It's the future. That's all I know.'

'Vee?' Gabrielle interjected.

'What?'

'That didn't feel like a timepool, did it?'

'You're right,' said Veronica. 'It didn't. And what about you, K? Anything?'

K didn't respond. Veronica snapped her fingers in his face.

'Nothing? Alright, we'll go back and have another look.'

'No!'

K stood up suddenly and grabbed Gabrielle's arm. The women looked at him, alarmed.

'You won't get back that way,' he pleaded.

'Then how?' asked Veronica. 'How do we get back?'

K hung his head. 'I don't know.'

'K,' said Gabrielle, 'why not explain to us what just happened? What exactly it is in there? Maybe we can work out a way to get home together.'

'No one was supposed to go in there,' K replied. 'No one but King Lud.'

'What?' Veronica asked. 'What do you mean?'

But K had already turned away and was making his way up the side of the crater.

Carter sat in his office. He had watched the day fade, saying to himself every few minutes that he would get up and turn on the lamp, but he had kept putting it off until the only light came from the streetlamp outside. It was enough to read his watch by, and that was all he needed. He pulled it out of his waistcoat pocket and pressed the button to flip open the cover. Five minutes since he last checked. He snapped it shut, returned it to his pocket, and thought again about the lamp. He recognised it well enough, this inactivity. It was what he always did when he wanted to put something off, some action, some decision, or, all too often, some deeply unpleasant thought. It was his hopeless way of trying to freeze time.

Where had they got to?

At the top of the crater stood the white chalk skeletons of what had once been buildings. Veronica, Gabrielle, and K sat down, exhausted from the climb. Gabrielle felt a stale, acidic taste in her mouth from inhaling the dust they had kicked up during the ascent; she rested against a wall, and tried not to think of her thirst. The stones shifted with her weight against them, slight as it was. K slumped to the ground, and put his head in his hands as he had done before. Veronica sat opposite him, cross-legged.

'So if it wasn't a timepool,' she said, as if their conversation had flowed uninterrupted by the trudge out of the crater, 'what was it?'

K moved his hands slightly, to reveal one of his eyes. He peered at her warily.

'You've heard about the ravens?' he replied, his voice almost a whisper.

'Ravens?'

'The ravens at the Tower of London?' Gabrielle interjected.

K nodded, and took his hands away.

'You know the story about them?'

'I think everyone does,' said Gabrielle. 'If they ever leave the Tower—'

'—The Kingdom will fall,' Veronica broke in impatiently. 'What's that got to do with this? With King Lud?'

K looked at her with the closest expression to reverence that she had ever seen on his face. It was, she thought, quite disconcerting to see him look so sincere.

'King Lud,' said K, 'is like the ravens. He was the king who founded London. The city was named after him. And that chamber we were just in—that was where he was buried.'

'Buried?' said Veronica. 'I thought Lud was just mishmash of ancient legends, like King Arthur. More a story than a real person.'

'Yes,' said K, 'and that's the source of his power.'

'What power? And why does it matter anyway, if he's dead?'

'He isn't dead,' K said sharply.

'I thought you said—'

'I said he was buried,' K replied. 'I didn't say he was dead. At the end of his reign, Lud was put in that chamber.' He gestured down into the crater. 'He retired there to continue dreaming up the city.'

'But that would make him hundreds of years old,' said

Gabrielle.

'Thousands,' said Veronica.

K waved their questions off, and fell silent again.

'Look,' said Veronica. 'Supposing the story is true. What happens if he's missing?'

'What happens to the dream,' asked K, 'when the sleeper awakes?'

Carter walked briskly through the gloomy streets of Shad Thames, his footsteps echoing off the cobblestones. He imagined for a moment that he caught movement in one of the darkened doorways, a swimming patch of dimness. He tapped his stick on the ground and started to whistle an old marching tune to warn whoever it was that he was game for whatever they could throw at him. Still, he picked up speed, and was glad of it when he turned into the narrow alley and found the door with the dull brass plaque next to it.

PHAETON — IMPORT — EXPORT

He rapped once, firmly, with his stick.

It was getting dark quickly, and bitterly cold with it. The heat drained rapidly from the earth as the sun vanished; it didn't so much set as snuff out like a candle. Veronica thought of a legend she had once heard, about the end of days: that a wolf would swallow the sun, and that the universe would turn to ice.

They were walking through the ruins of the city aimlessly now, simply trying to keep warm. Their way was lit by a strange glow that came from the crumbling stones themselves. Gabrielle was trying to keep K talking.

'There was something you said earlier. Something about

King Lud still being alive. How? Is there something in the chamber that prolongs life?'

'In a sense, yes,' said K. 'But not in the way you think.'

'Time runs differently, doesn't it?' Veronica said, suddenly.

'You're right,' said K. 'Nobody knows why it was built. Some people think that it's a sort of prototype time-travel device. You can leave the chamber at any time, but it only opens up from the outside at certain points, usually every couple of centuries. Time runs much more slowly inside the chamber than it does outside. Hundreds of years could pass out here, whilst to the person inside it's no time at all.'

Gabrielle gasped. 'So that's what happened to us. Veronica, we must have been there for—what, five, ten minutes?'

'Maybe more.'

'So when are we?'

'Very, very far into the future,' said Veronica. 'And, for all we know, stranded. Where Mailfist and K were perfectly happy to send us.'

K stopped walking and whirled around.

'Look,' he said, angrily, 'it was a miscalculation.'

'What?'

'Mailfist thought you'd go down there, take stock of things in less than a minute, and get out again. He never thought you'd spend so long that you ended up this far into the future.'

'We only stayed in there so long because of you!' Gabrielle exclaimed.

'Yes,' said K, sheepishly, 'I didn't agree with Mailfist. I thought his plan was too risky. I went into the chamber in the 16th century so I'd be able to warn you, and maybe even stop Lud from being kidnapped.'

'Well done,' said Veronica. 'That worked out very nicely, didn't it?'

'What have you done with them?'

'I'm so sorry, sir, he just barged in! '

'Did K tell you? Did he tell you what I'd do if anything happened to them?'

Mailfist carefully replaced his bone china cup in its saucer and looked at the two men: Jim Carter, twice the height and size of the clerk who was usually so good at manning the desk outside the office and repelling unwanted visitors.

'That's quite all right,' he said to the clerk. 'Leave this to me.'

The clerk scowled, nodded curtly, and walked out of the room.

Mailfist smiled at Carter. 'I'm terribly sorry about that,' he said. 'Perhaps you'd care to join me for some tea?'

Carter swept his stick across the table top, sending cups, saucers, pots, milk, and sugar lumps flying.

'What's that?' said Gabrielle.

The three of them stopped and listened, shivering with cold. It was the sound of tiny stones skittering along a hard surface. Veronica looked around to see where the noise was coming from. She noticed that a wall just ahead of them was shaking, loose fragments from the top tumbling downwards like the spray of a waterfall.

K stepped towards it and put his hand on the glowing surface. He turned his head back towards them, and looked as if he was just about to ask a question when the whole structure shattered and collapsed.

In the darkness beyond, a pair of lamps shone like the eyes of a great monster approaching through the darkness. The sound of the stones breaking apart was drowned out by the deep bass rumble of heavy machinery, and the whine and grind of smaller metal parts scraping against each other.

Veronica felt the hairs lift on the back of her neck. It was just an instinct, not even a conscious thought, but—

'Get down!' she shouted, and pulled Gabrielle to the ground. She looked up and saw K diving to avoid a streak of white flame that leapt out of the darkness, hissing and spitting. It hit just to the left of them, opening up a hole in the ground.

Even though the flash only illuminated the distant machine for a second, there was no mistaking the dark segmented body, the ungainly, hunched appearance, the wheels enclosed by a thick set of metal treads that bit into the earth.

They were looking at a land ironclad.

FOUR

'If you know of a nearby timepool,' Veronica shouted to K as another bolt of energy shot overhead, 'this would be a good time to mention it.'

K peered cautiously over the rim of the crater at the machine.

'It seems to have stopped for a moment,' he said. 'It's appraising the situation. And no.'

'No what?'

'I don't know of a nearby timepool. In fact, I don't know exactly when we are, so even if a timepool opened up in front of us now, we wouldn't have any idea where it would lead.'

'If you're not going to be helpful,' said Gabrielle, 'we're just going to have to take our chances.'

She began to stand up, but Veronica pulled her back down.

'Look!' Veronica pointed. There was a ridge of earth that led off to one side. 'Cover. Let's go!'

The three of them kept low and scurried away as a search-light swept across the ground in front of them. They heard the scrape of the ironclad's turret swivelling around, accompanied by a high, whining sound that Veronica assumed must be the guns charging.

There was another flash of light, and a deep concussion as the ground behind them exploded into a fine mist. The air around them crackled and buzzed. They broke cover and ran for their lives.

'Don't tell me you haven't felt it,' said Mailfist.

'Felt what?' asked Carter.

'You can play the fool with everyone else if you like, Carter. But don't do it with me. We know each other too well for that.'

Carter sighed.

'Yes,' he admitted. 'Things are—I don't know—loosening around me. It's like when you sense a storm coming. Sometimes you feel it before there's even a single cloud in the sky.'

Mailfist nodded. 'And our skies are not exactly clear, are they? Go on.'

'There was something Veronica said. Something Mortimer told her—you know, the ironclad man. He said it just before he died. That the Empire was coming.'

Mailfist got up from his seat, and turned to look out of the window at the Ministry's machinery.

'Well,' he said, 'that's something she neglected to mention to me.'

'You can't complain,' Carter replied, sharply. 'You've hardly played fair with her.'

There was a knock at the door.

'Come in!' shouted Mailfist.

The door opened, and Carter's assistant walked in. He paused as he caught sight of the broken crockery on the floor.

'Ignore that!' snapped Mailfist. 'What is it?'

'Sir, it's about K.'

'The time is out of joint.'

'What?' Veronica looked at K, but he turned away again.

The three of them were sitting in a deep hollow in the ground. They had waded through a marsh and down a slope into a landscape pockmarked like the surface of the moon. White stones were scattered around, glowing dimly like dying stars.

'Something's occurred to me, K. Don't the Ministry tag their agents?'

K nodded and felt around his collar. He produced a brass chain that glinted in the light; there was a round pendant at the end. He flipped it open to reveal a compact clock face.

'Synchronised to the Ministry,' he said. 'For all the good it'll do.'

'They'd just leave you?' said Gabrielle.

K nodded. 'We're on our own,' he said. 'Mailfist would never—'

The ground began to vibrate.

'Gabrielle, look over there,' ordered Veronica. 'Let's work out where they're coming from, at least.'

Gabrielle and Veronica raised their heads over opposite sides of the crater.

'Vee!'

'What?'

'Three from this side.'

'Same here.'

'Vee, we're surrounded!'

Mailfist led Carter out of his office, through the main hall, and into a curved corridor that led deeper and deeper into the Ministry. The machinery shimmered and whirled in its glass housing.

'I really shouldn't be doing this,' he said.

'I'm not going to argue with you,' Carter replied. 'But why does K mean so much to you?'

'It's not that he means so much to *me*,' said Mailfist. 'It's—'

He checked himself, but it was too late.

'That's it,' said Carter. *'Come in Agent K, your time is up'*? He needs to be in the right place at the right time, or—'

Mailfist strode ahead to a large bronze door. He turned a thick wheel set halfway up its length to unlock it.

'Is it soon?' asked Carter. 'K's moment?'

Mailfist continued to ignore him, pushed open the door, and hurried through. Carter followed him in. He was just about to ask Mailfist the question again when he was struck by the sheer enormity of his surroundings.

The room was a vast oval, with a curved ceiling holding a map of London made of what looked like gold leaf, framed in thick, polished glass. As he watched it, the map rippled like a reflection on the surface of a lake. The floor was taken up with glass cabinets containing cogs, cables, chains, and dials, all ticking away in perfect synchrony.

In the centre of the room was a raised dais: a brass rail halfway up formed a great curve. An innumerable number of watch faces of every conceivable shape and size were set into a panel attached to the rail. Some were large pocket-watches, some small sundials, some glass displays with the time displayed in red glowing digits. In the centre was a huge lever set into the ground, like a massive brake. Mailfist was already standing on the dais as Carter approached, scrutinising the clock faces.

'Come on up,' said Mailfist. Carter stepped up onto the dais. He noticed Mailfist's finger was resting on one of the smaller faces, a tiny dial no bigger than a thumbnail.

'This is the one,' said Mailfist. 'This is K's.'

Mailfist pressed the dial. The machine hummed, and there was a sound of water sloshing back and forth from above. The men looked up: Carter saw the map of the city expand, old structures crumble away and new buildings rise; the city spreading further and further outwards, swallowing towns and villages as it went.

The image began to flutter.

'That's not right,' said Mailfist.

'Alternative versions of the city,' said Carter. 'One on top of the other.'

'It's worse than I thought,' whispered Mailfist. 'I've never seen this sort of turbulence.'

The image finally resolved to a desert of rubble and craters. Towards the centre, almost imperceptibly, a ripple spread from a tiny point of light out toward the edges of the frame.

'That's him!' shouted Mailfist. 'Good God!' He tutted and shook his head. 'Far, far away.'

Mailfist rolled up his sleeves, placed both hands on the lever, and looked at Carter.

'If you wouldn't mind,' he said. 'It has been a while since this was last used.'

Carter gripped the lever and braced himself.

'I really shouldn't be doing this,' Mailfist repeated.

'Of course not,' Carter replied.

The two men forced it forwards. There was the sound of breaking glass.

'Surrender now,' said the voice from the ironclad, 'and you will not be harmed.'

'Do you believe that?' asked Gabrielle.

'Of course not,' said Veronica. 'K?'

K shook his head.

'Good. Consensus. Fight to the death. Only—'

'Only what?'

'I don't know. He sounds—*scared*. Now why would they be scared of me?'

'Surrender now,' the voice said again, 'and you will not be harmed.'

'Yes, yes, you said.' Veronica moved towards Gabrielle and took her hand.

'This is it, Gabs. I'm sorry.'

'That's quite all right.'

Gabrielle leaned forward and kissed Veronica.

'I'm ready,' she said.

FIVE

'Hold fire!' said a voice.

'What?' Veronica exclaimed. 'You?'

'Sorry about this, Veronica, but it really is time to give up. That's your problem: you never know when to stop.'

Veronica turned to K. 'What do you know about this?' she demanded.

K raised his hands. 'Nothing, I swear!'

Veronica reached out to grab him just as the nearest ironclad exploded in a ball of orange flame. The blast wave threw the three of them to the ground.

'What was that?' asked Gabrielle.

They scrambled to their feet and peered over the edge of the crater.

In the light of the burning ironclad, they saw a mass of bodies emerging from the hollows of the earth; slender, insect-like figures, moving swiftly and silently. Some were aiming weapons at the ironclads: others were crawling over the surfaces of the machines, pulling off weaponry effortlessly, or tugging open hatches and dragging out the occupants.

'The Nameless!' Veronica shouted.

'Watch out!' shouted K, pulling them both down. An ironclad, spinning desperately in an attempt to fling off its assailants, was firing its cannon wildly. They ducked as it shot a bolt in their direction, cutting a deep gouge in the rim of the crater.

'Marvellous!' shouted K. 'Saved from the ironclads only to die in the crossfire!'

Veronica put her arm around Gabrielle.

'I'm so sorry, Gabs,' she said. 'This is all my fault.'

'It's not, Vee. It's not. It was my idea to go back to St Paul's.'

Veronica shook her head.

'Oh my dear,' she said. 'You don't know the half of it.'

Above the crackle of weapons, the grinding of the machinery, and the roar of the explosions, there came the sound of breaking glass.

'No!' said K. 'What the hell is Mailfist—?'

They were sprayed in a shower of displaced earth as the wall of the crater collapsed around them. The mist cleared. They saw something standing just a few yards ahead: something that had definitely not been there before. It was a massive structure, its shape strange and irregular, like an engine taken out of its housing. Blasts of energy from the battle smashed and warped its glass and bronze parapets.

A door at the front swung open. Jim Carter, smoking a cigar and looking nervously at his pocket watch, emerged.

'Carter!' shouted Veronica.

Carter looked up and frowned, as if he had spotted someone arriving late for a theatre date after the play had started.

'Britton! Gabrielle! We don't have all bloody day!'

He beckoned for them to come in as the building took another hit. He staggered and grabbed onto the glass doorframe to steady himself.

'And bring your friend!'

Veronica, Gabrielle and K ran towards the door of the

Ministry. The air was hot and thick with smoke. Carter shepherded them in; as he closed the door, Veronica grabbed him and kissed him once on the cheek.

'First time for everything,' he said, then turned and thumped the wall of the corridor. 'Let's go!'

The ticking of the Ministry sped up until it sounded like the buzz of an angry wasp: and then again there was the sound of breaking glass.

Mailfist was already back in his office when they arrived, trying to sweep the broken crockery under the table with his foot.

'I see you've been talking about us,' said Veronica.

Mailfist nodded. 'Quite. Do take a seat.' He searched around on his desk until he found his small silver bell. He had just picked it up to ring it when his assistant walked in with a fresh tray of tea and toast.

'Excellent,' said Mailfist. 'Shall I be mother?'

Veronica, Gabrielle, and K sat in a semicircle around his desk, whilst Carter stayed leaning against the wall.

'How long were we there for?' Mailfist asked.

'Not too long,' said Carter.

'Good, good.' He turned to Veronica and Gabrielle, dabbing at his forehead with a napkin. 'The Ministry isn't designed for this, you know. She's supposed to move at a consistent rate, not break through the fourth dimension like a battering ram—'

'When was that, Mailfist? How far forward did we go?' asked Veronica.

Mailfist sighed. 'A long way. I don't even like to think about it. But that's not even what worried me the most. London will fall, Veronica; it has several times before, and it will again. But that version of it was something that should never have existed.'

'So why is it there?'

'It's not. Or rather, it's not constantly there. London is in flux, Veronica. There's a battle going on right now for its future. And we aren't even sure who the key players are yet. You have just been to a future in which . . . someone—'

'The Empire?'

'Someone,' Mailfist repeated, firmly, 'has got the upper hand.'

'How?' asked Gabrielle. 'It can't be because of King Lud.'

'I'm sorry, Miss Pendleton. It can. Lud created the city. Not just by laying a few foundation stones, or building a road, or setting up a dock. Far more than that. London isn't like other cities: London was made from dreams. Lud's dreams. The old legends aren't just stories. They're real. We're the ones who are fictional: Lud's fictions, to be precise. If he's not there, under the city, dreaming about it, dreaming about all of us—'

'Things are falling apart,' said K. 'They've deposed Lud, so they can gain total control of the city.' He looked at Mailfist. 'I'm sorry, sir. I took matters into my own hands. I tried to stop them, but I failed.'

'K,' said Mailfist, sadly, 'we will discuss this later.'

'So what changed your mind?' K asked. 'Why did you come for us?'

'Later, K,' Mailfist repeated. He gazed down into his nearly empty cup, and swirled the tea leaves around as if divining the future.

'Look,' said Veronica, 'I have no idea what this is about, but it isn't getting us any closer to sorting things out, is it?'

Mailfist jerked his head up and looked at her distractedly.

'Oh my dear Miss Britton,' he said. 'I couldn't possibly impose—not after—'

'Mailfist, you protest too much.'

'Veronica Britton!' thundered Carter. 'You are not spending another moment on this case. I won't have it, do you hear me? And you, Mailfist, stop encouraging her.'

Mailfist flushed scarlet. 'I wasn't—'

'I think you were, actually, in your usual roundabout sort of way,' said Veronica. 'But it doesn't matter. The point is that the Empire—whatever it is—is very bad for all of us. And the Nameless don't seem to like it too much, either. We don't know who's behind it—'

'I thought you recognised—' Gabrielle interrupted.

Veronica shot her a warning glance. 'We don't know who's behind it,' she repeated. 'Still, there's a clear way we can interfere with their plans. We can find King Lud, restore him to his proper place, and make sure he's kept safe in the future.'

Mailfist nodded eagerly.

'One problem,' said Carter. 'If you go in search of him—if I allow it—how are you going to find him? He could be anywhere. They might have killed him, you know.'

'He's right,' said Gabrielle.

'No,' said Veronica. 'Lud's alive. I know it. Look, if they were going to kill him, why not just send an assassin into the chamber to do it? Why go to the trouble of dragging him out? I think they didn't want to end his life just like that. They wanted to depose him. They wanted to show who was in charge.'

Mailfist nodded.

'Very well, Miss Britton. But that still leaves us with the problem of how to find him.'

'Child's play. We know that K went into the chamber in the 16th century, correct? And Lud was still there?'

K nodded.

'And we know that Gabrielle and I found K alone in the

chamber when we entered in the early 21st century. So that means there's only a period of four hundred years or so when Lud would have emerged onto the streets of London. And I'd guess that he would have stayed in the immediate area — just in case an opportunity arose to get back. I've found people before with far less than that to go on.'

'She's right, you know,' said Carter.

'She is,' Mailfist agreed. 'Mr Carter, might I engage the services of your agent again?'

'Agents,' Gabrielle interjected.

Carter stepped forward to Mailfist's desk and put his hand out.

'Time and a half,' he said.

'Indeed.' Mailfist shook his hand firmly.

'Good work,' said Carter, wiping away the crumbs and marmalade Mailfist had transferred onto his palm. 'Miss Britton, Miss Pendleton, time to go.'

In the 21st century, St Pancras was — as it always had been and always would be — noisy, dirty, and chaotic. 'Do you know,' Veronica said, as she and Gabrielle stepped off the Euston Road and into the comparative tranquillity of the red-brick courtyard of the British Library, 'that Boudicca's supposed to be buried under one of the platforms at King's Cross? And that's not all. They unearthed the bones of a mammoth not far from here in 1690.'

'No,' Gabrielle replied. 'I wonder how it got there.'

'Remind me to tell you sometime.'

Gabrielle stifled a yawn as Veronica placed a substantial pile of books in front of her.

'What are we looking for?' she asked.

'Anyone who fits Lud's description,' Veronica replied.

'Which is?'

'Old, eccentric. May have tried telling people he was really King of London. Probably made a spectacle of himself.'

'That hardly narrows it down.'

Veronica nodded. 'True. So let's get going.'

Gabrielle opened the first book, and began to read. It was a relatively recent publication, from the late 20th century: a compilation of London's famous characters. The first page she turned to had a photograph of a man wearing a sandwich board, extolling the virtues of a low-protein diet in controlling undesirable passions. The next described Tiddy Doll, the extravagantly dressed gingerbread seller from the early 19th century, who fell into the frozen Thames and could be observed, arrested at the point of death, for many days thereafter.

Veronica, meanwhile, was flicking through an oversized volume of London street scenes. She put her boots up on the green leather surface of the desk, and the man sitting opposite tutted from behind his laptop.

Gabrielle finished her book, and returned to the collections desk for the next batch of material. The librarian behind the desk, a slender man in a pinstriped three-piece suit who had an extravagantly long beard, lifted the set of books with surprising ease. Just as she was turning to go, he placed another volume on top of the pile she was carrying.

'I thought this one might be useful,' he explained. 'I took the liberty of ordering it up from the stacks.'

Gabrielle thanked him and returned to Veronica. Veronica lifted the book the librarian had picked out, and began to glance through it.

'Who gave you this?' she asked.

Gabrielle pointed in the direction of the desk. The librarian was standing there, looking across eagerly.

N.P. BOYCE

'Oh, him?' said Veronica, and gave the man a wave. 'We get along very well. Funny, really. He wishes he had been born in my time, and vice versa.' She turned the page carelessly, paused for a moment, and turned it back.

'Wait a minute.'

She threw down the book in front of Gabrielle. The *bang* rang around the reading room: from all sides came mutters of disapproval.

'Gabrielle,' said Veronica, 'what do you make of this?'

Gabrielle looked at the open book, a collection of Hogarth's engravings from the 18th century. She was familiar with the artist; Carter had had a similar book in the house when she was younger, one that he had specifically forbidden her to look at, containing as it did scenes that were quite unsuitable for a young lady's eyes. Naturally, Gabrielle had memorised every single image. This one, however, was new to her. It was a scene from Ludgate Hill, with the dome of St Paul's Cathedral in the background — Wren's building, which was still only a few decades old at that point.

It was night, and the street was populated by the usual crowd: a tavern door had been flung open, and the landlord was throwing out a pair of rowdies; a hopelessly drunk young man was being led along the street, his guide about to betray him to a gang of thieves waiting around the corner with evil-looking cudgels in their hands. The focus of the engraving, however, was a set of figures just to the right of the frame. A brazier was burning, its light picking out a collection of what looked like street-dwellers.

Standing over the brazier, lit dramatically, was an old man in tattered robes. He wore a crown whose jewels had long since been plucked out, and whose points were bent and broken. He was addressing the crowd: his long white hair was wild and tangled, his expression was stern and intense, and his hands were caught in the middle of some extravagant gesture. Even from the engraving, one could see that there was something different, something arresting about this man. Some of the crowd were gazing with rapt attention; some were laughing; others were asleep, their mouths open, their faces pinched and weary like those of the dead. The caption read:

Every Inch a King

'That's him,' said Gabrielle.

'No doubt about it,' Veronica replied. 'I'll get a copy made. Then we'll see if we can find him. This print is from 1751. There's a timepool near Waterloo — down in the Cut — that comes out around then. The only problem is that it means we have to go via the 1980s. Not my favourite decade.'

'What's it like?'

'Horrid. Grey, with the occasional outbreak of violence.'

'Hmm.'

'Still, it's worth it to get to the 18th century. The 18th is fun. Dangerous, but fun.'

It was night when they got to their destination, and bitterly cold. They walked briskly along the north bank towards St Paul's. The air near the river smelled ripe, the odour of London from the years before the Thames became clean.

Some streets they walked through were apparently deserted, whilst others were alive with activity; some were halfway between the two, an unexpected movement in the shadows revealing a group of the dispossessed huddled together for warmth, or the eerie glint of several pairs of eyes looking out from an apparently derelict house.

They had just turned the corner from one such street when

they heard the man's voice.

He was standing next to a brazier, exactly as he had been portrayed in the engraving. He looked thinner, however, and more ragged: his white hair was lank, falling almost to his shoulders. He was dressed in robes of a moth-eaten brown fur — maybe bearskin — that hung off his body. The man's crown, too, was in a worse state of disrepair, battered and caked with dirt: only the thinnest edges of metal glinted in the firelight as he spoke.

He was addressing a mixed crowd: some old, some young, mostly street-dwellers like him. There were, however, one or two who appeared better dressed, and were attended by bodyguards. His voice was cracked and high, but still carried well.

'My children,' he said. 'I call you that, for you are all my children. A king is a father to his subjects, is he not? Well, my children, I recognise all of you, although I dare say none of you recognise me. I knew you before you were born, before your parents were born, before your parents' parents. I looked across the sea, and saw your ancestors in the places where they lived: I brought them here. *Come*, Lud told them, *come to a city that belongs not to a single country, but to the whole world.*'

There was a titter from someone in the crowd. Lud turned and stared at the culprit — one of the young men of fashion — imperiously.

'You laugh, sir. Well, you are free to laugh. You have the upper hand at the moment, eh? Well, I tell you this: you have it for now, but it will not last for long. Oh, I know you, sir, I know you very well. I have seen the moment of your death, diseased and in penury. I have seen your grave, the marker washed clean by London rain, the patch overgrown with weeds and thistles, your memory lost forever.'

The young man shouted an obscenity at Lud and stormed off, his bodyguards in tow. Veronica and Gabrielle darted into the space his departure had created in the crowd. Lud lifted his hand to his crown and raised it a fraction of an inch.

'At last,' he said. 'Veronica Britton. I have been waiting for you.'

'We're here to take you home, sir,' said Gabrielle. Lud smiled at her. 'Of course,' he said. 'You were part of my dream, too.'

'Come with us,' said Veronica. 'We'll put things right.'

'Oh you will, will you?' said Lud. 'Well, you might, at that.'

He stepped forward and presented his hand. Gabrielle took it, and led him away.

'You know where my chamber is?' he said. 'It's quite close by.'

'Indeed,' said Veronica.

'And you have identified a time point when it is open?'

'About 250 years from now.'

Lud chuckled. 'Good,' he said. 'That means my tea will be about ready.'

They were now in a street where the only light came from the dim lantern of a watchman in the distance. The river swashed gently in the background.

'Oh, you should have seen London in my day,' he continued. 'There has always been something soft about this city, something mutable. When I founded it, the very mist, the very earth was rich with the seeds of time.'

They approached a narrow archway: a figure emerged from the shadows, dressed in a coat of dark velvet and carrying a cane.

'Miss Britton,' the porter said, 'Miss Pendleton. Sir. A very good evening to you. If you'd like to step this way—'

There was a chattering noise in the darkness, the sound of irregular tapping like mice scurrying behind a skirting board, with mechanical trills and screeches breaking in intermittently. Veronica stepped forward and felt resistance: she reached down and found a door handle. She turned it, and the door opened stiffly.

A man stood outside, dressed in a grey charcoal suit. His hair was short and neatly combed; his face had the same, hard-to-place features of every other porter.

'Sorry about the door,' he said, in a brisk, business-like manner. 'They've just had a new carpet put down. It catches on the bottom edge, you see. A real pain. Would you like to come with me?'

Lud reached out and touched the man's face. In the fluorescent light, his hands looked pale and dirty; they were calloused and covered with cuts and scratches. The porter didn't flinch.

'Good lad,' said Lud. 'Your brother, the one we just met, he was a fine lad, too. You're all of you fine lads.'

The man smiled at him, but didn't reply.

'Ah,' said Lud, 'and you know when to hold your tongue, too. All the better, eh?'

The porter led them down a narrow stretch of corridor, and into an open-plan office. It was late in the day, and people were winding down. Through the tinted glass, one could see the streetlights coming on outside. Nobody so much as glanced at the strange group making their way towards the exit.

'How—?' asked Gabrielle.

'I can be pretty persuasive,' said the porter.

They walked through a well-furnished lobby, with a black leather suite and a large glass table. The receptionist buzzed them out without even looking up.

'I'm sorry, sir,' said K. 'I disobeyed your orders. I accept—'

Mailfist shook his head sadly.

'There's no need to apologise, K. And anyway, that isn't why you're here.'

K looked up. Mailfist turned away, unable to meet his gaze, and got up from the desk. The office had now been cleared, and a fresh breakfast tray brought in. For once, it was untouched.

'You know very well,' said Mailfist, 'why I broke every rule in the book and came to retrieve you.'

K said nothing. Mailfist looked out of the window, the reflection of the machinery glimmering off his face.

'I wish,' Mailfist said hesitantly, 'that there was another way. You have done such service, K, but the time is fast approaching.'

K shrugged. 'But there isn't another way, is there?' he said.

'It has to happen,' said Mailfist. 'There is nothing anyone can do. Not even me.'

SIX

Veronica, Gabrielle, and Lud made their way along the tube tunnel.

'Do you know,' asked Lud, 'how I discovered this chamber?'

'No,' Gabrielle replied.

'Back in the old days, there was a barrow at the far end of my village,' said Lud, 'a tomb from some time long before our own. I forbade my people from interfering with it. Good seldom comes of such things. Then one day, a boy went missing. Not a very pleasant boy, nor a particularly clever one: but he was one of my subjects. So all of the men and women set about looking for him. We couldn't find him anywhere. He had, it was said, been seen playing on the barrow; but then again, he had also been seen playing near the river. I assumed he had drowned. There was no more we could do.'

Lud put out a hand and leaned against the curved wall of the tunnel, breathing heavily.

'Are you all right?' asked Veronica.

'Of course I am,' said Lud. 'I simply need to catch my breath.'

'We can rest for a little while,' said Veronica. 'But not too long. We've already wasted a couple of hours waiting for the trains to stop running so we could get you down here safely. I don't want to leave it much longer.'

Lud smiled.

'I understand,' he said. 'Would you like me to go on with my story?'

'Yes, please,' said Gabrielle.

Lud took a deep, wheezy breath.

'The boy did turn up in the end,' he said. 'When we had all but forgotten about him. When I had become an old man, and his mother was long dead. He came running into the great hall, his cheeks flushed, not looking a day older than when he had last been seen. And that was true, you know, he really *wasn't* a day older. He told us that he had fallen through a hole in the barrow, and scrambled straight out again. He said it was midday when he fell in, but dark when he emerged; he wondered if he might have had a bump to his head, and been unconscious without knowing it.'

'But you thought differently,' said Gabrielle.

'You know,' added Veronica, 'we really should go now.'

Lud sighed impatiently, stood upright and began to shuffle forward. Veronica took his arm.

'I knew then,' said Lud, 'what my destiny was to be. I had been worried, you see, about my city. I was approaching death. I still am. The answer to my problems lay in this chamber. Inside, I could dream out all the days of my city.' He paused. 'They want every part of this city,' he said. 'The people who took me. Every part that is, or was, or will be. They wanted to make me an exile in my own kingdom. Do you know I almost forgot how to dream?'

Gabrielle found her legs becoming suddenly heavy: the stale air of the tunnel was oppressive, and she was struggling for breath.

'Veronica,' she said, forcing out the words, 'we're near.'

'Good,' Veronica replied. 'The sooner the better.'

'What's that?' asked Lud, pointing at something on the wall.

Veronica turned to see. A point of red light was glowing on the brickwork next to her: she put her hand out to touch it and it skittered away.

She swung her head back in time to see the man pointing the gun at them. He fired suddenly: the bullet ricocheted wildly along the tunnel.

'Veronica!' shouted Gabrielle.

'I'm fine,' she replied. 'Lud?'

'He wasn't hit.'

'Get down!'

The man fired another shot. The women and Lud huddled together on the ground.

'This is one of those times when I really wish you'd think about carrying a gun!' hissed Gabrielle.

'Point taken.'

'Who's he?' asked Lud. 'Is he one of the ones who kidnapped me?'

'Probably.'

Lud made to stand up. Veronica and Gabrielle tried to stop him, but he shook them off with a strength that surprised them.

'Put down your weapon!' he shouted. 'You dare to draw upon your king?'

Gabrielle waited for the shot. She looked up and saw Lud striding towards the man. And it was the strangest thing, but Lud no longer looked ragged, or carried himself like an old man. The years seemed to have fallen away from him in an instant: his hair flowed like a lion's mane, and his robes appeared heavy and luxurious. His voice, too, was different, no longer reedy and tremulous, but deep and assured.

'You are my subject,' Lud said. 'You may be disloyal, but you are still my subject.'

'Stay back!' the man shouted. 'Stay back, and you won't

be harmed.'

Lud chuckled. 'You presume to dictate terms to me?'

'It's the women,' said the man. 'My orders —'

'Ah,' said Lud. 'The women? You think I'd give Veronica Britton to you?'

He was standing face-to-face with the man, reaching out towards the gun.

'Veronica Britton has a purpose,' said Lud. 'One you can barely comprehend.'

He grasped for the gun. The man wrenched his hand away, leapt to one side, and pulled the trigger just as another figure appeared and dragged him to the ground. The report was muffled, and there was a startled cry. Gabrielle and Veronica got up and scrambled towards the two figures fighting on the ground, but before they got there, the gun went off again.

One man lay, quite still, on the ground; another crawled on all fours towards them.

'Veronica?' said a voice that was familiar, though faint.

'K?'

K looked up at the women, and turned his head, painfully slowly, to check on Lud. He settled his weight back, so that he was kneeling up. Lud stepped forward and placed his hand on K's head as if delivering a blessing.

'My good and faithful servant,' said Lud.

K bowed.

'No time,' he whispered. He looked at Veronica. 'Get him back. Now!'

'Gabs,' said Veronica, 'you stay with K. Look after him. I'll be back in a moment, and we can get him to a hospital.' She took Lud's arm and led him towards the opening to the chamber.

Gabrielle knelt down next to K. She put his head in her lap, and held his hand. It was clammy to the touch.

'I have caught,' whispered K, 'an everlasting cold.'

'Goodbye, Miss Britton.'

Veronica and Lud stood at the entrance to his chamber. The surface rippled and black tendrils darted out, catching on their hair and clothes.

'The chamber is about to close,' Lud continued. 'I had better go inside now. I would not want your friend's sacrifice to have been in vain.'

'He's not dead yet,' said Veronica.

'No,' Lud replied softly. 'No, of course not.'

'I'm sure you'll be safe here from now on,' said Veronica. 'The Ministry will make sure of that.'

'I'm not sure I have faith in the Ministry,' said Lud. 'But I have faith in you, Miss Britton.'

He held out his hand. Veronica took it and curtseyed.

'Oh no,' Lud said, pulling her up. He shook her hand firmly, and patted her on the shoulder. 'I would ask you to join me, Miss Britton. To see out all the days of this city together. But I am afraid that will not be possible. Miss Britton, you have a great destiny to fulfil. I shall be watching.'

Before Veronica could say any more, Lud turned and walked into the doorway. The dark strands crisscrossed over his back and enveloped him. There was a noise like stone scraping, grinding, and meshing together. Then he was gone, and in the place of the opening was a gleaming slab of dark rock whose curves aligned perfectly with the wall of the tunnel. The chamber had resealed itself: and who knew how long it would be before it opened again?

Lud dusted himself down and looked around the chamber. It was much as he had left it: indeed, the fire was still burning, and the drink he had been brewing was steaming away. He leaned over and inspected it, worried that it had stewed in the pot. The colour was a pleasant tan, the smell rich and inviting.

'Perfect,' he said. 'Just the right amount of time.'

He decanted some into an earthenware cup, sat down in his armchair, and took a long, refreshing sip. Then he put it to one side, and set himself dreaming again.

'Gabrielle?'

Gabrielle started suddenly, and K let out a deep groan.

'I'm sorry,' said Veronica. 'How is he?'

'I think he's dying.'

Veronica crouched down and looked at K. His pale face shone with sweat in the torchlight, and she saw that the front of his black jerkin was glistening with blood. His eyes were closed and he looked almost peaceful. Veronica realised, for the first time, just how young he really was.

He opened his eyes slowly and looked around.

'Veronica Britton,' he said.

'K,' Veronica replied, 'we're going to have to carry you. There's a hospital not far from here. We can get you help. They can patch you up properly these days.'

K shook his head.

'No,' he said. 'No help.'

He raised his left hand weakly, and scrabbled at his collar with his blood-stained fingers.

'What is it, K?' asked Gabrielle.

'Unbutton,' K replied.

Gabrielle gently unfastened the top few buttons to reveal a brass chain. She pulled it out. K's pendant watch looked undamaged; but when she opened it up, she saw it had stopped. It felt cold and heavy in her hand.

'Time's up,' said K.

'No,' Gabrielle protested. 'K, what can we do? We must be able to do something!'

'It's too late,' said Veronica.

'Please,' K whispered, 'just take me home.'

'It doesn't seem right,' said Gabrielle.

'I know,' Veronica replied. 'But right or wrong doesn't come into it. This is how it has to be. K's death is a fixed point. It has to happen at a specific time and place. If it doesn't—well it could cause some serious damage.'

'How?' Gabrielle asked. 'How can one person more or less make such a difference?'

'You'd be surprised,' Veronica replied. 'Careful!'

The women shifted to one side to let a horse and cart pass along the narrow street. K was propped up between them. He was drifting in and out of consciousness now, his feet occasionally moving instinctively one in front of the other as if trying to help them on their way.

The sky was brilliant with stars: a pale, silver light shone through the gap between the buildings, whose upper storeys were built so far out into the street that they almost met in the middle. The ground beneath their feet was slippery, and the women had to fight to keep their balance.

'Almost there,' gasped Veronica.

At the end of the alley, a comforting orange light glowed in a translucent window. The door next to it was open; they stumbled through and into a warm, dimly lit room. K seemed to revive a little as they crossed the threshold.

The room was poorly ventilated, and thick with the tang of wood smoke. Tables, chairs, and benches were scattered around; they were filled, but not with the usual crowd. True, some were dressed in Elizabethan clothes like K's, but others were in costumes more in keeping with Roman,

Medieval, Regency, or Victorian periods, to name but a few. One, a young woman with bright red hair, was dressed in a catsuit straight from the 1960s. The only thing they had in common was that all were clad in black. There was a low rumble of conversation that stopped as they entered, as if they were expected. The occupants of the room all rose: the men removed their hats.

'Ministry agents!' hissed Gabrielle.

A stout middle-aged woman rushed forward and touched K's cheek. She ran the back of her hand gently across his skin.

'Oh, Kit!' she gasped. 'Is he dead?' She turned to Gabrielle, tears beginning to well in her eyes. 'What happened?' she demanded. 'What did they do to him?'

'Easy now, Eleanor.'

A man wearing a dirty white apron stepped forward and took the woman's arm. 'Poor K,' he said to Veronica. The man — evidently one of the barmen of the tavern — was dark-haired and bearded, his skin reddened with drink and heat from the fire. But beneath it, he was, unmistakably, another identical sibling of the porters and clerks of the Ministry.

The barman took hold of K under the arms. 'Gently,' he said. They lowered him to the ground; Eleanor took off her cloak, rolled it up, and put it under his head. The barman disappeared for a moment, and then returned with a pewter cup of wine. Gabrielle dipped a handkerchief in it, and held it to K's lips. They moved, very slightly, as he tasted it, and his tongue poked out of the corner of his mouth to catch the drops on his beard. He smiled absently, as if waking from a pleasant dream.

'What year?' he muttered.

'1593,' Veronica replied. 'You're in Deptford.'

'I knew it,' K replied. 'I'm home.'

Eleanor sobbed. K opened his eyes, but seemed not to see them.

'Is that Eleanor?' he whispered. 'Oh Eleanor, I'm sorry it had to be here, in your house.'

'Rather here than anywhere else,' she replied. 'Everyone's here, Kit. Everyone.'

'Good,' K replied. 'How fitting.'

He coughed suddenly, and groaned with pain. Gabrielle took his hand.

'Veronica,' K said. 'I will see you again. Or rather, you'll see me.'

'What?'

'It's not happened yet. For you,' he replied. 'It's something to look forward to.'

He was again racked by coughs. He slumped back, closed his eyes, and sighed.

'Death isn't so bad,' he said. 'It's the only point when all of the possibilities of one's life are finally set in stone.'

His head went limp, and lolled back.

SEVEN

Veronica knew that Gabrielle was upset: she had managed to toast half a dozen slices of bread to perfection over the fire, without burning a single one.

'I'm so sorry,' Veronica said.

Gabrielle looked at her distractedly.

'About K,' Veronica added.

'We could have saved him,' said Gabrielle.

'No we couldn't.'

Gabrielle put her teacup down.

'K's death was preordained,' Veronica continued. 'It was always going to happen in that room, on that night. By working for the Ministry, he got to dictate the terms, at least a little bit. It's more than most of us can hope for.'

Veronica got up, and knelt down next to Gabrielle. She was crying freely, her tears glistening in the light from the fire.

'I don't understand,' she said. 'What's the point of anything? If it's all predestined, why bother?'

'Oh, Gabs.' Veronica sat on the arm of the chair, and put her arms around Gabrielle. 'You might as well say that fish are destined to stay in the sea. We exist in time, that's what we're made for. That's the only reason anything means anything: because everything comes to the end at some point.'

Gabrielle nodded. A lock of hair came loose from behind her ear: Veronica tucked it back into place and kissed it.

'You know what?' said Gabrielle. 'The strangest thing is that I didn't even like him all that much.'

'He wasn't easy to like,' Veronica agreed.

'What about the Empire?' said Gabrielle, wiping at her tears with her sleeve.

'What about them?'

'They're still around.'

'Of course they are,' said Veronica. 'But we stopped them from deposing King Lud. We stabilised reality. Not a bad day's work, although — technically — it took place over thousands of years.'

'What about the future? The one we visited? Is that real? Is that what's going to happen?'

'It's one possible future,' Veronica replied. 'What we did today made sure it isn't the only one. I can't pretend the future of this city is all good, Gabrielle. But there are so many futures — so many possibilities. There are versions of this city where the buildings are made of crystal and ice. There are versions that exist underwater. There are some where the very stones of the pavements sing to each other.'

'Then there's the one ruled by the Empire.'

'Yes,' said Veronica softly. 'Then there's that one.'

'What do they want?'

'Control,' said Veronica. 'Why, I've no idea.'

'And the Nameless?'

'They're no friends of the Empire. That's for sure. On the one hand, it means we're not alone. On the other, the fact that the Nameless have even noticed them terrifies me. It means we have to take the Empire very, very seriously indeed.'

Gabrielle nestled down, and Veronica stroked her hair

gently. They looked into the fire for a while: it was burning low, and would need another shovelful of coal soon to stop it from going out entirely.

'Vee?' said Gabrielle.

'Yes?'

'Who was it?'

'Who was who?'

'Out there in the future. The voice from the ironclad.'

'Oh.'

'Were you hoping I'd forgotten?'

Veronica got up and walked over to the window. She lifted the drapes and looked at the street outside. A thick greenish fog had descended, one that pressed against the window-panes. For all she could see, they might have been the only people alive, in the only house left standing in the city.

'Yes,' she said, 'I was hoping that.'

'So who was it?'

Veronica let the curtain fall, but didn't turn around.

'Forget about it. It was a mistake.'

Veronica walked around the back of Gabrielle's chair and sat down again. Gabrielle handed her a piece of toast.

'Thank you,' she said.

'Vee—?'

'You're not going to forget about it, are you?'

Gabrielle shook her head.

'All right,' said Veronica. She took a big bite out of her slice of toast: Gabrielle had covered it with thick layers of butter and strawberry jam, just the way she liked it. She washed the sweetness down with the dregs of her tea, feeling the combination fill her with a pleasant warmth. Then she spoke again.

'Gabs,' she said. 'I think that whoever the Empire are, and whatever they're trying to do, it may be—at least partially—my fault.'

'What do you mean?' asked Gabrielle. 'How can it possibly be your fault?'

'How much has Carter told you about me?'

Even in the dying firelight, Veronica could tell that Gabrielle was blushing.

'He said you were engaged once,' she said.

'Did he say who to?'

'He said an agent. A Ministry agent.'

Veronica nodded. 'His name was John. John Doyle. Code-name D.'

'Carter said that he was lost. That he went on a mission one day, and never came back.'

Veronica raised an eyebrow. 'Really? Is that what he said?'

'Well isn't it true?'

'Yes,' Veronica replied, 'and no.'

'So what *did* happen to him?'

Veronica poured herself another cup of tea. It was luke-warm and bitter.

'I loved him,' she said. 'That's what happened to him.'

'And that was him? In the future? He's with the Empire now?'

'It sounded like him. But I have no idea how it could be. It can't have been John, Gabrielle, because I killed him.'

PART THREE

The Dead Letter

ONE

Veronica was woken by the sound of someone knocking at the door of her flat.

She slipped quietly out of bed, put on her blue silk dressing gown, and tiptoed out of her bedroom into the hallway. She looked briefly into the spare room, where Gabrielle lay asleep.

The knocking started again. Veronica closed the door gently and crept along the hall. She crouched down and looked at the chink of light at the bottom of the door: two feet were silhouetted there. She put her ear to the wood. The person on the other side was shifting their weight from foot to foot, making the floorboards creak.

'Miss Britton!' a man's voice said suddenly. 'Miss Britton, I need to talk to you.'

Veronica unlocked the door and opened it a crack.

'Frayn!' she hissed. 'What on earth do you mean calling around at this time? I've had rather a trying day.'

The man who stood in her hallway was dressed in clothes that were probably very expensive and fashionable when they were bought, but were now threadbare and shabby. It was as if he had got himself perfectly outfitted a couple of decades before, and then decided that the issue of dress was not one worth bothering with again until the clothes were practically falling off him: which, Veronica knew, was precisely the case. He was holding a large wicker basket in one hand. Veronica caught a flash of movement within.

'Eh?' said Frayn, stroking his chin.

'Frayn,' whispered Veronica, 'it's the middle of the night.'

'Is it?' Frayn reached into his waistcoat pocket and pulled out a watch. He put on a pair of round spectacles that were tied around his neck with a ribbon, and looked at it.

'No, no,' he muttered. 'That one's no good. That one hasn't worked for years.'

He put down the basket, dug deep into the pockets of his overcoat and pulled out another watch, holding it to his ear to make sure it was ticking.

'That's more like it,' he said, and looked at the time.

'Good heavens!' he said. 'I had no idea. I really am so sorry. I've been wandering the streets for — well, it seems like hours. In fact, now that I think about it, it must have *been* hours. You see,' he replaced the watch and put his hand to his forehead, 'I've had a little bit of a shock.'

'You'd better come in,' said Veronica. 'But be quiet. My friend's asleep. And don't forget your basket.'

Frayn sat down without removing his coat, putting the basket down roughly next to him. A miaow of protest and the sound of claws scratching against wickerwork came from within.

'I must apologise again for the intrusion,' said Frayn. 'Only I didn't know who else to turn to. You know, Miss Britton, I've been thinking. And I've realised that over the years, you're the only person I've ever met who I can really trust.'

'Hadn't you better let Hodge out?' said Veronica. 'She sounds like she's getting terribly tetchy in there.'

'What? Oh, of course, of course. I suppose the sooner she gets to know your rooms the better, eh?'

Frayn pulled back a bamboo rod that held the basket closed, and flipped open the lid. A marmalade cat sprang out, miaowed once, and looked quizzically at her owner.

'Here we are, Hodge,' said Frayn. 'This is Veronica Britton's flat. You remember Miss Britton, don't you?'

The cat skulked around the back of her chair and started scratching at her carpet.

'Hodge,' Frayn pleaded, 'please don't do that my dear.' He smiled apologetically at Veronica. 'I'm so sorry, Miss Britton. She isn't normally like that. She's usually the most affectionate of creatures. I'm afraid the past 24 hours have been somewhat unsettling for the both of us.'

Hodge miaowed as if in assent, and then walked off to explore the rest of the flat.

'Ah, that's good,' said Frayn. 'It seems she's settling in already.'

'Settling in?' Veronica replied. 'What do you mean *settling in*?'

'I decided that you would be the best person to look after her,' Frayn explained. 'As I said, you're the only person I could ever really trust, Miss Britton.'

'That's very kind of you. But I can't look after your cat.'

'Oh, Hodge is very little trouble,' said Frayn. 'Just two meals a day and a warm fireplace. Speaking of which, I don't suppose you have any smoked mackerel? She loves smoked mackerel. It might be nice to give her a piece now.'

'Frayn,' said Veronica, 'why on earth have you come around here in the middle of the night to ask me to look after your cat?'

'I told you. You're the only person I trust. How many times have I said that now?'

'It's more the middle of the night bit I was wondering about. Do you have to leave town suddenly? Is that it?'

'Oh no,' said Frayn, 'I've never set foot outside of London, and I don't intend to now.'

'So why are you lending me Hodge?'

'I'm not lending her, Miss Britton. I'm giving her to you.' Frayn sighed and reached into another of his overcoat pockets. He pulled out a small black box.

'I'm here to give you Hodge,' he said, 'because I may not be around to look after her much longer.'

'What? Are you ill?'

Frayn shook his head.

'No,' he said. 'Here.'

He handed Veronica the box.

'It's from the future,' said Veronica, holding it up to the light. 'A recording device. Hold on.'

She examined the buttons, and pushed one that was marked with a triangle. The recorder switched on, and a voice started speaking. It was breathless and hoarse, but quite clearly Frayn's.

'I don't have long,' it whispered, 'so I'll have to be brief. They'll be back soon. You must keep the Dead Letter safe at all costs. That's what they want, and they mustn't get it. Tell Miss Britton – tell her – '

There was the sound of an explosion, and the recording stopped.

TWO

'We're going to be late,' said Veronica, as the carriage rattled up the hill towards Hampstead. 'What took you so long?'

'It wasn't me,' Gabrielle protested, 'it was her.'

Hodge, curled up in her lap, purred smugly.

'Her fur was untidy,' Gabrielle explained. 'She needed a good grooming.'

'Couldn't you have left her at home?' asked Veronica.

Both Gabrielle and Hodge shot her a sulky expression.

'No,' Gabrielle replied. 'She'd get lonely. And anyway, it would be odd to go to Frayn's, and not take her with us.'

'Quite,' said Veronica. They travelled on in silence for another few minutes before she spoke again.

'I couldn't help but notice —'

'What?'

'Since Frayn came around —'

'Yes?'

'Well, you've been sleeping in my spare room.'

Gabrielle smiled. 'I meant to thank you. It's really been very kind of you.'

'And once or twice — *not* sleeping in my spare room.'

'That's been very kind of you, too.'

'Gabrielle, have you moved in?'

'Would you like me to?'

'I—Gabrielle, could you answer the question?'

'Probably.'

'Probably?'

'Probably.'

'Right,' Veronica sighed, looking out of the window. 'Glad to have cleared that up.' She leaned out and called up to the driver. 'How much further?'

'Nearly there!' the driver bellowed.

Veronica ducked her head back in.

'He said that half an hour ago,' she whispered.

Gabrielle shivered. 'I think he's telling the truth this time. It's getting cold.'

'Hampstead,' said Veronica. 'Practically the back of beyond.'

The carriage sped through a set of rusting gates and onto a gravel driveway. It arced to the left, giving the women a view of a grand house framed in the window. It was a large, ungainly building: the centre was a tumbledown red brick structure, probably from Queen Anne's day. The roof and the two wings that framed it had obviously been added at a later date: though it was hard to say exactly when, because it was impossible to focus on them. They seemed, out of the corner of one's eye, to be in constant motion. Even if a single detail—a Georgian sash window, say, or a futuristic glass door—was discernible, it would transform itself into something else if you just looked away from it for a moment.

The night was cloudy and starless, but a bright glow came from the lawn. As they got closer, they saw that an aura of light encircled a single tree—an apple tree, in fact, its boughs heavy with fruit. Next to it stood a shabby figure, waving at them.

'Frayn!' shouted Gabrielle.

Frayn ran up to the women as they stepped out of the carriage.

'Good evening, ladies,' he said, his teeth chattering. He looked behind them and into the carriage anxiously. After a few seconds, Hodge emerged from its depths and ran over to the front door, where she pushed her way through an ornately-decorated silver cat flap and into the house.

'It's good to see you again, Frayn,' said Veronica. 'How are you bearing up?'

'Not so bad,' said Frayn. 'Of course, my little fund-raising evenings are always a little tense but this — well, this is of a different order of magnitude. It's never pleasant sitting around waiting to be murdered.'

Veronica nodded sympathetically. 'Yes. I know.'

Frayn produced a small black box from his coat pocket and held it up.

'Here it is.'

Veronica took it and pressed a button. Nothing came out but a low, barely audible hiss.

'It seems you're right,' she said. 'Where did you find this?'

'One of the rooms upstairs. On the fifth floor, or maybe the sixth. Anyway, it leads into some sort of office. Lots of people sitting around, gazing at screens. Interesting thing about the future, Miss Britton. Work or play, all they do is stare at screens. Anyway, this was lying on one of the desks. I thought it looked just like the one I found in the maze, so I picked it up.'

Veronica looked at the recorder thoughtfully, then handed it back. After Frayn's midnight visit to her flat, she had advised him to let her know when he found another of the recorders— or, more accurately, the same recorder from an earlier point in time. Such a finding, she reasoned, would indicate that the clock had started, and that the attempt on his life would be made soon. And here it was: in pristine condition, discovered on the morning of one of Frayn's dinners during which he scraped around for donations to keep his impressive — if ramshackle — collection of curios running. Frayn's life was not one of fixed points: she had done a background check, and discovered numerous possible deaths, some decades before this, some far into the future. So he could be saved, and the murderer — whoever it was — flushed out.

That, at least, was the theory.

'Do you think we could discuss this inside?' asked Gabrielle.

'Ah yes,' said Frayn, and took hold of the heavy door knocker. It was an immense block of iron, and he strained to lift it before letting it swing back and strike the metal plate. The door trembled and the echo reverberated in the still night air. After a few moments, the door opened an inch, and a rheumy eye framed by wrinkled skin peered suspiciously out of the gap.

'Steeple, my good man,' said Frayn. 'Any chance you could let us in?'

'You go on ahead,' Veronica said to Gabrielle. 'I just need to pop back into the carriage and get my umbrella.'

THREE

'What do you want?'

The shopkeeper had been waiting all morning to confront the character hanging around the front of his establishment. It was a chilly day outside, one that had started with freezing fog and was now bitingly cold with a darkening sky that promised snow. It was weather that, in combination with a heavy meal the night before, had made him feel decidedly dyspeptic.

Usually he tolerated people who just wanted a few hours' respite from the elements. This man, however, had gone too far: he was beginning to put the other customers off, ones who would actually spend their money. And that, the shopkeeper thought, was where one had to draw the line.

The man was dressed in a ragged dark robe; his hair was tangled and his face dirty. In fact, he would have given the impression of a wild character were it not for his eyes. They were pale, a watery blue colour, and there was a look of gentle unworldliness in them that almost stopped the shopkeeper in his tracks. He looked away from the man and spoke again.

'I'm sorry,' he said, 'but you can't stay here. I have a business to run. My livelihood, you know.'

The man nodded gravely.

'If you have no business here, then I can't allow you to stay.'

The man nodded again.

'I have,' he said.

The shopkeeper frowned.

'You have what?' he asked.

'I have,' the man said, anxiously, 'business.'

The man reached into the top of his robe and pulled out a folded piece of paper. He handed it to the shopkeeper carefully. It was heavy, smelled of smoke, and was slightly scorched at the edges. The shopkeeper took it over to the table at the rear of the shop and unfolded it, leaning over to examine it in the weak winter light.

A moment later, he stood back and drew a deep breath; he placed his hand experimentally on the sheet, and pressed against it as if expecting his fingers to go straight through. He looked up at the man, who was staring at him expectantly. There was a pang from his sternum, which he did his best to swallow back down and ignore.

Forcing some degree of control into his voice, the shopkeeper spoke.

'Did you come by this honestly?' he asked.

The man nodded.

'How much were you thinking of asking for it?'

'Some food,' the man replied, 'and something to drink.'

'Come, come,' said the shopkeeper, 'this paper is worth far more than that, man!'

He paused anxiously; his wife had always said that his kind heart would be his downfall, and she was, once again, about to be proved right.

'All I really need,' said the man, 'is something to eat.'

Before the shopkeeper could answer, the door at the front of the shop was flung open, letting in a blast of cold air. A cabman walked in, his hat pulled down firmly, and a scarf covering his nose and mouth. His high boots clattered on the bare boards of the shop floor.'Ah,' said the cabman, 'there you are. I heard rumours you were in the district.'

The ragged man looked back in confusion.

'Don't worry,' the cabman said, reassuringly, 'this happens from time to time. I'm the one who rounds up the waifs and strays.'

Still the ragged man looked blank, although the shop-keeper noticed a certain tension developing in his posture: he was getting ready to bolt.

'Come on,' said the cabman casually, and reached a gloved hand out to rest on the ragged man's shoulder.

The ragged man's jaw trembled and he stammered out his next few words.

'I—I don't remember,' he said.

The cabman shrugged.

'There's no need to remember,' he said. 'And there's no point in trying. I know what it is to be as you are now. If you come with me, you'll have a warm bed, food, and compan-ionship. There is little more a man can ask for in this cruel city, eh?'

The cabman turned to the shopkeeper, who found himself nodding in agreement.

'Very well,' said the cabman decisively. He clapped the ragged man on the back, and the shopkeeper—not entirely of his own volition—held the door for them as they walked out into the street. The cabman opened the door of a box carriage that stood outside; the ragged man got in and sat down. Then the cabman climbed up into his seat, took hold of his whip, and the vehicle pulled away into the crowds on the Charing Cross Road.

The shopkeeper went back inside, and straight away

noticed the paper still lying on the table. He took it up hurriedly and ran out into the street again; but the cab was long gone. He returned to his shop and examined the paper again. It was, he knew instinctively, a thing of great value: he had given nothing for it, not even the meal the ragged man had asked for, so to sell it on would be tantamount to stealing. There were many in his trade, he knew, who would be able to convince themselves that this was an act of God, a stroke of luck to be accepted with a clear conscience. But the shopkeeper wasn't that sort of man, as his ledger of accounts would show.

The shopkeeper decided he would keep the paper safe for the ragged man, who would undoubtedly return when he was in better shape. Though now that he thought about it, the man's face was not exactly a memorable one — the shopkeeper could recall that it had been dirty, and that there was a certain troubled vacancy in the expression, and that was about it. No matter. That was a problem for another day.

The shopkeeper folded the paper carefully and placed it in one of the volumes that was shelved behind the counter. Then, satisfied that he had done all he could for now, he sat down and waited for the next customer. The pain came again, a little sharper this time. It radiated all the way up to his jaw. Still, he was sure that it was nothing serious.

FOUR

The dining room was lined with paintings of long-dead Frayns and views of London from the vantage point of Hampstead Heath. Thick curtains were drawn across the windows to keep in the heat: a fire idled in the grate, and light came from a few candles in the middle of the table. The ceiling, Gabrielle noted, was very high: or at least, she assumed it was, because it wasn't actually visible. The walls simply stretched up and up into an indistinct, shadowy blur.

There were four guests sitting down to dinner with Frayn, Veronica, and Gabrielle: an elderly lady, who was nevertheless dressed in the latest fashion; a dark-haired man in his thirties who seemed to be having the time of his life; and an odd pairing, a bearded, bald-headed man in late middle age who stared rather severely over a golden pince-nez, and a young, pale girl who could have been any age between 16 and 20, who sat in sullen silence. The older man, Professor Bendrix, was describing his work with great enthusiasm as his soup grew cold: the girl, Hettie, had long since finished hers and was eyeing up his bowl as if waiting for the right moment to pounce.

'She was just wandering the streets, babbling about an explosion,' Bendrix said. 'So they brought her to the hospital thinking she'd been in an accident of some sort.'

'Gracious,' said the older woman, Mrs Thorne. It was one of the few interjections that anyone had managed so far. She turned to Frayn. 'You must give me the recipe for this soup, dear boy. Shame on you for keeping something this delicious to yourself all these years.'

'I'm afraid that won't be possible,' Frayn replied. 'It came out of a tin.'

'Oh.'

'They couldn't find anything wrong with her,' Bendrix continued, 'physically, that is. So they referred her over to me. My specialism, you see, is the art of Mesmerism. It's been shown that it can work very well in retrieving lost memories.'

'And did it work?' Veronica asked.

'Not quite,' said Bendrix. 'Even under the deepest levels of influence, Hettie was unable to remember anything about her past.'

There was a general murmur of sympathy from around the table, and a growl from Hodge, who had finished a plate of smoked mackerel laid out for her on a saucer on the floor and was evidently wondering if there was any more where that came from.

'However,' Bendrix continued, with the air of a man showing an invincible hand at poker, 'we did discover some most—ah—extraordinary abilities.'

'What abilities?' asked Gabrielle.

'She was able to talk and write with a far higher degree of intelligence than that with which I had previously credited her,' he replied. 'Indeed, she was able to discuss politics in some detail, and even express some considered opinions of her own!'

Veronica coughed, which Bendrix took to be an expression of disbelief. He nodded across the table at the young man, Nyman. Nyman looked back at him distractedly.

'It's the strangest thing,' said Nyman. 'I think I just felt a spot of rain.'

'Never mind that now, man,' said Bendrix impatiently. 'Tell them about the time you came to see Hettie.'

'It really was the most remarkable thing. I had lost one of my watches — not the most valuable item, but one of great sentimental value. The watch my parents bought for me, in fact, before I started in my first post. Back when I was a mere clerk.

'I'd searched high and low for it. Couldn't find it anywhere. I suspected it had been stolen, but it was hardly the sort of item one could call the police in over: and even if I did, where would they start? I talked the thing out with a friend at my club, and he mentioned that if I went to one of Bendrix's demonstrations at University College Hospital, there was a young woman there who might be able to help me. I thought, well, there's nothing much to lose other than a couple of hours of my time, so I went along.'

Bendrix nodded proudly. Hettie remained silent and indifferent, although Gabrielle noticed she had managed, with great sleight of hand, to swap her soup bowl with his, and had already consumed half of its contents.

'Hettie is a most sensitive subject,' said Bendrix. 'She falls into the trance state remarkably quickly. Sometimes I do not even need to perform the passes. Strong emotion, I have noticed, is one trigger, although I am sure there are many others that have yet to be identified.'

'Does it hurt at all?' Mrs Thorne asked Hettie. Hettie looked up from her soup and shook her head.

'Quite the opposite,' Bendrix said. 'She doesn't remember her trances.'

'Go on with your story, Nyman,' said Frayn.

'Well,' Nyman continued. 'He blindfolded her, and asked

her to list the contents of people's pockets. She got them all absolutely spot on. You'd be surprised what some people carry in their pockets. Anyway, when it came to me, she said that there was something missing. Bendrix asked her what it was, and she replied that it was a watch. She was right: I'd kept that watch in my pocket every day of my working life, and even though I knew it had gone, I kept putting my hand to the place it should have been whenever I wanted to check the time. Bendrix went on to ask her where it was, and she gave a description of a shop off the Seven Dials, of a man — who sounded suspiciously like one of my clerks — handing it over to a pawnbroker there. I didn't believe it at first. When the demonstration was over, I returned to my office and summoned the man to my room. He confessed everything: he'd got into trouble over some gambling debts, and had noticed my watch resting on my desk when I popped out for a moment. Decided to take it, win his money back, then redeem it for me.'

'A sad story indeed,' said Mrs Thorne. 'Gambling is such a scourge amongst the young these days. Why, only the other day, I was reading an account of—'

'Quite a feat, I'm sure you'll agree,' Bendrix interrupted, seemingly alarmed that the conversation about his prodigy was about to turn into one on the evils of gambling.

'Quite,' said Veronica. She was looking intently at Hettie, who stared back at her for a moment with incurious eyes before picking Bendrix's bread roll off his plate and eating it.

'One might say,' said Bendrix, grinning, 'that with girls such as Hettie, and doctors who know how to handle their powers, there will no longer be any need for detectives.'

'Possibly,' Veronica replied, still staring at Hettie as the sound of a light shower started up in the background.

It seemed remarkably clear and crisp, given the layers of fabric insulating the window panes.

'I say,' said Mrs Thorne, looking up, 'it seems to be raining.'

The others around the table followed her gaze. It was true: at the centre of the table, a fall of rain was sprinkling the candles, that flickered and hissed.

'How remarkable,' Nyman exclaimed. 'I knew you needed to do some repairs, but really, I had no idea—'

The room was suddenly filled with a blinding white flash. A few seconds later, a thunderclap shook the walls and made the plates and cutlery rattle.

'Oh dear,' said Frayn, raising an umbrella. 'A storm is coming.'

Veronica also opened her umbrella as the rainfall became heavier. Gabrielle snuggled up underneath. The servants, she saw, were taking oilskins out of one of the side cupboards and passing them around.

'Just a light one, I expect,' said Frayn, reassuringly, as the water fell through the holes of his umbrella and trickled down his face. 'It'll pass in a minute or two.'

The servants rushed over to the table, now dressed in their heavy waterproof overcoats and sou'westers, and held umbrellas over the guests. There was another flash of lightning, and the thunder followed closer this time. Gabrielle noticed Hettie flinch as if she had been struck. She looked around in surprise: her eyes narrowed, and a sly expression came over her face, as if she were taking careful note of everything and weighing up her next move. The lightning flashed again, and in an instant, she was back to her normal vacant state.

'I say,' said Bendrix, 'it's not dangerous, is it?'

'Oh no,' said Frayn. 'Not in the slightest. Just a dratted nuisance.'

There was a sudden gust of wind that turned his old umbrella inside out. He fiddled with the metal arms, trying to right them. The next gust blew the whole thing clean out of his grasp. The lightning and the thunder now struck simultaneously. It was as if someone had tossed a bomb into the room: guests and servants hit the floor, deafened by the blast. Gabrielle found herself eye to eye with Hodge, who had staked out a decent sheltered spot at the first hint of precipitation. The cat padded over and nestled into her arms.

There was a terrible sound of fabric tearing; the tablecloth was lifted up and flew into a wall, scattering metal, glass, and china along the way.

'Follow me!' shouted Frayn, clinging to the carpet to avoid being blown away.

The servants helped the dining party towards the door as the rain turned to ice cube-sized hailstones that fell with a ferocious clatter. Frayn, shielding his eyes from the lightning, placed a hand on the doorknob and tugged. The door swung open with a violent crash, revealing the tranquil setting of a well-lit drawing room beyond. Gabrielle felt Hodge spring from her and dash for the safety of the hearth; as the guests limped into the sitting room, Frayn handed them each a freshly-laundered white towel. Hodge rolled in front of the fire, toasting first one side, then the other.

'I'm terribly sorry about that,' said Frayn, as he dried his hair. 'It's never been quite that bad before. Sometimes it's all sunshine and soft summer breezes, you know.'

'Oh, Frayn,' said Mrs Thorne, and tutted like a nanny scolding a favourite child.

'I am not going back in that room,' said Bendrix. 'Are we, Hettie?'

Hettie shrugged and grinned.

'Phew,' said Nyman. 'That was — well, I've never seen anything like it before. A room with its own weather system!'

Frayn chuckled.

'I've lived here all my life, and the old place still surprises me. Always another door to open, you know. Always something new to explore.'

'Frayn,' said Mrs Thorne, 'it's impossible to be an explorer on an empty stomach.'

'What?' said Frayn. 'Eh — oh yes, I see what you mean. I was thinking we might want to go to the Abbey for the next course.'

FIVE

He was, he reflected as he hurried up Haverstock Hill in the gathering gloom, a man who had got himself into serious trouble.

He tapped the pocket of his overcoat to reassure him that the book was still there.

It was not.

He stopped and stood stock-still for a moment, gripped by sheer panic. He tried to think back to the tube, to his journey from the Charing Cross Road up to Belsize Park. Why had he put the book in one of his external pockets, where anyone could pick it up? After all, it was compact enough to fit into his inside pocket. So —

He pressed his hand against his chest, and felt the reassuring solidity of the book there. That was exactly what he had done: transferred it from his outer to his inner pocket without even thinking about it.

He wiped the sweat from his forehead and headed on up the hill. He knew, instinctively, that he was being followed: once or twice during his journey he had thought that he caught a glimpse of someone. He tried to think of what exactly he was going to do when he got home. Naturally, the best thing was to contact the Ministry straight away and have them send someone round. He had a telephone number scribbled in the back of his diary; from what he remembered, it was an old-fashioned number from the time before area codes. He would have to guess as to how it might have been modified over the years. Or possibly, when it came to the Ministry, things like telephone numbers didn't change. He would just have to try.

It had seemed like a joke when he first started at the Home Office all those years ago. His duties had included, according to a small paragraph right at the back of his contract, liaison with the Ministry of Chronic Affairs. It had turned out that no one in his department had ever visited the Ministry, met any of its staff, or indeed heard from them in living memory. Most people didn't even believe it existed. Yet here it was in his jacket pocket: a clear and present risk to the country that only they were equipped to handle. It was written on fragile paper and had been folded into a volume dumped in one of the one pound book racks on the Charing Cross Road, but it was potentially more dangerous than the atomic bomb.

He thought back to the time, just a few hours earlier, when he hadn't even known of the paper's existence; when his life had been safely, cosily dull. A simple routine of sleep, food, and work, with the occasional variation or excursion, of which his decision to browse the second-hand bookshops after leaving the office had been one.

He wondered what had drawn him to the book. He normally glanced into the barrows on his way into the shop, and had picked up a bargain or two from time to time. This volume, however, was not exactly one that caught the eye. Perhaps, he thought, it was not a coincidence that he had been drawn to it. Perhaps someone, or something, had meant for him to pick it up.

The book's spine was plain; a muddy brown leather binding whose title had long since rubbed off. He got the feeling that no one had so much as glanced inside it for many years: there was a brittle *crack* as he opened it, as if the spine had long since rotted away. A piece of paper fluttered down; he had picked it up and unfolded it.

What happened next was a blur. He tried to play it back in his mind as he quickened his pace up the hill. He had stumbled into the shop, pressed a ten pound note into the hand of the shopkeeper, and not even waited for his change. Then he had run, shaking and faint, down to Leicester Square tube station. The shock of what he had seen had been so great that it was as if he had been hit around the head: his ears were ringing, a high-pitched sound like someone drawing their finger along the rim of a glass. The sound was still there: he had the horrible feeling that it was actually coming from the paper itself.

He was so distracted by this thought that he nearly walked straight past the entrance to his flat. He retraced his steps, and put his hand in his pocket for his keys. He realised he had been pressing his hand firmly against the book in his inner pocket all the way up the hill, and that it felt unsafe to remove it, even for an instant. He stole a quick glance back over his shoulder, and thought he saw a dark figure darting quickly out of sight. Hurriedly, he turned his key in the lock, and stepped into the hallway.

As he did so, he tripped over something and sprawled headfirst onto his hall carpet, into the pile of unsorted junk mail and letters for long-gone occupants. He looked up and saw a flash of red fur as a bristled tail whipped silently away from the door. It could have been a cat, or possibly a fox. They were equally likely possibilities in London these days. He got up and closed the door firmly. Then he ascended the stairs to his flat.

The lights were on when he got in. Had he left them on this morning? He couldn't remember. No time to worry about it now. He sat down at the small writing desk next to the window in his living room, pulled out his desk diary, and flicked through the pages to find the number of the Ministry. He dialled the number, and as it rang he cradled the telephone in the crook of his shoulder, took a blank envelope from his drawer, and carefully folded the precious paper inside.

The phone was still ringing. He wondered if they were still working at this hour, although he had heard somewhere that the Ministry ran around the clock. Still cradling the phone, he wrote the Ministry's name on the envelope and sealed it: then he placed it inside a second envelope, on which he wrote

To be opened in the event of my death.

There was a click and a rattle as the person at the other end picked up. 'Hello,' said a voice; it echoed as if the person was bellowing into an old-fashioned mouthpiece.

'I need to speak—' the man consulted his desk diary again. 'I need to speak with—er—Mailfist. Urgently.'

'Might I ask who is calling?'

The man began to reply, but was cut off by a *snap* as the line went dead. He tried pushing the button in the cradle, but the phone failed to come back to life. Replacing the handset, he thought about what to do next. The only option was to go down to the Ministry in person: he had a vague idea that it was somewhere in Shad Thames.

The front door was suddenly forced open with a crash, and the man heard footsteps rushing up the stairs. He examined the window: he couldn't remember when he had last opened it. He pushed the catch open, and tried to raise the sash. It refused to move. He pressed at the edges to try and loosen it in the frame, all to no avail. It might be easier, he thought, if he had been able to let go of the envelope that he still held crumpled in his hand, but it seemed now to be stuck there with glue, as if it were some living thing that had latched on to him. He was still fiddling with the window when a group of men in black uniforms spilled into his living room. He turned slowly to face them. Their leader was a young man with pale, porcelain skin and coal-black eyes. His gaze was instantly drawn to the letter in the man's hand.

'Give it to me,' he said, 'and we'll leave you alone.'

The letter now trembled and burned in the man's hand. He had a sudden vision of London reduced to a vast plain of concrete, cement, and steel, all the elegant buildings and greenery gone, the river drained dry. A fiery place of labour and misery, and one that expanded outward, ever outward, encompassing first the south of England, then the north, then the remainder of the British Isles. It grew further still, under the oceans, its grey tendrils extending to spread the fires of its satanic industry to Europe, to the Americas, to the whole world.

'I'm sorry,' said the man, and shook his head. 'I will die before I let you get your hands on this.'

'Yes,' said the leader. 'You will.'

Whether it was the force of the bullet, or whether the man leapt intentionally through the window, no one could have said. But within an instant, the civil servant flew through a blizzard of glass and splintered wood, and out into the damp air of the gathering night. Time slowed down for him, and for a moment he thought that he was hanging suspended in the air, that some miraculous force had intervened. Then he felt himself tumble slowly, painfully slowly as if through a thick, viscous liquid, and down to the pavement below. And then he was past thinking, or feeling, anything ever again.

SIX

The garden was quiet. It was the wholesome silence of a type of life that asked nothing more than to go about its daily business undisturbed. The guests sat at a dinner table in the middle of the grass whilst Hodge chased a butterfly.

'Much more pleasant,' said Bendrix.

'Can't they see us?' asked Nyman, as two monks in plain dark robes walked through the cool, silent cloisters.

'Seen and not seen,' Frayn replied. 'They know we're here, on some level. On another, I suppose you'd call it a conscious level, they don't. If you draw attention to yourself, they'll talk to you for a little bit. But they soon forget.'

'I have observed the same phenomenon with Hettie,' said Bendrix. 'When I have her under the influence, I can persuade her that she has lost the faculty of sight; even though her eyes are open, indeed, even though they are reacting perfectly normally in response to the stimuli of light and movement, she is quite convinced that she cannot see a thing.'

'Oh dear,' said Mrs Thorne. 'That sounds most distressing.'

Hettie reached across, picked a roast potato from Bendrix's plate, and popped it in her mouth.

'You had better not say any more, Bendrix,' Frayn said. 'Otherwise Mrs Thorne will be setting up another of her charities. This time to address the plight of mesmeric prodigies.'

Mrs Thorne tittered, and put her hand in front of her mouth. Her fingers were slim, almost skeletal, lined with age and bedecked with onyx rings. Frayn winced and rubbed his left eye, as if struck by a sudden headache.

'I suppose that's invisible, too,' said Nyman, indicating a dark wooden door of the sort that lined the corridors of Frayn's house: only this one was set squarely into the wall of the cloister.

'Quite,' said Frayn.

'Where are we, anyway?' asked Gabrielle.

'My best guess is that this is the old Kilburn Abbey,' Frayn replied. 'At some point in the Middle Ages.'

'I've never heard of it.'

'I don't suppose you would have,' said Frayn. 'There aren't many contemporary accounts of it. It was destroyed, along with all of its records. Some sort of fire, I understand, though the details are vague.'

A sparrow alighted on the table and began to hop from plate to plate, looking for scraps. Hodge, sensing potential prey, sprang up and pounced on it. The bird flew just as the cat's paws scuffed its tail. Hodge sat up and chattered angrily as it escaped.

'Well,' said Frayn, reaching out to stroke the cat, who turned and gave him a playful nip, 'I think the second course was far better than the first. Now, shall we go for coffee? You'll understand that I'm a very modern gentleman: I don't believe in separating out the sexes. We'll go to a delightful place on the first floor. No, Nyman, there's no need to take your napkin.'

'I would like,' said Frayn, with the air of a pasha demanding a particularly opulent dish, 'two lattes, one hot chocolate, one mocha—' He turned to Veronica. 'That's a sort of blend of coffee and chocolate, you know. A great boon.'

'I know,' Veronica replied.

'Oh, and three plain coffees, without milk. And some cakes. Yes, some of those nice cakes with the coconut icing.'

'Isn't it marvellous?' Frayn whispered, as the young man in the green apron rang up their order behind the counter. 'The trick is to ask for what you want in one go, before they forget you exist.'

'Quite,' said Veronica, looking across at the rest of the party. It was raining outside, and the cafe was stuffy and overheated: the windows had misted up, making the street an indistinct blur of dark umbrellas and raincoats, with the occasional red cloud of a bus passing by. Mrs Thorne and Nyman shared a small sofa, whilst Bendrix, Hettie, and Gabrielle sat opposite. Hodge was curled up in Gabrielle's lap, fast asleep, her paws and ears twitching as she chased butterflies in her dreams. With the exception of Gabrielle and Hettie, the guests were as stiff and uncomfortable as if they had suddenly found themselves in the jungle surrounded by wild animals. Gabrielle was preoccupied with Hodge, whilst Hettie was examining a silver pocket watch. When Veronica caught her eye, Hettie slipped the watch away so quickly that she couldn't see where it had gone. A moment later, Bendrix went to check the time: as Veronica turned back to the counter, he had started frantically patting down his pockets.

'That'll be 25 pounds and 55 pence,' said the young man in the apron, reading the figure off the till and then glancing around from side to side, unsure of exactly who he was supposed to be addressing.

'Ah yes,' said Frayn, turning to Veronica and raising an eyebrow. 'I always forget that one has to pay. I don't suppose you'd have any of the relevant currency—'

Veronica sighed and delved into one of her belt pockets.

'You must remember to add this to my bill,' said Frayn. 'Expenses, eh?'

They returned to the others with the drinks and cakes.

'Rather rich,' said Mrs Thorne, sipping at her hot chocolate, 'but very pleasant. Thank you.'

Frayn gave her a little bow, and she giggled.

'You know, even when you were a little boy, you were quite the gentleman.'

'Frayn?' said Veronica, for he had suddenly turned white and was tugging at his collar to loosen it. 'Are you all right?'

'Oh yes, yes,' said Frayn. 'It's just a bit—well, a bit close in here.'

'Maybe you should go outside for a moment or two,' Nyman suggested. 'Take some air, you know?'

Frayn smiled at him mischievously, the colour returning to his cheeks.

'Why don't you go for a little stroll?' he asked.

'Eh?'

'Go on,' said Frayn, winking at Mrs Thorne. 'Just a quick turn.'

'All right,' said Nyman, intrigued. He got up, walked over to the door, and tugged at the handle. It was stuck fast. He tried again, with more force: nothing. He stood back to examine the lock and the hinges, just as another of the customers brushed past him, opened the door with ease, stepped outside, and put up an umbrella. Nyman darted behind them into the open doorway, only to bounce back as if he had hit a thick pane of glass.

Frayn laughed. 'Sorry, Nyman. I never can resist playing that trick.'

Bendrix tutted and muttered something disapproving under his breath.

Nyman returned to the sofa and sat down.

'Well, it defeats me,' he said. 'How does it work?'

'You should know, Nyman,' said Frayn.

'Me?'

'Yes. You've done a bit of prospecting in your time, haven't you?'

Nyman nodded.

'And you know how the ground shifts around. Sometimes quite violently, with eruptions and whatnot? So everything's pushed out of place, so you get layers that should be one on top of the other lying side-on instead, and so forth.'

'Yes, but I don't see —'

'This house,' continued Frayn, who had lapsed into the pedantic tone that he used when giving guided tours, 'is built on — indeed, partially constructed out of — just such an area. Only one composed of splintered time, rather than splintered rock. Many years ago, there was a great upheaval of some sort or another, which threw off all these little bubbles, or cells, if you like, of space and time.'

Mrs Thorne cleared her throat.

'I once visited a house in Dorset,' she said, 'in which the walls were made entirely of rock that held fossilised animals. Funny little bodies, and claws, and tails wherever one looked.'

'Precisely,' said Frayn.

He polished off the rest of his mocha with a noisy slurp.

'Ladies and gentlemen: if we're all finished, shall we look at the cabinets? I promise you the most exciting part of the evening is yet to come.'

SEVEN

She was a young woman, somewhere in her late teens or early twenties, wearing a black leather catsuit — something she'd seen on a television programme and liked, Mailfist imagined. Her hair was a shocking, artificial shade of red.

'J,' he said, 'it's good to see you again. Do have a seat. Tea?'

J glanced around the office with that strange look she had that was simultaneously distant and alert. How did K describe it? Yes that was it: 'Casing the joint.' Satisfied, she slipped into the chair and sat looking at him intently. Instinctively, his hand went to check his watch was still there. It was — for now at least.

'Thanks. I'm parched.'

Mailfist poured her a cup and handed it over. She took it in both hands and smiled at him with the winning grin that he suspected had got her out of all sorts of trouble in the past. He cleared his throat.

'You're here, J, because I have a mission for you. One of the utmost importance.'

'Goody. Tell me more.'

Mailfist handed her an envelope.

'The full details are within. In essence, it's a reconnaissance mission.'

J sighed and played with the ends of her hair.

'I've been receiving some disturbing reports recently, J. The clerks thought it was the machinery at first, but everything's been tested and it seems the Ministry is working as well as she ever was. There's no doubt about it: something is very amiss in the state of space and time somewhere in North London.'

J rolled her eyes.

'It looks,' he continued, 'as if there has been — for want of a better word — an explosion somewhere around the medieval period. The ripples are making themselves felt at this moment; and they go backwards in time as well as forwards.'

'What do they think caused it?'

'The clerks? They have no idea. They doubt that any natural force could have produced it, but there's always an outside chance. I need you to go back, J, and look into it. Just look, that's all. Don't intervene, don't touch anything, and certainly don't steal anything. All I want is a written report on my desk in a week's time. I want to know what happened, how, why, and, if possible, who's behind it. Do I make myself crystal clear?'

J smiled and winked.

'I'll get right onto it,' she said.

'Good. See the technicians if you need any equipment. And dye your hair. That is, dye it again. Something more natural than one of your usual colours. Inconspicuous. Black should do the trick.'

'But I've only just—'

'Black, and that's the end of it. I don't want you burned as a witch.'

J uncrossed her legs and stood up. She replaced her teacup on the desk.

'Observation only, J. Remember that.'

J was already halfway out of the door. 'I will, sir.'

'Good. I expect to see you back here in a timely fashion.'

'Time is relative, sir,' said J, as she stepped out and shut the door firmly behind her.

Mailfist shook his head and poured himself a final half-cup of tea with the dregs of the pot. He splashed a little milk in and looked around for the spoon.

It was gone.

EIGHT

'This is new.'

Veronica pointed at a stuffed woolly mammoth that stood in a glass cabinet at the centre of the room. It was the first item Frayn had unveiled as he walked around pulling dust sheets off the exhibits.

'Yes,' said Frayn, pausing in his tracks. 'I have no idea how it got into the house. It made an awful mess downstairs, and then it escaped into the garden. Tore up the grass terribly, and completely ruined the cook's vegetable patch. Before I could do anything about it, the woman got her husband to shoot it with the old elephant gun he brought back from India.'

'Poor thing,' whispered Gabrielle, putting her hand on the glass.

'Indeed,' Frayn said. 'It hadn't harmed anyone. But there it was, dead in the vegetable patch, and I thought we might as well make use of it. Tough meat, though. I don't recommend it.'

Frayn continued around the room, uncovering the exhibits. It was a vast hall with a stone floor; its walls were lined with dark wood, and thick, rough beams supported the whole structure.

'The Frayn Collection,' said Frayn, 'exists to enlighten and to entertain. It has been in the family for a long time. I have tried to audit the number of rooms in this house, and found the job impossible: it appears the total is still rising. So we will be making new discoveries, I hope, for many years to come.'

Gabrielle walked over to one of the cabinets and looked inside. The plaque at the top simply said 'Light'. It was filled with all sorts of devices: Davey lamps, battery-operated torches, tallow and church candles, and some small, cube-shaped objects that emitted a clean, steady glow. Hodge, too, pressed her nose up against the cabinet, as if carefully examining its contents. Gabrielle looked down at the cat. There was something different about her: coming back to the Frayn collection seemed to have given her a new lease of life. From being the placid lap cat Gabrielle had been looking after, she had turned into a lithe, alert creature.

'We receive thousands of visitors every year,' Frayn went on, 'from all over the world. If I were to charge them an entry fee, I would be a rich man indeed. If I tried to unlock the secrets of the — er — more advanced artefacts, I would be as wealthy as — well, maybe as wealthy as you, Nyman.'

Nyman smiled. He was gazing into a cabinet labelled 'Vessels': one that held clay beakers, jewelled goblets, and Styrofoam coffee cups.

'But I've never charged anyone to see my collection,' said Frayn, 'and I never will. As for the technology — I allow myself a little bit of speculation as to its use and function, but I never go any further than that. There are, of course, some things I would never put on display.'

'Yes, Frayn,' said Bendrix, sharply. 'I've been meaning to talk to you about that.'

'What's that, girl?' Gabrielle asked, kneeling down to look at Hodge, who held something in her mouth, something pale and limp like a dead bird. Bendrix ignored her.

'You want my money,' Bendrix continued, 'but what good will mankind get from it? What good will *I* get from it, eh?'

'This museum doesn't run itself,' Frayn replied. 'There is the business of exploration, identification, cataloguing. Then there is the cost of the upkeep of the building and, needless to say, security . . .'

Bendrix looked over at Gabrielle and Veronica, who were both kneeling down next to Hodge, trying to get her to release the damp piece of paper clasped in her jaws.

'You mean paying private detectives to look after cats?' Bendrix snorted.

'Her coat's damp,' said Veronica. 'Gabrielle, why is her coat damp?'

'Looking after this house isn't some sort of hobby, you know,' said Frayn. 'Nor is it a source of income. It's a solemn duty. People come here to learn. It is a humbling experience, to see the richness of London time. Clears their minds of any sort of prejudice or sense of superiority over others.'

'Fine words,' said Bendrix. 'But think of how much good could be done with some of the objects here.'

'Much good,' Frayn replied, 'and much evil. Who is to say which is which?'

'The Dead Letter,' said a voice that was clear, prim, and authoritative.

'What?' said Veronica, turning to see who had spoken.

'The Dead Letter,' Hettie repeated, marching towards Hodge.

'Nobody move!' Bendrix hissed. 'She's in a trance!'

He approached her timidly, almost on tip-toe. He touched her elbow, but she shook him off.

'Don't you dare touch me!'

'Perhaps it's best if you leave the child alone,' said Mrs

Thorne.

Hettie knelt down next to Hodge, and stroked her in a long, elegant gesture from her ears to the very tip of her tail. Hodge gave out a throaty growl of pleasure and arched her back.

'Thank you,' Hettie said, and took the paper in one hand.

'Hettie,' said Bendrix, softly. Hettie looked around to see Bendrix and Mrs Thorne standing behind her. Hodge spotted them too, gave a high trill of distress, snatched the paper back, and darted away, weaving around the cabinets and out of the room.

'Veronica Britton.'

They all turned again to look at Hettie. She was staring at Veronica, as if she had suddenly recognised an old friend.

'You must keep the Dead Letter safe at all costs. That's what they want, and they mustn't get it. Tell Miss Britton — tell her —'

Hettie suddenly went limp and collapsed in a heap. Nyman ran to catch her.

'Well you're her doctor,' he said to Bendrix. 'What do you recommend?'

'Rest,' said Bendrix, hurriedly. 'She needs to recuperate. Sometimes she sleeps for as long as 48 hours after her trances. Frayn, could you ring for the servants?'

'I'm afraid not,' said Frayn.

'Why not?'

'They've left. I sent them away.'

'Why, man?' said Nyman. 'Whatever for?'

'It's — ah — their one night off a year. They have a special ball to go to. It's — traditional. Yes, it's traditional.' He looked around shiftily.

'Well in that case, it's up to us. Bendrix, you take her legs. Mrs Thorne, I wonder if you could accompany us?'

'Certainly,' Mrs Thorne replied. The two men carried

Hettie out of the room. Mrs Thorne cast an anxious glance at Frayn as she left.

As soon as they had gone, Frayn walked over to the mammoth cabinet and leaned against it, his eyes closed.

'Oh my word,' he said. 'Miss Britton. Miss Pendleton. Did you hear what she just said?'

'Quite,' Veronica replied. 'Look, we need to find Hodge and get that bit of paper back.'

Frayn shrugged. 'We can look,' he said. 'But that cat knows this house better than I do. Sometimes she goes missing for weeks at a time. I'm sure she has all sorts of adventures.'

'Weeks?' said Gabrielle, dismayed.

'Sometimes,' Frayn repeated. There was a scratching noise at the door. 'On the other hand,' he said, 'sometimes it's just a couple of minutes. Coming, dear!'

Frayn walked over to the door and opened it. Hodge strode in and miaowed at them.

'Dear, dear,' said Frayn, kneeling down to tickle her under the chin. 'Did the nasty man shut you out?'

'The paper's gone,' said Veronica. She raced over and knelt next to the cat. 'Where did you put it?' she asked. Hodge stared at her, and for one moment looked sincerely as if she was about to answer the question. Then she miaowed again and trotted over to Gabrielle, who picked her up.

'Gosh, girl, you're heavy!' she gasped. A look of surprise crossed her face. 'Veronica,' she said, 'Hodge's fur is dry.'

'The way I see things—' Veronica started.

Frayn held up his hand.

'Better wait for a moment, Miss Britton.'

There was a faint rattling noise in the distance, and a breeze of stale air. A moment later, the train rushed past them in a blaze of electric light.

'Sorry,' said Frayn. 'Please continue.'

'Frayn,' said Veronica. 'I'll never understand why you chose this room as your study.'

Veronica, Gabrielle, and Frayn were sitting in an abandoned underground station. The floors were covered in thick, luxuriant rugs, and a set of shelves, chairs, and a green leather-topped writing desk had been installed. Light came from a single bulb housed in a stained glass lampshade, the sort that would become fashionable sixty or so years in the future. Only the walls hadn't been touched: they still carried fading advertisements for Strand cigarettes, Horlicks, Bovril, and days out in the country. It would have been a perfectly cosy little hideout were it not for the tube trains that screamed through every three minutes.

'Mainly comfort,' said Frayn. 'I never could sleep as a boy: my room was — is — above this room. I used to like hearing the trains rattling through below. Made me feel like I wasn't alone, you know.'

He opened one of the drawers in his desk and took out a half-full bottle with a hand-written label.

'Could I offer you ladies a drink?' he asked.

'Yes,' Veronica and Gabrielle replied, simultaneously.

Frayn fished around in his drawer, and pulled out a chipped teacup. He wiped it out with his handkerchief.

'I'm sorry,' he said, filling it to the brim, 'you'll have to share.'

The whisky — wherever and whenever it was from — certainly had a kick to it. Gabrielle coughed, spraying Hodge, who licked her fur appreciatively.

'So, Miss Britton,' Frayn said, leaning back in his chair and taking a deep swig from the bottle, 'the servants are safely away. The would-be murderer has been lulled into a false sense of security. Means, motive, opportunity, and all that.

The only question is: who is it?'

'It's hard to tell,' Veronica replied. 'I have some ideas, but nothing solid. How long have you known these people?'

'Mrs Thorne, of course, since I was a boy. She was widowed at a young age, and sort of attached herself to the Frayns. Never had any children of her own, you see. I say, is it warm in here?'

'Not particularly.'

'Odd. Anyway, Nyman has given us quite a bit of money over the past few years, and I've known Bendrix on and off for a little longer. He used to live around these parts.'

'I don't know why you invited him,' said Gabrielle. 'He seems beastly.'

'Beastly and rich, unfortunately.'

'And what about this girl he has with him?' asked Veronica. 'I could swear I've seen her somewhere before.'

'I think the poor thing is as much a mystery to herself as she is to anyone else. Bendrix might not be the ideal guardian, but falling in with him is hardly the worst thing that could have happened to her. Look, I don't want to put you under any pressure, Miss Britton, but—'

Frayn delved into the desk drawer again as another train rushed past. Its occupants sat reading newspapers and listening to personal stereos, their minds elsewhere. As the rattle died away, Frayn pressed the button on the scuffed recorder.

'I don't have long,' said the voice, 'so I'll have to be brief. They'll be back soon. You must keep the Dead Letter safe at all costs. That's what they want, and they mustn't get it. Tell Miss Britton—tell her—'

A shot fired, terminating the recording.

'So you see,' said Frayn, pulling the new, blank version of the recorder from his pocket and placing the two side by side on the desk. 'You haven't stopped me being murdered yet.'

'The Dead Letter is the key,' said Veronica. 'If only Bendrix hadn't scared Hodge away like that. Why, Frayn? Why must it be protected at all costs?'

Frayn was staring at the two recorders. 'I don't know,' he said. 'In fact, I have a horrible feeling that I might have given myself the notion.'

'What do you mean?'

'I found a machine with my voice captured on it, telling me the Dead Letter is hugely important. Maybe that's how I found out it was hugely important. So when the moment of crisis comes, that's the message I leave to be discovered and — oh dear, I'm feeling rather giddy again.'

'I'd try not to think too much about it,' said Veronica. 'Gabrielle, could you go over to the Ministry? Sound out Mailfist. I was hoping to keep him out of it, but I think the stakes are too high now.'

'Veronica, I —'

'Just get back as soon as you can.'

'Will you look after Hodge? Both of you?'

'Ah.' Frayn smiled. 'I see you've become as attached to her as I am.'

Hodge, asleep in Gabrielle's lap, swatted her paw at an imaginary mouse.

NINE

Veronica woke with a start. She was sitting in a heavy leather armchair outside Frayn's room, keeping watch. Or she was supposed to be, at least. She pulled out her watch and looked at its luminous hands: how long had she been asleep for? No more than a couple of minutes, she was sure of that. Yet even drifting off for 30 seconds could make all the difference. She simply had to stay awake. She felt light-headed and feverish; her throat was sore, and she wondered if she was beginning to catch a chill. It must have been the rainstorm earlier.

During her short sleep, she had experienced a strange dream composed of a patchwork of impressions: lutes playing, and the smell of a hog roasting; the squawk of station announcements; the howl of a rioting mob; hooves on cobblestones; a bird tweeting; and a pen scratching against paper.

Then there was one sound—a murmuring—that was still there in the background. She sat up in the chair, feeling the hairs rise on her scalp, the perspiration bead and cool.

The words were indistinct, but the tone and the rhythm were sickeningly familiar.

'That's what they want, and they mustn't get it. Tell Miss Britton—tell her—'

Veronica leapt out of the chair. Hodge, who had been

sleeping in her lap, sprang free and scurried away. The source of the voice, Veronica realised, wasn't Frayn's room; it was coming from down the hallway. She sprinted towards it, but before she could lay her hand on the door the whole corridor shook with the report of a gun.

Veronica kicked open the door and dived inside, hitting the ground and rolling. But the room was empty. A window was open: she ran towards it, but rebounded off an invisible barrier. Flung back onto the floor, she yelled in frustration. Her cry was answered by a stifled groan. Looking up, she saw, in a crumpled heap next to the wardrobe, the broken body of Frayn. She crawled over and knelt down next to him, resting his head in her lap.

'All my life,' he whispered, looking her in the eye. 'All my life.'

Frayn closed his eyes. He took a few more shallow breaths, and fell silent.

'Miss Britton? Is everything quite all right?'

Veronica looked up. Frayn stood in the doorway, holding a candle.

'I heard a heck of a racket. I wondered if — oh my goodness.'

Frayn staggered forward, nearly dropping the candle as he knelt down next to Veronica and his own recently deceased body.

'I say,' said Frayn, his voice trembling, 'would you mind awfully if we covered me — covered that thing up? It isn't very pleasant to look at.'

'Can you stand?' asked Veronica.

Frayn nodded and got slowly to his feet, supporting himself on one of the bed posts. Veronica whipped off the top blanket, and covered the body on the floor. Outside they heard Hodge scratch at the doorpost before moving off to patrol the hall.

'I suppose you made sure—' Frayn began, sitting down again.

'What?'

'I really am dead, aren't I?'

'It looks like you will be soon, if we don't work this thing out.'

Veronica examined the clock on the mantelpiece, and checked the time against her own watch.

'Frayn, why didn't you tell me one of these rooms was a version of your bedroom from an hour into the future?'

'I didn't know. When I explained to Nyman that the house was like a geological phenomenon, I was oversimplifying. Whatever the event that triggered this was, it's not settled down yet. New rooms are bubbling up to the surface the whole time. Nothing's settled. In fact, things seem to be getting less stable.'

As he spoke, he took the new recording machine from his pocket and examined it, pressing the buttons and letting the tiny wheels inside run backwards and forwards.

'That reminds me,' said Veronica. She knelt next to the body, lifted the blanket and examined the body as Frayn looked away. She eased the tape recorder from its hand, and covered the body back up. Then she rewound the tape, and pressed the 'play' button.

'That's what they want, and they mustn't get it. Tell Miss Britton—tell her—'

Frayn shuddered and covered his eyes.

'So now we have three of these things,' said Frayn.

'In a sense,' said Veronica. 'Your tape recorder—the blank one—becomes this one. Then this one somehow travels back in time and lands in your maze. Then you find it, and it ends up in your desk drawer.'

'Are you sure my death isn't inevitable, Miss Britton? Only it's looking like a done deal right at the moment.'

'Don't lose hope, Frayn. I've done my research. I'm going to have a quick look around, and see if there are any clues as to who shot you. Gabs will be back shortly, and then we can begin to piece it all together.'

Mailfist, dressed in a suit of heavy black velvet, finished applying a little marmalade to a slice of toast with a fussy precision.

'I meant to come and see you earlier,' said Gabrielle. 'We were terribly sorry about what happened to K. And so very grateful for what he did.'

Mailfist winced at the mention of his dead agent's name. He finished with the knife and put it gently to one side; then he took the silver spoon out of the marmalade jar, licked it clean and placed it next to the knife.

'One needs to watch these things,' he explained. 'Spoons have a way of going missing around here.'

Mailfist took another sip of tea, and washed it around his mouth. The *tick tock* of the Ministry echoed through his office.

'That's quite enough small talk. What time is it outside?'

Gabrielle checked her watch. 'Half past one.'

'Morning or afternoon?'

'Morning.'

Mailfist shifted in his chair. 'I don't know why you couldn't have come at a more reasonable hour,' he grumbled.

'It's a matter of some urgency,' Gabrielle replied. 'A man may die tonight because of the Dead Letter.'

Mailfist got up abruptly from his chair. He still held his teacup limply in his hand; its contents spilled over the carpet.

'The Dead Letter,' he murmured.

'Mailfist, what is it?'

'All I know about the Dead Letter,' he said, not looking at her, 'is that it is something very, very dangerous indeed. Many times I've heard things about it, here and there. One rumour was that it burned in the Great Fire. Good riddance, I thought.'

'It's still here,' said Gabrielle. 'I think I caught a glimpse of it tonight.'

Mailfist turned around. He looked pale and worried.

'You saw it? You must be mistaken. Who has it?'

Gabrielle took a deep breath.

'Mailfist, there's no easy way to say this. I think a cat's got it.'

There was a knock at the door, and Mailfist's secretary walked in carrying Hodge in his arms.

'Miss Pendleton,' he said. 'You were followed.'

'Well?' asked Frayn. He had shifted position slightly so that he now sat at the foot of the bed, facing away from the dead body. He had taken a small hip-flask and collapsible cup from his dressing-gown pocket and was treating himself to a drink. The fact that he had yet to offer any to Veronica only worsened her mood.

'Nothing,' said Veronica. 'I'm afraid whoever did this was a professional. I suppose I could try digging the bullet out of your body down there—'

Frayn winced, and poured himself another shot.

'Sorry, Frayn.'

Frayn drained the cup in one gulp.

'That's quite all right, Miss Britton. I accept that we cannot afford to be delicate at a time like this.'

'Anyway, it's possible the Ministry would be able to match it.'

'The Ministry.' Frayn sighed. 'Do you know how long and hard I've fought to keep their noses out of my business? It's all going to change now. Sometimes I wonder if I should have simply submitted to my fate.'

'Frayn,' said Veronica, 'the Dead Letter, whatever it is, sounds like something extremely dangerous. We know that whoever wants it—and I already have a pretty good idea who it is—would kill you for it. They wouldn't have any compunction about that, if I know them—but it does expose them to a certain amount of risk. I think that a lot more than the Frayn Collection is at stake tonight.'

Mailfist led Gabrielle through the glass corridors of the Ministry, Hodge at their heels. Periodically, the cat stopped, her eye caught by the motion of the machinery in the walls; she dabbed at the moving cogs experimentally once or twice, and then hurried along to keep up with the two humans.

'Where are we going?' asked Gabrielle.

'There's no way to explain what you're about to see,' Mailfist replied, 'so I'm not even going to try.'

'That's my father,' said Frayn. He had become drunk and maudlin, and was looking at the photographs in a frame on the mantelpiece.

'I think we need to get back to your room, Frayn. Your proper room, that is,' said Veronica.

'It's odd, isn't it?' said Frayn, running his finger over the glass. 'They're like little cells in time themselves, aren't they? Photographs, I mean. A bit of the light that fell that day, captured on a thin bit of paper, imprisoned forever. These were taken with a special type of camera that turned up in a photographic store. It's on the second floor, towards the back of the house. The most amazing invention. You just press the button on top, and the pictures come out ready-developed.'

'Come on. We need to be back before—'

'This,' said Frayn, pointing out a stern, bald-headed old man, 'was my father. He's still here, you know. One of the rooms downstairs leads out to a little patch of the Heath from about 25 years ago. Some days, when I go there, I catch a glimpse of the old man taking his constitutional. He walks past a line of trees, one that marks the boundaries of the cell. I shout his name, but he never notices, of course.'

Frayn pointed out another picture. 'This was me back in the fifties.'

The younger version of Frayn had a surprised expression as if someone had just crept up on him from behind. He was standing next to a younger, seated Mrs Thorne. She was looking at him affectionately.

'More like a mother to me than anything else,' said Frayn. 'And I suppose I was like the son she never had.'

'Frayn, this isn't the time for—'

'Oh!' Frayn put his head in his hands and slumped forwards. Veronica took him under the arm and jerked him upright.

'We have to get back to your room,' she said.

'To bait the trap, you mean?'

Veronica ignored his remark and got him to his feet. As they made their way out of the door, he held back for a moment.

'I say.' He gestured over his shoulder. 'You don't suppose *he* might still have a full flask in his pocket, eh?'

Mailfist swung open the vault door and stepped inside the room, followed by Gabrielle. The atmosphere was warm and moist.

'The light's supposed to work automatically. Never mind—one moment.'

Gabrielle heard a revving noise like a dynamo starting up, and in an instant the room was flooded with light. She started back in horror. She was standing in a room that stretched back as far as the eye could see. It was entirely filled with identical, inanimate figures dressed in plain black robes. At first glance they could be taken for waxworks: but looking more closely, one could make out the slight rise and fall of their chests, the minute flaring of the nostrils that indicated they were breathing. She took a few steps along the line. Their eyes, she realised, were following her.

'Good God!'

'I'm sorry, Miss Pendleton,' said Mailfist, dusting down the shoulders of one of the specimens in the front row. 'It is a bit of a shock if you're not expecting it.'

'What are they?'

'Don't you recognise them?'

'Of course.' Every man in the room was a replica of the porters and clerks of the Ministry, albeit clean-shaven and—in some way—unformed. Like the basic template from which all the variations she had met were taken.

'They're quite all right,' Mailfist said, reassuringly. 'And quite harmless.'

He took out his gold watch and started swinging it from side to side. 'Now,' he said, 'let's find out what's going on.'

'So what do we do now?' asked Frayn, sitting down on the bed. He was still drunk, but at least the short walk along the corridor to his room—his *real* room, as Veronica thought of it—had cleared his head a little.

'We wait. We intercept whoever the assassin is, and find out what they're up to.'

'What about Hodge?'

'She wasn't in the hall. I think she's probably taken herself off somewhere safe.'

Frayn was about to reply when they heard a floorboard creak outside.

'What should I do?' he whispered.

'Hide!'

Frayn crept over to the wardrobe, got inside, and pulled the door to after him.

'Oh my goodness,' Veronica heard him say. 'What on earth are you doing in here?'

Before she could ask what he meant, the main door handle rattled. Silently, she stepped across the room and flattened herself against the wall.

Mailfist shone a small torch into the eyes of the porter. He repeated the process at intervals along the line before he turned, satisfied, to Gabrielle.

'Well, Miss Pendleton, go ahead and ask.'

Gabrielle looked uncertainly at the identical men, all staring straight ahead with the same blank expression. Hodge ambled into the room and began to use one of the men as a scratching post. He didn't even blink.

'Which one of them should I address?'

Mailfist waved a hand carelessly. 'It doesn't matter,' he said. 'They should all know the answer.'

'I don't understand.'

'I think of them as the individual cells that make up a brain. Or the individual letters that make up a word.'

Gabrielle turned to the nearest man.

'Hello,' she said.

The man relaxed and smiled at her. He spoke pleasantly and fluently.

'Hello, Miss Pendleton. How delightful to see you again.'

Once he had spoken, he resumed his default position.

'Have we met?' asked Gabrielle.

The next man along the line spoke.

'We have. And we will again. Many times, and in many places. But now we understand you wish to ask us something.'

Mailfist nudged her.

'Go on,' he whispered.

'I wish to know what is contained in the Dead Letter.'

The men were silent as the Ministry clocks ticked away for precisely sixty seconds. Then someone spoke at the back of the room.

'On the 23rd of January, 1948, a man by the name of Matthew Judd stopped on the corner of the Charing Cross Road and New Oxford Street to buy a packet of cigarettes. His usual brand being out of stock, he decided to . . .'

Another began. 'On the 27th of April 2011, Pamela Louise wondered if the novel she was reading might actually be a biographical account of her whole life up to that point . . .'

'. . . 1598 a party of men made off with the timbers that made up the old Theatre and transported to the site where the new structure was to be built . . .'

'Miss Brattland woke from a troubled sleep on the night of April the 15th, 1809. She got out of bed and walked over to her window as the clock chimed three . . .'

'What?' said Gabrielle.

The door was nudged open a couple of inches, and a light ginger snout protruded through the gap. Hodge slunk into the room cautiously, looking over her shoulder. She kicked the door shut behind her with her hind paws. Veronica knelt down to face her.

'Where did you get to?' she asked.

Hodge emitted a muted growl in reply. Veronica looked

closer as she stepped out of the shadows. She was holding the Dead Letter in her mouth.

'Good girl,' said Veronica, her other hand closing around the letter. Hodge inclined her head slightly to one side, and then stopped, her ear pricked as if she had just heard someone approaching. She lifted her paw and, with a smooth, professional gesture, scratched Veronica on the back of her hand. Her claws were razor sharp.

'Ow! Veronica cried. 'You little—'

She reached out and picked the cat up. Hodge wriggled and squirmed in her arms.

'Come on, girl,' she said, 'calm down.'

The floorboard outside creaked again, this time with a heavier tread. Hodge mewed in alarm. Veronica ran over to the wardrobe, opened the door and flung in the cat without looking.

'Sorry, Frayn,' she said. 'Can you keep her quiet?'

The door to the room was kicked open. Veronica heard the click of a gun being cocked, and saw its polished barrel gleam in the candlelight. She ducked as the first shot was fired, hitting the wardrobe door. She leapt forward and tackled the would-be assassin, who sprawled backwards into the hallway, the gun flying to one side. Veronica rolled again, snatched up the gun and pointed it at—

Nothing. She caught a glimpse of a dark figure vanishing around the corner and down the stairs. She was just about to give chase when a horrible thought occurred to her.

Veronica returned to the bedroom and looked at the wardrobe, which now had a hole right through the middle of it.

'Frayn!' she shouted. 'Frayn, are you—?'

There was no reply. Bracing herself for the worst, she turned the handle and opened the door.

Mailfist walked ahead of Gabrielle and Hodge down the corridor of the Ministry. He was keeping a furious pace, and the machinery seemed to have speeded up to keep time.

'I can't believe you just did that!' he shouted, without looking back at her.

'How was I to know?' gasped Gabrielle.

'You've broken my library!'

'I'm sure they'll stop eventually.'

'Eventually? And when might that be?' He took his watch from his pocket, consulted it, and flung it down to swing on its chain as he ascended the spiral staircase to the main hall. 'Half an hour. And they're still going strong. They could be at it for weeks. Months!'

'Well don't you have some sort of emergency switch? Can't you turn them off and on again?'

'Pah!'

Mailfist opened the doorway to the main hall and stepped inside. Hodge scampered after him, keeping low as if hunting birds. Gabrielle followed, breathless, a few moments later.

'Oh dear,' she said.

The clerks had frozen in position. Some were bent over papers writing, others lifting cups of tea to their mouths. One or two had frozen mid-stride as they were walking across the office and had fallen to the ground, stiff as waxworks. The cacophony they were making rolled around the office.

'It was cold on the morning of April the 7th, 1380, as Nathan Pinnock made his way to the courtyard of the George Tavern in Southwark to begin his pilgrimage . . .'

'Fire, fire everywhere. They burned all they could see, then came back to turn over the ashes for any survivors . . .'

'As he was descending the escalator, the call came for a doctor to attend an emergency in the station . . .'

Hodge jumped up on one of the tables, and began to wolf

down some half-eaten toast. Mailfist turned to Gabrielle, his face turning first red, then very pale with anger.

'Miss Pendleton,' he said, 'please show yourself out.'

'Well,' said Bendrix, looking at his watch and then at the clock on the mantelpiece, 'this is quite intolerable.'

'I'm hungry,' said Hettie, sullenly.

'I'm very sorry, my dear,' said Mrs Thorne, patting her hand, 'we'll just have to be patient.'

Nyman got up, walked across the breakfast room, and looked out of the French windows at the lawn.

'At least it's a nice morning,' he said. 'Well, apart from over by the apple tree. Looks like night over there.'

'Five minutes,' said Bendrix. 'I will give him five minutes. Then, Hettie, you and I are leaving. And he shan't see me, or a penny of my money, ever again.'

'What I don't understand,' said Mrs Thorne, 'is where the servants are. They may have been away last night, but why weren't they back this morning? Do you imagine someone's told them not to come?'

'Some sort of practical joke, you mean?' said Nyman.

'Yes, I suppose so. I can't think why else anyone would do such a thing, can you?'

Hettie shrieked suddenly and jumped out of her chair as something shot out from underneath and headed for the door.

'What?' shouted Bendrix. 'Oh. It's only that blasted cat.'

Hodge, seeing the closed door, turned around and miaowed loudly.

'Poor thing,' said Mrs Thorne, reaching out to stroke her. 'Look, she's wringing wet.'

Hodge scurried back over to the door, sitting down as if expecting someone.

'Was it raining last night?' said Nyman. 'Anyway, I thought she spent most of the night—'

The door opened, and the cat darted through the gap. The next instant, Gabrielle ran in holding Hodge in her arms.

'Veronica?' she said.

'Miss Britton evidently has a more pressing engagement elsewhere,' said Bendrix, curtly. 'As has Frayn.'

'I say,' said Nyman, 'do you need any help?'

Gabrielle shook her head. 'I need all of you to stay in this room.'

'On whose authority?' Bendrix demanded.

Gabrielle didn't answer. She walked out and closed the door behind her. A moment later, they heard the key turn in the lock.

Gabrielle put down Hodge, and made her way up the stairs towards Frayn's room. She stopped halfway up and knelt down to examine the carpet. She pulled a magnifying glass from her pocket, and inspected the pile more closely.

No doubt about it. There was a set of muddy paw prints.

She turned and looked at Hodge, who licked her front paw and began to wash behind her ears. Then Gabrielle continued up the stairs and along the corridor, following the prints. They led to a room whose door was half-open. She pushed it the rest of the way and entered.

On the floor, covered by a blanket but still recognisable, was a body. Gabrielle ran forward to examine it. As she approached, however, she felt lightheaded, and saw the air in the room ripple like a heat haze. When it resolved, the body had gone. Hodge was crouched where it had been, scratching at the carpet.

Gabrielle frowned and looked up. She had seen something out of the corner of her eye; something glowing with that

peculiar aura that told her it didn't belong there. She realised that the picture frame on the mantelpiece was glowing
brightly, almost as if it was on fire. She picked it up and ran
her hand over it.

'Miss Pendleton?'

She dropped the frame. It fell to the floor and shattered.

'It's all right, Miss Pendleton. It's only me.'

Nyman stepped into the room.

'How did you get out?' asked Gabrielle, kneeling down and
pocketing the photographs from the broken frame.

'Hettie,' Nyman replied. 'It turns out she's handy with a
hairpin and a lock. I say . . .'

He walked over to the wardrobe, whose door was hanging
open, and ran his finger around a hole in the centre.

'Ragged around the edges,' he said. 'And it looks pretty
fresh.'

Gabrielle stepped over to examine it. Then a thought
struck her, and she reached through the clothes that hung
in the wardrobe. Nothing. She could feel a cold, solid wall
behind.

'What did you expect to find?' asked Nyman.

'Shh.' Gabrielle shut her eyes, closed the door, and rested
her hand lightly on the wood.

A collection of images crowded in on her all at once, like
multiple exposures on a photographic plate. She tried to
focus, let one layer of events float to the surface, but it was
almost impossible. Too many branches of time and space
were growing, hydra-like, from this one spot.

She ducked instinctively as something swung towards her
face. It was a branch: a branch from one of the overgrown
hedges in the maze. And there was Veronica, running ahead
down the path, catching her dress. The image was replaced
by one of Frayn sitting up in bed as someone made their way

down the hall to his room; speaking a few words into a tape recorder as he got up to face an intruder. A bullet hit him and he staggered backwards, falling to the floor: falling but never hitting it, dissolving as he went. Then he was hiding in the wardrobe: this time, he recorded his message and looked up, seemed to recognise someone — moved forward, and . . .

There was a jerky black-and-white image of a girl dancing in a nightclub, men in top hats and monocles looking on appreciatively. Then a darkening street, a window shattering, a body falling.

'It's no good,' said Gabrielle, opening her eyes. 'I can't make sense of it at all.'

Frayn might have mentioned, thought Veronica, that there was a doorway to the maze inside his wardrobe. And he could have made a better effort to maintain it, at that. She had to stop every few paces to untangle herself from the hedges, which could have done with a good pruning.

Then again, Frayn didn't change his clothes that much. A disruption in the fabric of space and time, if located in his wardrobe, could easily have escaped his notice for a while. The question was what time period this maze existed in. It was night — that much was clear, at least. But was it in the past, or the future?

There was a flash of movement just ahead of her, near the ground. Her eyes had adapted to the darkness now, and so she was able to recognise it for what it was.

Hodge. She stopped, turned around, and looked back at Veronica. She opened her mouth and miaowed quietly as if to urge her on. Veronica took a few steps forward. The walls suddenly opened out; she was standing at the entrance, with the lights of Frayn's house glowing in the distance. Three humans — and one cat — were making their way across the lawn.

The cat was, of course, Hodge; the humans were Gabrielle and Nyman, chasing after Hettie. Gabrielle looked like a ghost. Her face was deathly white — covered with dust and, on one side, an alarming streak of blood. Veronica ran forward to help them, only to rebound off an invisible barrier set across the entrance to the maze. This, she realised, was the boundary of this particular time bubble. She turned around to retrace her steps, but Hodge — the version that had been leading her through the maze — bounded in front of her and blocked her path.

'Okay,' said Veronica, 'you're the mistress around here.'

'When did you last see Frayn and Veronica?'

Nyman's answer was drowned out as another train rushed through the office.

'Miss Pendleton,' he said, 'surely there's somewhere more convenient to interview us?'

'I like it here,' said Gabrielle.

Nyman crossed his legs and leaned back in his chair.

'I last saw them when we left the display. I helped carry poor Hettie to her room. It had been quite an evening.'

Gabrielle nodded. 'And what did you do after that?'

'I went straight up to my room. I had some correspondence to look through. Important business that couldn't wait.'

'And did you hear or see anything unusual?'

'Just the cat.'

Hodge, drowsing in Gabrielle's lap, opened a single eye and twitched an ear.

'You mean Hodge?'

'Yes. She scratched at my door, so I let her in. She spent all night sleeping at the foot of my bed.'

Gabrielle frowned and looked down at Hodge, who swiftly closed her eye and went back to sleep, or at least, to feigning it.

'You've got to be joking.'

Hodge stood proudly in front of a door set back into one of the hedges. She miaowed, strutting back and forth and rubbing against it. Veronica stepped forward, opened it, and walked inside.

'And that's the last time you saw either of them?'

Bendrix examined his nails in an exaggerated display of boredom.

'Quite sure, Miss Pendleton, quite sure. I trust this concludes matters. We need to leave soon.'

'Only one or two more questions. But no one's leaving yet.'

'Miss Pendleton, Hettie is exhausted following the events of last night and this morning. She needs rest.'

Hettie didn't react to hearing her name. She had taken her necklace off, and was examining it in the dusty light of the office.

'Might I have a look at that?' asked Gabrielle.

'Is it really necessary?' asked Bendrix.

'It may be.'

'Hettie!' Bendrix snapped his fingers and gestured towards the girl. She handed the necklace over to Gabrielle.

It was a gold locket, hanging on a length of thin black ribbon. Gabrielle flipped it open. Inside was a watch.

'She was holding it when she was found in the street,' said Bendrix. 'She doesn't like to let go of it. You're lucky she's let you look at it for this long.'

Gabrielle looked down again at her hand. The necklace had gone. She turned to Hettie, who had already put it back on.

'Who exactly are you?' she asked.

Hettie shrugged as another train roared through the office.

Veronica found herself in the main hallway of Frayn's house. It was cool and dark, but outside the windows the sun was blazing. The doorbell rang, and a servant shuffled into the hall and opened the front door. Veronica stepped back into the shadows: above her, she could hear footsteps thundering down the stairs.

'Good to see you again, young man!' The visitor's voice was that of a woman: confident, perhaps even a little strident.

'Who are you?' said another voice. It was Frayn, but much younger. He was still a boy.

'You remember me,' said the visitor. 'Mrs Thorne, your old friend. Why, only last week you told me that if the sun came out, I should jump in a carriage and come around to see you. So here I am.'

'I'm sorry,' said Frayn.

Veronica felt something move against her leg, and started. She looked down. Hodge, a young, thin version of Hodge, looked up at her.

'You remember,' said Mrs Thorne. Her voice was still rich and sweet, but Veronica detected an element of steel in it.

'I — I think I remember,' said Frayn. 'It's just . . .'

There was a thud as he collapsed and slid down the stairs.

'Oh dear,' said Mrs Thorne. 'The poor boy's fainted. I dare say he's been running around too much in this heat.'

Veronica stole a glance around the edge of the stairs as Mrs Thorne and the servant stepped up to tend to the fallen boy. She saw a flash of red fur in the sunshine; it was Hodge, pawing at Frayn's scalp in an attempt to revive him.

'Shoo!' said Mrs Thorne, brushing the animal off. 'Would you put this creature outside?'

The servant obeyed, plucking the cat from the fallen boy,

although she wriggled and howled in protest as he did so. He walked over to the front door, and deposited Hodge as gently as he could on the front step.

'Go on,' he said. 'Plenty of rats out there. Go and catch us one, eh?'

Veronica heard Hodge's plaintive mewing as the door was closed in her face. There was a tug at her dress, and she looked down. To her surprise, Hodge was there, looking up at her just as she had before. The cat turned and walked off down the hallway just to the left of the stairs, as Mrs Thorne and the servant picked up Frayn and carried him to his bedroom.

The cat padded a few yards along the corridor, then turned around and miaowed insistently. Veronica followed her quietly. Hodge was standing outside one of the doors, rubbing her cheek against it. Veronica reached out for the handle. The whole thing was rattling on its hinges.

'Did you notice anything unusual last night?' asked Gabrielle.

Bendrix stroked his beard. 'I noticed many unusual things, but I assume you mean after Hettie and I retired to our rooms?'

'Please go on.'

'Nothing whatsoever. Oh, apart from that animal.' He pointed at Hodge, who stared back at him coldly. 'I woke in the night in the most awkward position, to find that it was making itself comfortable at my expense.'

'Me too,' said Hettie.

Bendrix turned to her and raised an eyebrow.

'What do you mean? She bothered you first, did she?'

'No,' Hettie replied. 'She slept on my bed all night.'

'Hettie, I think you're mistaken,' said Bendrix firmly. 'She has these fantasies sometimes,' he explained to Gabrielle.

'She went through a period of telling a story about a man in black.'

'He's in pieces,' said Hettie, as if this explained everything.

Veronica stepped onto a moving surface. She swayed to one side, reached out, and stabilised herself on a metal pole that ran from floor to ceiling.

She was, she realised, in an underground train carriage, probably late at night. It was half-full, and the passengers were subdued: either dozing, or reading the scraps of newspaper left behind from earlier in the day. By the look of their clothes and the advertisements on the walls, she had turned up at some point in the 1980s.

She picked up Hodge, who was curling around her legs.

'Why have you brought me here?' she asked. 'Where's Frayn, eh?'

The cat jumped out of her arms and landed in the lap of one of the passengers, a sleeping young man. He shifted a little in his seat and mumbled, but didn't wake up. Hodge stepped down to the floor of the carriage and miaowed. Veronica followed her as she walked over to one of the empty seats and stepped up on her hind legs to look out of the window.

'Oh yes,' said Mrs Thorne. 'She came into my room. But her fur makes me sneeze. I had to put her out.'

She reached out to take another sip of tea, and Gabrielle noticed deep scratch marks on her forearm.

'That looks painful,' she said.

'Oh, it's nothing,' Mrs Thorne replied. 'High spirits, that's all.'

'I suppose so. But you'll have known Hodge for some time, of course.'

'I suppose so, my dear.'

'Tell me, when did Frayn get her?'

Mrs Thorne smiled nervously and drained the rest of her teacup. She fiddled a little with the brooch on her dress. Gabrielle was sure she heard a faint chattering noise, like that of a telegraph machine.

'I'm sure I don't remember, my dear. Do you mind if I have a little more tea? It's rather dusty in here, isn't it?'

'I'm afraid the pot's empty,' said Gabrielle. 'Would you mind taking a look at this?'

She handed over the photograph of Frayn and Mrs Thorne.

'What is this, dear?' asked Mrs Thorne.

'Don't you remember it?'

Mrs Thorne squinted at the image.

'The light's so terrible in here, I really can't tell.'

Without looking up, she grabbed the empty teapot with her free hand, and swung it around to hit Gabrielle in the face.

Through the window of the tube carriage, Veronica saw that Frayn's office was in disarray. The table and chairs were on their sides, and papers and books were scattered around. The light bulb was swinging back and forth, illuminating two figures struggling on the ground. One was Gabrielle, bleeding from a head wound: the other was a surprisingly nimble Mrs Thorne.

'Gabrielle!' she shouted.

One or two people looked up from their papers and stared at her briefly. A young couple giggled. Within a couple of seconds, everyone had forgotten about her again. She banged on the window as the train rattled away down the tunnel.

As the train rushed through the office, Gabrielle broke free from Mrs Thorne's grasp, grabbed a book from the shelf, and hit her squarely on the forehead with it. Mrs Thorne reeled for a moment, but kept coming. Gabrielle ducked as she lunged at her. Mrs Thorne sprawled behind her on the platform, sending Hodge running for cover. Gabrielle turned in time to see her pulling a small silver pistol from her boot and aim it. She dived and knocked Mrs Thorne's arm as she fired. The shot went wild and knocked out the light. In the darkness, Gabrielle heard the pistol flying from Mrs Thorne's hand and skittering across the floor. She was only distracted for an instant, but it was enough. Mrs Thorne grabbed her by the throat. Her nails were sharp and tore into Gabrielle's skin, forcing her back to the edge of the platform.

There was a rumbling noise in the distance that at first she mistook for the blood rushing in her head. Then she felt the gasp of air from the tunnel and, looking to one side, realised she was looking directly into the headlights of an oncoming train.

TEN

'Miss Britton!'

Veronica recognised the voice immediately. She swung around from the window to see Frayn standing behind her in the tube carriage. He was holding yet another version of Hodge in his arms.

'Frayn?'

'It's so good to see you're safe. Come on!'

'Frayn,' she said, 'I have to get back to the house.'

'Why?'

'Gabrielle's in trouble. Mrs Thorne's the one, Frayn. She's the assassin!'

'Yes. Good work, old girl. Quite. Excuse me.'

Frayn staggered back and collapsed half-in and half-out of the doorway. Veronica ran over, hauled him through, and closed the door behind them.

They were in a darkened room. The air smelled of cigarette smoke: overhead, there was a suffusion of brilliant white light. She heard the rustle of paper and the whisper of conversation. Then a piano started playing a jaunty, raunchy tune. She looked up in the direction of the noise. There was a screen at one end of the room; on it, a young woman in a figure-hugging outfit, her hair neatly bobbed and eyes defined with deep black rings of kohl, was smiling and gyrating. She heard a voice.

'You must keep the Dead Letter safe at all costs. That's what they want, and they mustn't get it. Tell Miss Britton — tell her —'

She pulled the tape recorder out of Frayn's pocket and stopped it running.

Gabrielle closed her eyes and waited for the train to hit. She hoped that it would be quick. Suddenly Mrs Thorne released her grip and let out a cry that drowned out even the rush of machinery as the train sped up to the platform. Gabrielle rolled out of the way, and scrambled to her feet. In the strobe lighting of the passing carriages, she saw Mrs Thorne trying to shake off the ginger cat that was clinging grimly to her head and clawing at her face. Mrs Thorne stumbled blindly to the edge of the platform; she put her foot out to stabilise herself, but it got caught between the carriage and the platform. In an instant, she was under the train. Hodge sprung free and cowered at Gabrielle's feet.

'Thank you, girl,' said Gabrielle as the train whipped away into the darkness. Hodge padded out in front of her and began to guide her to the door, miaowing every few yards to indicate the way.

'Oh, my goodness,' said Frayn. 'I feel awful. Did I faint?'

'Yes,' Veronica replied. 'It seems to happen when Mrs — well, you know, when *she* comes up as a topic of conversation.' She handed him the tape recorder.

'So you recorded your message?' she said.

'Yes,' he replied. 'I got rather nervous in that wardrobe. Thought I'd record something just in case. And, well, that was what popped into mind. I've heard it so many times, you see. Anyway, just as the shot was fired, my clever little cat helped me to escape. A very circuitous route, but . . .' He trailed off and looked at the screen.

'Mrs Thorne isn't what she seems,' said Veronica. 'I think that, despite appearances, last night was the first time you met. I noticed you looked rather uncomfortable around her. Now the very mention of her makes you sick.'

Frayn leaned forward and pressed his hands against his temples as if in pain, but nodded for her to continue.

'I think her plan was to kill you last night, then go back in time and get to know you from childhood. You would have absolute trust in her and name her as one of your executors, and a trustee of the collection. So she — and her employers — would have free rein to search the Frayn Collection from top to bottom to retrieve the Dead Letter, whatever it is.'

'It's doesn't seem *real* anymore,' said Frayn, 'when I think of Mrs — of that woman now. It's like remembering a book I read, or a play, or one of those things.'

He waved at the screen, where the heroine, now in a dressing gown but still immaculately made up, was pacing back and forth in a hotel room, tearing a telegram into little pieces.

'I therefore believe that Mrs Thorne has met her end. Gabrielle must have defeated her, setting up the paradox. I now remember something that never happened. That sort of thing always makes me feel ill. Your companion is safe, Miss Britton. At least for now.'

'Still,' said Veronica, 'we should get back.'

'Agreed,' said Frayn. They stood up and shuffled out into the aisle. Facing them were two dozen pairs of cats' eyes, glowing in the darkness.

'I think,' Frayn whispered, 'that my cat has other plans.'

Gabrielle staggered into the drawing room and collapsed into the nearest chair. Her dress was torn and dusty, her face caked with blood and dirt. Hodge ran in after her, mewing with concern.

'Good God!' Bendrix exclaimed.

'Where's Mrs Thorne?' asked Nyman. Gabrielle didn't answer.

'Come on,' said Nyman, 'is she hurt?'

'What are you asking questions for?' said Bendrix, roughly. 'Can't you see the woman's had a tremendous nervous shock? She needs brandy. Have you a flask?'

Hettie put her hand on Nyman's shoulder. 'She's dead,' she said, softly.

'Eh?'

'Nyman!' Bendrix shouted. 'I'm talking to you. Now, do you or don't you have one?'

'What?'

'A hip flask, man.'

'Oh. Yes, of course.'

Nyman took out a small silver hip flask, unscrewed the cap, and handed it to Bendrix.

'Not for me, you fool! For her.'

'Of course. Sorry.'

Nyman gave the flask to Gabrielle. She sipped at it and coughed. Then she raised it to her lips again and drank deeply.

'I say,' said Nyman, 'steady on.'

'Don't stop her,' said Bendrix. 'Every nervous system is different. It could be that Miss Pendleton's is so excitable that to quell it requires an enormous quantity of brandy.'

'True,' whispered Gabrielle.

Bendrix knelt down next to Gabrielle and took her wrist gently, feeling for her pulse.

'Slowing down,' he said approvingly. Gabrielle started up from the chair, nearly knocking him over.

'Leave now,' she said, urgently. 'We need to leave now.'

'Miss Pendleton,' said Bendrix, 'you've evidently been through a terrible ordeal. You need to rest.'

'It's not safe,' she said. 'That brooch of hers was some sort of transmitter. She activated it. We need to get out of here and head for the Ministry. It's the only place we'll be safe. I'll send a message to Carter on the way, and also to Mailfist—tell him to expect—'

'Gabrielle Pendleton!'

The three of them turned to Hettie. She was standing tall, her eyes glistening with confidence and liveliness.

'She's slipped into a trance again!' exclaimed Bendrix. 'She must have been startled by Miss Pendleton's appearance.'

'Well can you get her back out?' asked Nyman.

'I'll try.'

Bendrix took out his pocket watch and waved it in front of Hettie's face. She snatched it out of his hand effortlessly, and made it disappear into her sleeve. The light in the room began to fade, and the walls started shaking.

'What's going on?' said Nyman.

'Another indoor storm brewing,' said Gabrielle. 'If we're lucky, it'll give us a bit of cover.' She ran over to the French windows and laid a hand on the bolt to unlock it just at the glass shattered and a squadron of armed men in black uniforms forced their way into the room.

The sky was darkening, and the rain had begun to fall. Veronica and Frayn huddled for shelter in the doorway next to the little house off Haverstock Hill. Hodge, in her many different forms, was gathered around them. There were young, slim, acrobatic cats that started at every noise, and were constantly glancing from side to side; assured, confident cats with a few years on them, who looked at you through narrowed eyes;

and old cats, slow on their feet, their fangs blunted and their eyes dull. Only they were all the same cat, Hodge, at every stage of her life from kittenhood to her declining years. And Veronica suspected that she was only seeing a fraction of the total number.

'Miss Britton?'

'Yes, Frayn?'

'I've always known she had a secret life. I mean, all cats do, that's part of their charm. I just never suspected that there were quite so many of her.'

'I think,' said Veronica, 'that she has become far more than just a cat.'

Frayn shifted a little in his wet slippers, which made an unpleasant squelching sound.

'She does seem to show rather more purpose and intelligence than the average cat,' he ventured.

'She's been exploring your house for a very long time now,' said Veronica. 'That's what cats do, isn't it? They like to know the limits of their territory. Only this cat doesn't have any limits. Frayn, I don't think the barriers around your time bubbles are completely impermeable.'

'You don't?'

'No. I think there are gaps around the edges. Gaps about the width of—I don't know. A cat's whiskers, perhaps.'

'Oh.'

'She's gone through those barriers, Frayn. She's able to bring all the versions of herself together at a single point in time. You know the Ministry frowns on that sort of thing? For humans, that is. I don't think anyone's tried it with pets before.'

'What's happened to my cat, Miss Britton?'

'All these different Hodges are able to operate as a single mind. A collective organism. I think she knows exactly what's going on.'

Frayn wiped his damp hair from his face, and adjusted the ruined collar of his dressing gown.

'If only she could talk, Miss Britton.'

'Indeed. And it's because she can't that she's led us here. She needs to show us something.'

A hunched figure hurried past them, his head bowed, his hand clenched around the inner pocket of his jacket. One of the cats peeled off to follow him. The man walked on a few paces, stopped, and doubled back on himself, shaking his head. As he approached a front door just a few yards away from them, he continued to look warily up and down the street. For a moment he seemed to catch sight of them, but then he shook his head again and put his keys in the lock. The man opened the door, and with a last glance over his shoulder, stepped forward. His legs became tangled with the cat at his feet, and he tripped and fell headlong into the hallway.

'Is that what she's brought us here for?' asked Frayn. 'To see her tripping someone up? Collective intelligence or not, she has a rather basic sense of humour, eh?'

The front door slammed shut, leaving the cat outside. A moment later, a light came on at the window in one of the upper floors.

'When did you get Hodge?'

'Oh, years ago. Too long ago to remember. Turned up in the maze one day, looking lost. Slip of a thing she was, but a good mouser.'

The group of cats around their feet huddled closer. Veronica saw, out of the rain and dusk, a group of men approaching. She gasped and stepped back a few paces.

'It's him!'

'Who?'

'Someone who shouldn't exist.'

Doyle's skin was pale, his eyes black and cold. He was, like the half-dozen other men he led, dressed in a smartly-cut black trenchcoat. He was holding a device in his hand — a small, circular object with a brass case. It looked like a ship's compass; indeed, he seemed to be taking a bearing from it. One of his men asked him a question: he waved impatiently to silence him, and stopped in front of the doorway. Then he nodded to another of his agents, who took a small brass tube from his pocket and held it in front of the lock. There was a crackle and a shower of sparks. Doyle banged roughly on the door then, without waiting for a response, marched through followed by his team.

'We should help!' exclaimed Frayn. He stepped forward and rebounded off an invisible barrier.

'Nothing we can do,' said Veronica. One of the cats at her feet hissed contemptuously as the last of Doyle's agents entered the building.

'Where is she?'

'Where is who?'

'You know perfectly well. Where is Veronica Britton?'

'Who am I speaking to? I can't be expected to answer if you won't even show me your face.'

The man standing over Gabrielle took off his balaclava, leaned down, and pushed his face into hers.

'My name,' he said, 'is Doyle. Does that mean anything to you?'

She recoiled.

'What is it?' he demanded.

'Nothing,' she said, although a phrase Veronica had once shown her in a poem was playing through her mind: *the skull beneath the skin*. Looking at this man was like seeing both skull and skin simultaneously.

'I saw you not long ago during a particularly nasty skirmish with the Nameless. Are you in league with them? Why did they come to your rescue?'

'I don't know.'

Doyle tilted his head to one side. 'That, I can believe. But as for where Miss Britton is . . .'

'She's disappeared.'

'Really? Like my agent? I don't suppose you'd know anything about that? Mrs Thorne, she called herself. The last thing I received from her was a distress signal. Now why would she call for help?'

'I have no idea.'

'You don't seem to know much, do you? Well, know this: you've got yourself mixed up in something I want very, very badly indeed. I don't suppose you've heard of it—it's called the Dead Letter.'

'The Dead Letter?' Bendrix interjected. Gabrielle kicked him under the table.

'So,' said Doyle, 'you know about the Dead Letter, do you?'

'Not a great deal,' said Bendrix hurriedly. 'I mean, I heard a little about it. It may not even have been *the* Dead Letter, it may just have been *a* dead letter. . .'

Doyle smiled. 'Sorry. I think we must have misunderstood one another.'

'Yes,' said Bendrix, a smile of relief creeping over his face. 'We must have.'

Doyle nodded to one of his agents, who stepped up and with a single movement broke Bendrix's right index finger. Bendrix cried out in pain and hunched forward.

'Good,' said Doyle. 'We understand each other. Next question. Where is the Dead Letter?'

Bendrix cursed under his breath. Doyle nodded again, and this time his agent broke the man's thumb.

'Stop it!' shouted Gabrielle. 'He doesn't know!'

Doyle ignored her. 'Let's have one more go,' he said.

Bendrix's head was still bowed. His voice, when it came, was almost a whisper.

'Miss Pendleton,' he said.

'Yes,' Gabrielle replied.

'This creature appears to want this so-called Dead Letter very much. It seems to be important to him.'

'I'm afraid so.'

'Then I assume it would put him in a position of considerable advantage were he to obtain it.'

Gabrielle hesitated. 'Yes, Bendrix,' she said, 'it would.'

Bendrix looked up. The colour had returned to his face, and he looked just as bullishly sure of himself as he had the previous evening.

'In that case, sir,' he said, looking defiantly at Doyle, 'I will never, ever tell you.'

Doyle sighed and shot him through the heart.

The sound of the gunshot mingled with the crash of glass as the man burst through the window and fell to the street below. All was quiet for a moment. Then the cat that had been trailing the victim's footsteps earlier trotted out of the shadows, and, without stopping, picked the envelope clasped in the dead man's hand up with her teeth. The group of cats tensed up as footsteps thundered down the staircase, and Doyle's agents ran out into the street and over to the body. Then the cats scattered in all directions.

'Miss Britton,' said Frayn, 'I think the cats are wise.'

Doyle returned his pistol to its holster and regarded his handiwork.

'Take it away,' he said to his men. Two stepped forward,

lifted Bendrix's body out of the chair, and carried it from the room.

'Now,' he said to Gabrielle. 'Let's try again.'

There was a rumble of thunder from the ceiling. A black storm cloud was gathering.

'Come on, Miss Britton,' said Frayn, stepping out into the street.

'Just a moment longer,' said Veronica. 'They shouldn't be able to see us, anyway.'

The men had finished their inspection of the body. Doyle was berating them as he took the brass compass-like device out of his pocket and checked it again. He shook his head as he looked at its display. Then he looked up. He was staring precisely in their direction, though not seeing them. He called one of his men forward. The man took a pair of binoculars with smoked black lenses out of a case and held them up to his eyes. He lowered them hurriedly and pointed at Veronica and Frayn.

'Run!' said Frayn. The two of them fled back down the street and towards the doorway that led out of their time bubble. The slap of boots on the wet pavement, and the sound of Doyle shouting followed them.

'Stop!' he yelled. 'I know you're there!'

Frayn got to the door first and flung it open.

'After you!' he shouted.

'No,' said Veronica. 'You're the client.'

'No, no, I insist!'

Veronica grabbed Frayn and flung him in headfirst. As she followed him, a lithe ginger cat leapt through the open doorway.

'She doesn't know anything,' said Nyman. Doyle ignored him.

'The choice is yours, Miss Pendleton,' he said. 'You can tell me everything you know about the Dead Letter and Veronica Britton. Or I can shoot someone else.'

'Why not search the house?' Nyman interrupted. 'Why can't you just leave us alone?'

'A good point,' said Doyle. 'In fact, that was my original plan. But Miss Britton and Miss Pendleton have complicated things. And I have no idea when Miss Britton will be back to cause trouble. So it's much easier if you just tell us.'

He nodded to the man guarding Nyman, who leaned forward and, almost tenderly, broke his right index finger. Nyman turned pale, and the sweat stood out on his forehead, but he didn't make a sound.

'Oh,' said Doyle. He sounded disappointed, and reached for his gun again.

'For God's sake,' said Gabrielle. 'Just stop!'

His hand came up empty, and the next moment Hettie stood before him, the pistol in her hand, pointing it directly at his forehead.

'My men will shoot if you pull that trigger,' said Doyle.

'They might miss,' Hettie replied. 'I won't.'

The thunder rumbled again, and a bolt of lightning licked down and singed the carpet.

'Let us go, Doyle,' said Gabrielle.

The lightning flashed again. Hodge began to howl, and ran for shelter under Gabrielle's chair as hailstones began to fall.

'No one is leaving this house,' said Doyle, 'until the Dead Letter is found.'

'You'll find it,' said Hettie. 'You'll have it, and you'll let it go.'

There was an explosion and everything went white. Gabrielle was flung to the ground: when she looked up, the table had been split in two, and the troops were scattered around the room. There was a metallic smell in the air, and the French windows had been shattered in the blast. The thundercloud roared again, and forked lightning hit the remains of the table, blasting it to splinters. Someone grabbed her from behind, someone with firm, wiry hands. She struggled to throw them off. 'Miss Pendleton!' a voice shouted over the ringing in her ears. She turned around and saw Nyman.

'Come on!'

Hettie lay across Doyle, out cold.

'We can't leave her!' said Gabrielle.

'We won't.' Nyman took hold of Hettie and hoisted her up. They hurried towards the French windows as behind them they heard the first groans of the waking men. Gabrielle kicked the door open, and they made their way out onto the darkened lawn.

'A moment, please, just one moment. I'm really not used to this sort of thing.'

Frayn collapsed into one of the nearest cinema seats.

'Just a second, then,' said Veronica. 'I'm pretty sure they can't follow us in here, but I don't want to wait around and find out.'

She sat down next to Frayn. Hodge jumped into her lap and purred.

'What do you think she was trying to tell us?' asked Frayn, reaching out to scratch the cat under the chin.

'We've just seen the Dead Letter, Frayn,' said Veronica. 'I think that poor man died holding it in his hand. He was trying to protect it. And Hodge — all of her — has taken on that burden now. She's been passing it around all of the different versions of herself, scattered around the various rooms of your house.'

'An army of cats,' murmured Frayn.

'I think that you haven't been looking after her all these years. She's been looking after *you*. Frayn, I think that Hodge is the most valuable item in your entire collection.'

'Oh,' said Frayn, fondly, 'I've always thought that.'

Hodge shifted across to Frayn's lap, and — although the wet dressing gown looked nowhere near as comfortable as the fabric of Veronica's dress — settled down and allowed herself to be fussed.

'What I don't understand,' he continued, 'is this: if they could see us, why couldn't they see the door?'

'I think that's another of Hodge's gifts. I think it's not just that she can get through gaps. I believe she's actually able to manipulate the doorways.'

'Goodness me, she *is* a clever girl.'

'Yes. I think she sealed the door behind us. But we still need to be getting along. We have to make sure the Collection is safe, and keep the Dead Letter out of the Empire's hands. How do you feel?'

Hodge jumped from Frayn's lap. He stood up and stretched.

'I'm ready to go back. If nothing else, I could do with a change of clothes.'

'Good,' said Veronica, rising to her feet.

Hodge led them around to the door that led to the underground carriage.

'Ah,' said Frayn, looking over his shoulder at the screen, on which the actress from earlier was now lamenting wildly. 'She's beginning to regret tearing up that telegram! Thought a prince could never truly love a showgirl. So sad.'

'Come on!'

With Hettie propped up between them, Gabrielle and Nyman hurried across the lawn. It was pitch dark all around, except for the area around the apple tree that glowed with the comforting light of dawn.

'Where to?' asked Nyman.

'The gates!' Gabrielle panted.

They headed for the driveway, and sped towards the entrance. They rounded the corner of the driveway, into the shelter of a line of trees. Their shoes crunched on the gravel. Between them, Hettie stirred and groaned.

'What's the connection?' asked Nyman.

'What?'

'In what way is the Dead Letter connected with the Ministry?'

'Look,' said Gabrielle, 'we're nearly there.'

They rounded the final bend. The gates stood slightly open.

'Turn back!' cried Hettie.

There was a clatter and a high-pitched whistling noise that Gabrielle recognised from the day she had spent in the London ruins of the deep future.

'Get down!' she shouted. The three of them dropped to the floor. There was a rush of heat, and the line of trees next to them burst into flame. Hettie scrambled to her feet.

'Hettie!' shouted Gabrielle. She heard the scrape as the ironclad positioned outside the gate turned its turret to fire again. Hettie stepped out of the path of its energy beam at the last possible second, holding up her hands as if to warm them. Nyman pulled her back to the ground.

'What were you thinking, young lady?' he said.

Hettie rolled over on her back. She was smiling and her eyes were glittering.

'They can't touch me,' she said. 'Nothing can touch me.'

She held up a fob watch. Nyman checked his pockets.

'What?' he said. 'How did you—?'

'No time.' She got to her feet and ran off.

'Where's she going?'

'Just follow her!' Gabrielle sped after Hettie, who broke through the trees and out onto the lawn. The two of them crashed through the branches. Behind them they heard shouts, the chatter of radios, and the crack of gunfire.

Hettie was running down the slope that led to the maze. Gabrielle and Nyman followed close on her heels as she approached the entrance. There was a figure there, one that seemed to be flickering in and out of existence. It was a woman in a dark dress. As they approached, the woman made as if to leave the maze and join them, but was thrown back by an invisible barrier. It was at that point that any doubt left Gabrielle's mind. She had just seen Veronica.

Veronica, Frayn, and Hodge left the train carriage, and entered the maze. It was a little darker and colder than when Veronica had been there last, and they could hear the sound of heavy machinery and men shouting to one another in the distance. Bright lights shone through the chinks in the hedge.

'They're looking for someone,' said Frayn.

'We need to get back to the house in the present. *Our* present,' said Veronica. 'Can you remember where the door is that leads back to your wardrobe?'

'Of course,' said Frayn. He turned around confidently, took one step, and fell over. Hodge, who had tangled herself up in his feet, stepped back and looked at him.

'I think she's trying to tell us something again,' said Frayn. 'Quite.'

Hodge padded away in the opposite direction. They followed her.

'She was here,' said Gabrielle. 'Veronica was right here.'

She knelt down next to Hettie, who had collapsed just

inside the entrance to the maze. She was murmuring as if in the middle of a bad dream. Suddenly her eyes snapped open.

'Where is it?' she asked.

'What?' Gabrielle replied.

'The Dead Letter.'

'Can you get up? We need to move.'

Hettie shifted and propped herself up on her elbows.

'Ah!'

She sunk back to the ground and curled up into a ball, clutching at her head.

'Hettie,' said Gabrielle, alarmed, 'what is it? What's wrong?'

Hettie groaned. Gabrielle put a hand out to comfort her. The physical contact sent a jolt through her like a bolt of electricity. She staggered back, and reached out for support. Her hand made contact with stone. She realised she was standing in a dingy, bare room. A man in a black robe was bent over a desk, scratching away with a quill at a sheet of paper. She strained to look over his shoulder and saw—it was hard to say exactly what she saw. It was like looking into a deep, clear pool of water, her eyes having to adjust to the different levels within.

The scratch of the quill got louder. She opened her eyes to see Hodge tugging at her sleeve. Hettie, who had regained consciousness, was standing above her.

'Come on,' she said briskly. 'Get up!'

Veronica and Frayn stepped out of the wardrobe cautiously. Hodge crept out of the room ahead of them, went into the corridor, and then returned purring softly.

'I think that's the all clear,' said Frayn. 'Where to now?'

'When I went through the maze on the way to meet you, I saw Gabrielle, Nyman, and Hettie running across the lawn towards me,' said Veronica. 'I think that time bubble was set only a short distance into the future. So the maze is our best bet if we're going to find them.'

'What about Bendrix. Did you see him?'

'No.'

'Oh dear. I didn't care for the man, it's true, but—'

Veronica was looking out of the window. She could see the flash of torches held by men scouring the grounds.

'You know, Frayn, it's interesting.'

'What is?'

'Every one of the time bubbles is an area close to your house. The abbey, the coffee shop, the tube station—North End, isn't it?'

'Yes,' said Frayn, 'but I don't see quite what you're getting at.'

'And new rooms are appearing the whole time?'

'They are indeed,' said Frayn. 'Faster and faster.'

'I've just been thinking about how this house was formed. About the event that caused it. We're at the epicentre of an explosion in time and space. I'm just wondering if it was a natural event or not.'

'Eh?'

'Those men out there. The Empire. When I've come across them before, they've been trying out technologies far in advance of their time. Things they might not be entirely able to handle.'

Frayn, busy laying out a dry shirt and trousers on his bed, looked up.

'Hm?' he said, distractedly.

'I wonder,' said Veronica, 'if tonight we're going to find out how your house came to be.'

ELEVEN

'Hettie?'

'That isn't my name. It was one they gave to me.'

Gabrielle stood up. Her temples were still aching, and she rubbed them with her fingertips.

'So what is your real name?' she asked.

'J.'

'Just J?' said Nyman, peering nervously through the branches of the hedge at the torchlight darting around the lawn outside.

'You're a Ministry agent,' said Gabrielle.

'Correct. And you're Gabrielle Pendleton. Mailfist told me about you.'

'What did he say?'

'He said I should deny everything if I saw either you or Veronica Britton.'

'I see.'

'Don't worry. I never listen to him anyway.'

J looked around.

'So where are we?'

'Frayn's garden,' said Gabrielle, 'in the maze.'

'Ah yes. Of course we are.'

'How much do you remember?'

J tilted her head back and closed her eyes.

'Dribs and drabs. That doctor, the one who treated me like his pet. Where's he?'

'Dead,' Gabrielle replied.

'Oh. I hope I wasn't the one who killed him?'

'No. It was the people who are after us now who did that.'

'Good. Well, not good.'

'What about before?' asked Gabrielle.

'Before what?'

'Bendrix said you were found wandering the streets, having lost your memory.'

'Oh,' said J, '*that*.' She stopped and patted herself down.

'What is it?' said Nyman.

'I had a spoon. One of Mailfist's. I took it from his desk. Don't tell me I've lost it! I hate losing things.'

'That's hardly the most important thing right now,' said Gabrielle.

J frowned. 'I really liked that spoon,' she said, sulkily.

Veronica and Frayn opened the window that led out onto the garden.

'Are you sure it's safe?' Frayn whispered.

'Probably not,' Veronica replied, sitting on the window seat and leaning out. 'But it's crawling with Empire troops downstairs. There's no way we can get away through the front door.'

'Can't she help?' asked Frayn, pointing at Hodge, who was stretching down from the window frame and testing the strength of the thick growth of ivy beneath.

'How? You expect her to carry you down by the scruff of your neck?'

'Couldn't she make us a door?'

'Either she can't, or she won't,' said Veronica. 'They amount to much the same thing in a cat. Anyway, this was the escape route Mrs Thorne used after she shot you. Before we changed the timeline, of course. So it should be strong enough. Look, Hodge is having a go.'

The cat scrambled out of the window, and began to descend to the garden.

'We'll have to be quick, though,' said Veronica. 'I'll go ahead, and catch you if you slip. How does that sound?'

Frayn regarded her sceptically. He had changed his clothes, and was now dressed in Turkish trousers, a paisley shirt, and a velvet smoking jacket and cap.

'I am considerably heavier than you, Miss Britton,' he said.

'Don't worry,' she replied. 'It really isn't that far to the ground. And the rose beds look nice and soft.'

She turned around and let herself slide gently out of the window into the cool night air, taking a firm hold of the ivy.

Doyle sat cross-legged on the floor in the midst of the wreckage, with a pair of binoculars and a partially disassembled compass in front of him.

'Report,' he barked, as one of his men approached.

'We've searched the grounds, sir,' the man replied nervously. 'There's no sign of them.'

'Really?' said Doyle, adjusting one of the compass's screws. 'And have you looked in the maze?'

'No sign there either, sir.'

'I've heard interesting things about that maze,' said Doyle. 'I've heard that it's very easy to get lost.'

He replaced the back of the compass and flipped it over. It lit up and began to tick. He picked it up and moved it experimentally from side to side.

'Come on,' he said.

As he descended the last few feet, Frayn lost his footing and grabbed wildly at the ivy. It tore off in his hands and he fell heavily onto his back.

Veronica helped him to his feet.

'Are you hurt?' she whispered.

Frayn straightened his smoking jacket.

'Just had the wind knocked out of me, that's all. Miss Britton, I don't suppose we have any choice?'

'What?'

'We couldn't just go and get help for Miss Pendleton and the others?'

'Frayn, we *are* the help.'

'I thought so.'

'How well do you know your way around the maze, Frayn?'

'As well as anyone. Only . . .'

'Only what?'

'I'm afraid it's rather a changeable beast. It seems to redesign itself the whole time. If there's a centre to it, no one's ever found it. My great-uncle, it's said, decided to find it one day. Went in with a climbing-rope tied around his waist.'

'What happened to him?'

'The servant holding the other end of the rope got worried after a day or so and gave the rope a sharp tug. It was stuck on something, so he went in and had a look. It was tied to a particularly stout branch. My great-uncle was never seen again.'

'I see,' said Veronica. 'Well, we'll just have to chance it.'

'And sometimes at night,' said Frayn, warming to his theme, 'there's a terrible howling noise, like the cry of some primordial creature — oh, I say.'

Veronica and Hodge were already stalking silently towards the maze.

'Was that thunder?' asked Nyman.

The sound of their pursuers abated for a moment. They,

too, must have heard it: a low growling noise, like a great beast about to strike.

'So what do we do now?' asked J. She was pacing restlessly back and forth.

'We wait for Veronica,' Gabrielle replied.

'Those soldiers, or whatever they are, haven't been able to find us,' J replied. 'Why do you think Veronica will?'

'She will.'

'Sweet.'

The rumbling came again, louder, and closer this time. Hodge sat back and howled.

'She's frightened,' said Nyman.

'No,' said Gabrielle, leaning in closer and examining the animal. Her ears were back and her eyes closed, 'I think she's summoning it. Whatever *it* is.'

Veronica, Frayn, and Hodge crept into the entrance of the maze. There was a heady, lush smell in the air of vegetation after a rainstorm, and the leaves looked waxy and heavy in the moonlight.

There was a deep bellow that made the hairs on the back of Veronica's neck stand on end. It seemed to come from all around: she looked over her shoulder at the entrance to the maze, only to find that it had vanished, and had been replaced by a hedge covered in thick blossoms.

'I see,' she said. 'No way but onwards.'

'Isn't that always the case?' said Frayn. 'Like time itself, really.'

'Perhaps you could explain something to me, lieutenant,' said Doyle, glowering at his subordinate as they stood outside the maze.

'Yes, sir.'

Doyle took a stick, stepped forward and walked along the length of the hedge, beating at the leaves. The cries of lost soldiers came faintly from within.

'When your men searched this maze, did no one think to make note of where the entrance was?'

'Sir — it seemed — well, it just seemed obvious. It was right here.'

'Quite.'

Doyle gestured for another of his men to come forward.

'If you would?'

The man lifted his binoculars, and flicked a switch on top.

'Do you see anything?' asked Doyle.

'No sir. Wait a minute.'

The captain pointed just to the left of Doyle.

'There, sir. There's a gap right next to you.'

'Excellent,' said Doyle. He turned to the lieutenant.

'A simple modification,' he said. He leapt forward confidently into the hedge and immediately got caught in the branches. A moment later he struggled back out, brushing leaves and petals from his clothes.

'Get axes!' he shouted at the captain and lieutenant. 'Axes, saws, and fire!'

There was a horrible sound from within the maze, a ferocious yowl accompanied by the terrified shouts of the Empire troops.

Veronica and Frayn emerged into a small clearing.

'Where's Hodge?' said Frayn, looking around. 'We were right behind her a moment ago.'

The cat emerged from around the corner, sat down and started washing. She was followed by another cat, a younger version, who strolled up to her, sniffed her, and joined in the grooming.

'You've got yourself a little friend,' said Frayn. 'How charming.'

Three bedraggled figures followed in her wake. Before Veronica could react, one of them ran up and embraced her.

'Vee!'

'Oh, Gabs!'

The women held each other tightly.

'Just let me look at you,' said Veronica. She loosened her hold and regarded her companion. Gabrielle's hair was matted with blood and dirt, and her face was streaked with sweat. Her dress was in tatters. She was beautiful.

'Veronica Britton!'

Veronica swivelled around to come face to face with J.

'I thought I knew you,' she said.

'I had red hair then,' J replied.

'Of course. So how did you come to be here, J?'

'I honestly have no idea.'

'Was it Mailfist? Has he known about the Dead Letter all along?'

'The Dead Letter?'

'Veronica,' said Gabrielle, 'I think she really doesn't know.'

There was another terrible, shattering howl from all around them. The two versions of Hodge sat up together and mewed in unison.

'Mailfist took me to some place where they keep all of the spare porters and clerks,' Gabrielle continued. 'I asked them what was in the Dead Letter.'

'What did they say?'

'They didn't answer. Or rather, I thought they didn't. They just gave me a random set of times and places, and what all sorts of people had been doing there and then. I only realised what it meant when I got back here. They were literally giving me a description of what was in the Dead Letter. Line by line.'

Veronica gripped her arm.

'Gabs!'

Gabrielle nodded.

'I'm sorry, Vee,' she said. 'I think that's what it is.'

'What *are* you talking about?' Frayn butted in. 'I have a right to know. It is my cat carrying this thing around.'

'The Dead Letter,' said Gabrielle, 'is a map. It's a map of both time and space. More than that, even. It's a map that shows the interconnectedness of every event in the city. The way, say, a Roman soldier dropping a coin leads to a woman missing her bus 2,000 years later.'

'So why does that matter?' said Nyman.

'Why does it matter?' Frayn exclaimed. 'Listen to yourself, Nyman. The key to all of time and space in this great city of ours!'

He staggered a little and sat down heavily.

'Why,' he said. 'It's unthinkable. It's just unthinkable.' He ran his hands through his hair and shuddered.

'The Empire are preparing for war,' said Veronica. 'They've already scavenged future technology to build their ironclads and God knows what else. They even tried to depose King Lud–'

'King Lud?' scoffed Nyman.

'Remind me later, and I'll tell you all about it. If there is a later. Anyway, with the Dead Letter they'd have won before a single shot was fired. They'd know everything that had happened or would happen anywhere. There would be no way they could be beaten. There wouldn't even be anywhere to hide.'

'What I don't understand,' said Frayn, his voice shaking, 'is how anyone managed to come up with the damn thing in the first place.'

J coughed.

'Actually,' she said, 'it's starting to come back to me.'

Her eyes widened suddenly and she dropped to the floor. The hedge behind her burst into flame.

'We need to get out of here!' shouted Veronica.

The cats ran over to the hedge behind her and started scratching.

'What is it, ladies?' said Frayn, getting up to investigate. Gabrielle got there before him and tugged at the branches to reveal a dark wooden door. She turned the glistening brass handle and opened it.

'It's our only chance!' she shouted. They ran through just as the first troops stormed into the clearing. Nyman brought up the rear; he closed the door as the howling started up again in the darkened maze.

TWELVE

The door the cats had taken Veronica and her companions through led to a cold, clear winter's day in the maze. The ground was hard, and there was a hint of frost on the hedges. Nyman listened in at the closed door.

'What can you hear?' asked Veronica.

'Not much,' he replied. 'Just the howling of that ghastly animal, if that's what it is.'

He smoothed his hair back; despite his many trials, thought Gabrielle, he was still looking remarkably well-groomed. And what about his finger? She had heard the *snap* of it breaking earlier, but he hadn't complained once.

'What happened to Bendrix?' asked Veronica.

'They shot him,' said Gabrielle.

'I thought as much.'

'Vee, the man who killed him—their leader—he seems to know you.'

Veronica turned to J abruptly. 'So why did Mailfist send you here, if not for the Dead Letter?'

'To look into an explosion. A huge detonation in time and space. He wanted to know more about it.'

'And did you find out?'

J shook her head. 'If I did, I can't remember. I think I got caught up in it, though.' She looked down at the cats, who were sitting at Nyman's feet, poised for action.

'What is it?' asked Gabrielle.

'That cat. I think she was there. Someone else, too. Someone I know...'

'Hush!' said Nyman.

He was pressing his head to the door again.

'What is it?' asked Veronica. 'What do you hear?'

'Something ticking,' Nyman replied, a moment before an explosion ripped a small hole in the wood immediately next to him. He fell back in a plume of smoke and debris, clutching at the side of his face.

'Nyman!' Gabrielle ran to his aid as J stepped over his body and examined the door. A gloved hand holding a gun was thrust through the hole. She ducked to one side, grabbed it, and twisted the wrist back until the weapon was dropped. The hand withdrew, and J picked up the gun and fired a few shots back. There was a cry of pain from the other side.

'Hodge!' said Veronica. 'Do you know another way out of here?'

The cats turned simultaneously and looked at her, like mirror images of one another. Then they got to their feet and trotted away down the corridor of the maze, weaving and curling when they reached the end as if feeling their way around an awkward gap in an invisible wall.

'Hodge!' Veronica shouted after them helplessly.

'I don't understand it,' said Frayn. 'Hodge would never abandon me. She's very loyal, you know. For a cat, anyway.'

Veronica ran after the cats as their tails disappeared around the corner. She hit the barrier that marked the edge of the time bubble and bounced backwards.

The door flew open, and a grenade was thrown in. J kicked it back out. She was thrown backwards by the force of the explosion, skidding to a halt next to Gabrielle and Nyman, who was still holding his face in his hands.

'Sorry,' she said, scrambling to her feet.

The door was now reduced to a few torn fragments of wood. Beyond, Gabrielle could see smoke, flames, and the outline of a squadron of soldiers charging towards them. Then they were upon her and her companions. She tried to cling to Nyman. 'Stop, he's hurt!' she shouted, but they ignored her. She swung a punch, but someone took hold of her arm and twisted it behind her back. She was hauled over to join the others, and forced to kneel in line next to Veronica.

'I'm sorry,' she whispered.

'Me too,' said Veronica.

'There's nothing you could have done,' Gabrielle replied.

'That's not what I'm sorry about,' said Veronica, turning her head slightly so that they could look at each other. 'I'm just sorry we didn't have more time together.'

'Me too,' said Gabrielle. She leaned over slowly toward Veronica, only for a hand to reach out and grab her by the chin. It was Doyle.

'What charming company you keep, Veronica,' he said. He let go of Gabrielle, stepped over to Veronica, and crouched down, bringing his face right up to hers. Gabrielle thought she saw Veronica flinch, as if smelling death on his breath.

'A kiss before dying?' he hissed.

There was the sound of a slap, and he fell backwards. The guards struggled to get Veronica's hands back behind her. Doyle got up, and brushed down his uniform. He inhaled deeply and threw his head back.

'You should have stayed dead,' said Veronica. She struggled to get to her feet again. The guards pushed her back to the ground. Something fell from her pocket and bounced on the gravel pathway.

'What's this?' said Doyle. He picked it up. It was the tape

recorder. 'Is it important?'

He pushed the button, and it played Frayn's message.

'Oh well,' he said. 'Too late now.' He flung it over the hedge.

Doyle nodded to the man behind Gabrielle. She felt cold metal pressed against the back of her head, and a jolt as the trigger was cocked.

'If you hurt her, Doyle —' said Veronica.

'What? What will you do? I tried to do this the easy way, Veronica, but you put paid to that. Now I control the Frayn Collection, as well as its owner.' He nodded in the direction of Frayn. 'He can help us. We can make it worth your while, sir,' he added.

'I don't know who you are,' said Frayn, 'but you are not welcome here. I demand you leave immediately.'

Doyle laughed. He turned back to the man holding the gun to Gabrielle.

'Kill her,' he said.

Gabrielle closed her eyes. The air shook and the ground trembled with a furious roar. 'It's coming through the walls!' someone shouted.

Gabrielle opened her eyes again as the man behind her cried out and fell to the ground clutching at something around his neck. She heard the sound of the other men screaming as they, too, succumbed to the tide that had overwhelmed them. She took a moment to realise what it was. Then something landed on her shoulders and nestled its nose into her ear.

'An army of cats!' she shouted, and stood up. The cat sprang from her and leapt onto Doyle's head, digging her claws in. In an instant, a dozen other animals were on him, biting and scratching vigorously.

Gabrielle looked around for her companions. Veronica grabbed her arm.

'Come on!'

They ran over to J, who had one of the older versions of Hodge sitting on her shoulders. The cat was miaowing and hissing.

'I think she's directing fire,' she said.

The cat sprang from her suddenly and wrapped itself around another of the soldiers. The ground seemed to bubble and swell around them with the mass of animals. They heard Frayn crying out; looking through the struggling figures, the flashes of black cloth and red fur, they saw him on his back, being carried along on the sea of cats. The animals deposited him neatly at Veronica's feet. He got up and straightened the cap on his head.

'Time to leave, I think,' he said.

'Where's Nyman?' asked Gabrielle.

'Miss Pendleton, I'm quite all right.'

Nyman had appeared suddenly at her elbow. His clothing was tattered, his collar torn, and the front of his shirt charred and blood-stained, but his face was unmarked, his hair still neatly smoothed down. Gabrielle looked at him, bewildered.

Veronica led the way through the press of bodies towards the door that led from the crisp winter's day to the dark night of the present. As she stepped through the door, Gabrielle saw her stumble and fall to her knees. She hurried over to help her up. Veronica was clutching at her side, and her face was pale.

'It's a scratch,' she was saying, as if trying to reassure herself. 'A scratch.'

Gabrielle leaned down to help Veronica up. Veronica put out a hand that was covered in blood.

'Oh, Vee!'

Veronica got to her feet and took a few uncertain steps forward.

'Good,' she said. 'Good.'

'What's the matter?' asked J.

'Nothing,' said Gabrielle.

They made their way out into the night. The maze seemed empty at first, but as their eyes adjusted to the darkness, they could make out the occasional cat scampering back and forth, keeping low. Gabrielle felt a tug at her skirt, and looked down. A very small and thin version of Hodge, no older than a few months, was trotting alongside her, dabbing her front paw at the hem of her dress. She leaned down, scooped the cat up, and carried her the rest of the way out of the maze.

The apple tree was swathed in a dense pillar of fog, glowing from within like the essence of a hazy autumn day. They made straight for it, past the ironclads which were wheeling around helplessly, their lights and viewing slits obscured by dozens more cats.

Once they were safely inside the fog, the five of them slumped to the ground. Frayn picked a few russet-brown apples from the tree and handed them around.

'We're lucky,' he said. 'They're just ripe.'

'So what do we do now?' asked J. 'Hide out till they give up?'

'No,' said Veronica. 'We have to find the Dead Letter.'

'How?' asked J. She took a large bite out of her apple, and rubbed its flesh along her hair, which began to change colour from black to its usual shocking red.

'I think this little cat is the key to everything,' said Veronica, pointing to Hodge, who was stretching and regarding her disproportionately large paws with an expression of great seriousness.

'Hodge?' said Gabrielle.

'Yes,' Veronica replied. 'She led us back — or rather,

forward—to see what had happened to the Dead Letter.'

'What did you see?'

'We saw Empire agents killing a man who had found it. Hodge picked it up before they could get to it. She's been passing it around between all the different versions of herself.'

'Then it's lost for good,' said J. 'It could be anywhere.'

'J,' said Veronica. 'You said earlier that you had seen Hodge before. Can you remember anything else about her?'

J stared at the kitten, frowned, and clutched at her temples. 'Ow!'

'What is it?'

'It hurts.'

'Perhaps I can help,' said Gabrielle. 'I picked something up before—some sort of residual energy, I think. J, might I?'

She extended her hand. J shrank back.

'I won't hurt you,' said Gabrielle, and pressed her palm against J's forehead before she could answer.

The two women flinched as Gabrielle made contact. She was plunged into blackness, and for a moment thought she had lost her sight. Then she saw a thin crack of light immediately in front of her. She put her face up against it, and saw a figure in a dark robe, the same one as earlier, bending over a page and writing. A thin kitten—Hodge—played in the light that fell from a narrow window. She had something bright in her paws, something that clattered as she dabbed it across the stone floor.

The man paused in his work. He got up, went over to the cat, and with infinite gentleness stroked her and took the object from her. He examined it. It was a small silver spoon. He regarded it for a moment longer. Then he started, as if he had heard something. He walked across the room and over to the door which Gabrielle was behind. As he did so, his face exploded into a million tiny replicas of itself, like the images in a kaleidoscope, and stretched back into infinity.

Everything went black again, and then she saw another face that she recognised. A woman peering in through a narrow window. A woman with red hair.

Doyle crawled grimly over the blood-stained gravel, through the burned foliage and out of the maze. He tried to find his voice, to bring his men to order, but panic had set in and they were fleeing in disarray.

By the time he got out onto the lawn, the ironclads where turning around to leave. Stragglers were clinging to the outside of the machines. He stood up slowly, stumbled as he tried to put the weight on his right foot, and realised one of the tendons must be damaged. He limped across the lawn, waving his arms and trying to stop the retreat, but to no avail.

Doyle realised they must think he was dead; some, he knew, would be actively wishing it. He had got used to the permanent feeling of exhaustion he had experienced since he returned from the dead; got used to feeling like he was a piece of wire stretched out thinner and thinner, forever at the point of snapping. But now it was simply unbearable. The grass of the lawn looked inviting. He imagined lying down in its cooling softness, falling into a deep sleep and never moving again, just sinking further and further down into the earth where he belonged.

He forced himself to look away; he was, after all, fooling himself. Since he had died and risen, he had not enjoyed a single moment of sleep. There was only one thing that drove him on, one hot, bright point of hatred that gave him strength.

Veronica Britton.

'It's no coincidence,' said Veronica. 'J and the Dead Letter were both there at the same time.'

'And the spoon,' said Gabrielle, weakly, rubbing at her forehead.

'Well, never mind about the spoon for now, dear,' said Veronica.

'No,' said J, holding her head in her hands and rocking back and forth. 'The spoon is important. I took it from Mail-fist when he wasn't looking. It was a really nice spoon.'

Veronica stood up and thumped the trunk of the apple tree.

'Will you two please stop talking about the spoon?' she shouted.

'Vee,' said Gabrielle, hesitantly, 'it's one of the last things I saw.'

J looked up. 'Yes,' she said. 'I dropped the spoon as I was running to hide in the cupboard.'

'Could we go back a little bit?' said Frayn.

'I traced the source of the explosion back to Kilburn Abbey,' said J. 'I got in, and had a look around. The monks were in a bit of a state. It turned out that one of them had had a vision. He said he'd seen the beginning and the end of days. So he had locked himself away in his cell with his cat, and started writing. They were worried about him.'

'How did you get them to talk to you?' asked Veronica, sus-piciously.

'I didn't. I hung around and listened. Lots of good hiding places in old monasteries. Tapestries, dark corners, that sort of thing. Anyway, I worked out where this monk was — the one they were talking about — and I decided to see what he was doing.'

'And what was he doing?' asked Veronica.

'He was writing,' said Gabrielle. 'He was writing out the

Dead Letter.'

'Oh dear,' said Frayn, wringing his velvet smoking-cap.

'What is it?' asked Gabrielle.

'I've just been thinking. It all fits together, doesn't it? I mean, the monk, the Dead Letter, Hodge here, the spoon—and the Abbey.'

'You mean the place we had dinner last night?' said Nyman.

Frayn nodded. 'You'll remember I told you it was destroyed in some sort of fire. Some people even say an earthquake. Well, suppose—just suppose for a moment that the disaster which befell the Abbey, and the eruption in time which formed the house—the eruption that's still going on, you know, hence all the new rooms—'

'And the explosion that Mailfist sent me to look into. . .' continued J.

Frayn nodded. 'Exactly,' he said. 'All one and the same thing.'

'But the explosion hasn't happened yet,' said Veronica. 'Or rather, it has, but not yet in the time bubble that contains the Abbey inside your house.'

'It's going to happen soon, though,' said J. 'Very soon indeed.'

'How can you know that?'

'Because I saw myself,' said J. 'I remember now. I was there. I mean, I was there, obviously, as I was then. But another version of me was in the Abbey around the time of the explosion, peering in through the window of the monk's cell. I think it was me as I am now.'

'How could you tell?'

J pulled out a strand of her hair and examined it. 'I used a dye I picked up in Camden in the late 22nd century. Citric acid-sensitive. You just rub it with a lemon, or an apple, and it changes from black to red. Neat.'

'So?'

'The version of myself I saw back then had red hair. I think that's where we go next tonight, Veronica — back to the Abbey. Just at the time the explosion happens.'

'And that's where the Dead Letter will be!' Veronica exclaimed. 'We need to go now. We can cut this whole thing off at the source.'

Nyman peered through the mist. 'It's beginning to lift,' he said. 'It's almost dawn. And it looks like — no, it can't be.'

'They've cleared off!' said Frayn, fanning at the air. 'Defeated by my brave little cat.' He picked up Hodge and placed her on his shoulders, where she snuggled down, content.

'Then let's take our chance,' said Veronica. 'They may come back.'

The group walked out of the mist and into the new day. The lawn was charred and churned up; the maze was now a dark, smouldering wreck. The rising sun shone blood-red on the broken fragments of the windows through which Gabrielle, Nyman, and J had escaped the previous night.

Gabrielle took Veronica's arm, and they walked side by side.

'Vee, you need to get your wound seen to. I can take things from here.'

Veronica shook her head. 'You know me, Gabs. I like to see things through to the bitter end.'

THIRTEEN

The monk stood examining the silver spoon in the light from his narrow window. He tilted it around so that it twinkled and shimmered. It looked oddly familiar to him: but why should it? He had never owned such fine things as this; and as for the treasures of the abbey, he was perfectly content to let others look after them. He was happy enough with his books and Pangur, his cat.

He stopped suddenly and looked out of the window. It was the strangest feeling, but he was convinced that he was being watched. The harder he looked, however, the more he began to question himself. He turned away from the window. There — there it was again. In the corner of his eye: a face looking in at him. Was it a man or a woman? He suspected the latter, but when he looked back, it had gone.

The cloisters were said to be the site of bizarre apparitions. Not long ago, one of the brothers — a quiet, level-headed fellow — claimed to have seen a group of beings in strange garb enjoying a feast in the middle of the gardens, attended on by servants. The announcement had provoked consternation: what exactly was the nature of these visitors? The monk had searched the archives of the monastery at the time, and had discovered several such accounts occurring throughout the history of the establishment.

The monk had been sceptical. Then the visions had come to him. It was only a few nights ago: he had woken up from a shallow sleep, but the usual jumble of impressions that came from troubled dreams hadn't gone away. The strange, multiplying details had persisted into the waking world. He had tried to dismiss them, but the pressure was simply too much. He could see and hear so many things in his internal world that the external began to seem pale and vague. Writing down what he saw— or rather, channelling it into this strange pictogram that he barely understood —was the only thing that seemed to help.

And yet in doing this, he felt furtive, as if it were something forbidden. He thought of the serpent, and the fruit of the tree of knowledge, and wondered if he, too, had been beguiled.

Pangur pricked her ears and tensed up. He listened carefully. Yes, there was something there. A sound —a very subtle sound—of someone shifting his or her weight, fabric brushing against wood. That was no apparition. It was coming from his closet. He paced over, grabbed the handle, and flung the door open. There was a woman there. She was young, slight of build, and dark-haired.

'Hello,' she said. 'I think I'm lost.'

Her eyes widened and a look of bewilderment spread across her face.

'Oh my God,' she said. 'It's *you*.'

The drawing room, like the garden, was in disarray, covered in fragments of wood and broken glass, the carpet torn and scorched.

'Oh dear,' said Frayn, taking off his smoking-cap and scratching his head as if he had no idea where to begin. 'Oh dear, oh dear.'

He walked over to the mantelpiece to examine the clock

that stood there. Its metal casing and face had melted, and were trickling over the edge. Nyman put his hand out and touched it. The surface yielded slightly as he pressed it.

'It's still warm,' he said.

Frayn leaned in and listened intently.

'It's still *running*,' he exclaimed.

'We're near the explosion,' said Veronica. 'The shockwaves are getting bigger.'

Frayn turned to her, alarmed.

'I say, Miss Britton,' he said. 'What's going to happen? I mean, will my house still be standing at the end of it?'

'Frayn,' said Veronica. 'Your house is the *product* of the explosion. Only the abbey is going to be destroyed. And I don't think we have much time left.'

She led them from the room and into the hallway. A set of deep cracks in the walls radiated out from the doorway that led to the abbey gardens.

'Come on,' she said.

'Since when has there been a timepool here?' asked J. 'Do you know that I walked all the way from Blackfriars?'

The monk looked at her blankly.

J frowned. 'You really have no idea what I'm talking about, have you?'

She walked over to the desk and examined the monk's handiwork. She frowned, leaned in closer, and then staggered backwards as if teetering on the edge of a cliff.

'What *is* that? How did you do it?'

The monk shrugged.

'It came to me a few nights ago. I could see and hear everything, from the beginning to the end of days. There was so much there—too much, in fact. It felt like my brains were boiling in my skull.'

He traced the lines and figures on the page with his finger.

'This was the only solution,' said the monk, frowning. He started back in alarm and looked up.

'You're an agent,' he said, 'with the Ministry. You're here to investigate an explosion. Something that ripped out a massive amount of space and time and deposited it—'

He looked dazed.

'Where does this knowledge come from?' he asked. 'Why has it been granted to me?'

'I think,' said J, carefully, 'that you just happened to be in the wrong place at the wrong time. The explosion happens here, or very nearby, and for some reason, you've felt its first effects. Those are your visions. Those are what you've put on paper.'

She looked at the page again.

'You idiot,' she said, 'what on earth did you think you were doing?'

The cloister was cool and grey; the dinner table was still there, its chairs placed neatly upside down on its surface. Frayn picked one off and sat down. Hodge, who had been hitching a ride in one of the voluminous pockets of his smoking jacket, got out and began to prowl around.

'What now?' asked Nyman.

'I think it's down to Hodge,' said Veronica. 'She can find the earlier version of herself here, and hopefully retrieve the letter for us.'

'Miss Britton,' said Frayn, getting to his feet, 'I'm so sorry. I quite forgot my manners.'

'That's all right, Frayn,' said Veronica, wincing.

'But you're so terribly pale.'

Veronica staggered a little to one side, and Frayn put out his hand to steady her, catching her at the waist. He saw her injury.

'Miss Britton!' he exclaimed.

Veronica shook her head. 'It looks worse than it is, Frayn.'

Frayn pushed his chair forward insistently. She sat down slowly.

'It was one of these windows,' said J, walking around the border of the garden, and testing the invisible barrier of the time bubble with her fingers. 'Yes. This one. Definitely this one.'

As she spoke, Hodge sprang from the ground and crawled in through the window. J peered closer, trying to adjust to the gloom.

'Oh,' she said.

Gabrielle stood on tiptoes and looked over her shoulder.

'Quite,' she added.

Inside the monk's cell, the dark-haired, slightly younger version of J glanced up suddenly from the page.

'What was that?'

'Nothing,' said the monk, pointing at the floor beneath the window where the kitten had just landed with a soft *plump*. 'Just Pangur.'

J looked at the cat, and then around the room carefully.

'If that's Pangur,' she said, 'which cat is *that*?'

There was another small marmalade cat sitting on top of the open cupboard door, looking down at them.

'Ah,' said the monk. 'Now she hasn't done that before.'

J ran back over to the window and looked out. She saw—she thought she saw—just out of the corner of her eye . . .

'Come on,' she said. 'We're going out to the garden.'

'But why?' The monk held up his ink-stained hands. 'I have to finish the manuscript.'

'You've done quite enough,' said J, tugging the sheet of paper from the desk and deftly folding it into her pocket.

Doyle stood braced against the broken window frame in the drawing room. The shards of glass dug into his skin, but he was past caring. He pulled the compass from his pocket. The glass was cracked, the casing buckled. He shook it; it emitted a feeble ticking sound. Slowly, very slowly, he rotated it in his hands, and tried to locate the signal.

There was the sound of footfall in the cloister.

'Come on out,' said a familiar voice. 'I know you're there.'

J—the dark-haired version—strode across the lawn and up to Veronica's chair. She took a scrap of paper from her pocket and opened it up.

'Is this what you're here for?' she asked.

As she opened it, the air seemed to clear. Everything came into sharp focus, as a pure, high-pitched note rang out. The dark-haired J blinked and looked around.

'Good God!' she said as she caught sight of the red-haired version of herself. 'How did you get here?'

'You idiot,' said the red-haired J, 'haven't you destroyed that by now?'

'I haven't had a chance,' said dark-haired J, 'I've only just taken it off him.'

'Who?' asked Veronica.

The monk ran into the garden and looked around in amazement at the figures seated there. They, in turn, looked in no less amazement back at him.

'It's *you*,' said Veronica.

'Me?' he asked.

'Yes,' said both versions of J simultaneously. 'It's the original Ministry porter.'

The monk frowned. 'What do you mean?' he asked. 'Are you speaking of my future? That was the only thing I couldn't see . . .' He reached out to take the paper from J. She tugged it away. The monk snatched again, and J pulled back—

Nothing. She looked at the space between thumb and forefinger where she had just been holding the letter. Then she glanced over at the red-haired version of herself who shrugged. They both looked down at the ground.

One of the Hodges was slouching towards Veronica, holding the letter in her mouth, whilst the other circled her as if to fend off attackers.

'Good girl,' said Frayn. 'Time to do what we must do, eh, Miss Britton?'

He took a silver cigarette lighter from the pocket of his smoking jacket and handed it to Veronica.

'Best to do it quickly,' he said. 'Then everything can go back to normal.'

Veronica took the cigarette lighter, flipped open the lid, and struck the flint. The flame caught first time and flickered in the darkening air. Hodge stood up on her hind legs, and rested her front paws on Veronica's knee. With her free hand, Veronica reached for the Dead Letter.

Suddenly, Nyman scooped the cat away from her. Hodge hissed, writhed, and scratched him, drawing deep furrows in the skin of his hands. He didn't even flinch, but grabbed the Dead Letter and tried to wrest it from her jaws.

'What the devil do you think you're doing, man?' shouted Frayn, and attempted to grab the cat from him. Nyman threw him off effortlessly. Then he turned his attention back to the cat, holding her at arm's length with one hand as she tore fiercely at his arm. Yet as soon as a wound was opened, it healed up like a zip being fastened. His facial features, too, were in flux, smoothing themselves out. 'Trust me, Miss

Britton,' he said. 'You have to trust me.' Veronica rose from her seat and swiped the cat from his arms, but it was too late. Nyman had the paper. Before anyone could say another word, the door was flung open and Doyle staggered into the garden. He started back when he saw the cats; one of them leapt through the gap in the door and was gone.

'Don't move, Doyle,' said Nyman, pulling out what Gabrielle recognised as a Nameless weapon. Doyle stared at him for a moment. Nyman's face was now almost completely blank, pale reflective surfaces filling in where the eyes and mouth had been.

'So,' Doyle said, as if relishing the moment, 'you're one of the Nameless, are you?'

Nyman — now completely transformed into one of the Nameless — raised his weapon. Doyle's hand crept to his side-pocket. The Nameless fired as Doyle drew a small black cylinder and pressed a button at the end. There was a flash of brilliant red light, and the Nameless staggered backwards, his shot going wild and burning a hole in the door.

Gabrielle saw nothing but a scarlet blur before her eyes, and wondered for a moment if the discharge from Doyle's gun had blinded her. Gradually, she saw shapes and movement resolve. She could make out the figure of Doyle, standing in front of the door, frozen at the sight of his handiwork. The Nameless lay curled up on the ground; he looked as if he had turned to stone. The monk was kneeling over him. There was something strange and blurred about the monk's outline. When he shifted his arm, he seemed to leave a wispy trail of afterimages behind him, as if he actually possessed a dozen arms.

'Doyle!' shouted Veronica. 'What have you done?'

Doyle turned the weapon slowly over in his hands.

'It's never been tried before,' he said.

The Nameless's body shifted and crackled as bright blue flames danced over it.

'The Nameless,' said Doyle, 'they're beings partially composed of the fabric of time. That's why they can't be killed or hurt. Except by this.'

'A time compressor,' gasped both Js.

The monk looked up. 'You've killed him!' he shouted.

'Worse,' said Veronica, crawling over. Nyman's body flickered and dissolved into thousands of tiny, intense points of light. The Dead Letter fluttered to the ground, and the monk picked it up.

'This? You killed him for this?'

The monk tried to get up, but fell back as if someone were pulling him down. His image began to fragment and spin away in all directions. There were hundreds and hundreds of him.

Doyle turned and ran.

'What are you waiting for?' shouted Veronica. 'This is it! This is what causes the explosion!'

They ran for the doorway.

'Where's Hodge?' said Frayn.

They looked down just in time to see the cat struck by a bolt of energy.

'We have to leave her, Frayn,' gasped Veronica. 'This is supposed to happen.'

'Oh dear,' said Frayn, pausing fretfully on the spot as an arc of brilliant white light surrounded Nyman's remains, and the monk's voice dissolved into a cacophony.

'On the November the 20th, 1998, at eight in the morning, William Hogan decided he wouldn't go to work that day . . . On the evening of January the 15th, 150, Grumio Festina was preparing a meal for 20 guests . . . On the 16th of September, 2176, Katarina Darby declared that London was now an independent state . . .'

Gabrielle was never sure afterwards exactly what order things had happened in.

The red-haired version of J took hold of Frayn and dragged him towards the door.

Dark-haired J was struck by a bolt of energy that whipped around her ankle like a lasso, dragging her back towards the centre of the storm.

Frayn, Gabrielle, and J stood in the corridor. A light so thick it seemed like liquid spilled out of the hole in the door left by Nyman's gun.

The door swung open and the corridor was filled with light.

Veronica, on the other side, pushed the door closed, shutting herself into the cloister.

Gabrielle flung herself against the door, trying to force it open, trying to get to Veronica, but J and Frayn pulled her off.

There was the sound of thunder.

A little while later, Gabrielle, J, and Frayn sat by the drawing-room hearth with blankets wrapped around them, drinking cocoa in silence. A cat emerged from under Frayn's chair, and dropped a tattered envelope at Gabrielle's feet. She picked it up and read the front. The words were very faint, but just about legible.

In the event of my death.

She threw it on the fire without opening it.

PART FOUR

The Infinite Empire

ONE

If she stood on tiptoe at precisely the right angle, she could see out of the window.

It had taken time to perfect this. Time, fortunately, was one of the few things they had allowed her. She had been deprived of all sorts of other things over the years depending on their mood, such as a bed to rest on, more than the bare minimum of clothing, food, light, and human company. Time, however, her captors had been more than generous with, had let it roll over her in waves.

Now, at last, she felt herself running short of time. The strands on her hairbrush had turned from grey to white. She was growing muddle-headed; she had occupied herself during her imprisonment by writing a book in her head, a detailed account of a short but rich period of adventure she had enjoyed as a young woman. She had eked the details out slowly, recording not just the bare facts but every detail she could remember of the people she had met, what they had worn, what they had eaten; the sights she had seen in the city as she travelled from age to age as freely as one might slip through its streets. Now she was finding it hard to pick up the thread of the previous day's efforts, although the older memories remained sharp enough; sometimes she had to start again and repeat her work. Perhaps her mind was going;

or perhaps it was because her account, despite her deliberate slowness in construction, was now reaching a series of events she did not wish to remember: the coming of the Empire, the late 19th century waging war on all the other eras of the city, colonising London's entire history. Why, she wondered, had she ever imagined she could stand against it?

Her legs and back began to ache: she relaxed back down onto the soles of her feet. She never managed to catch more than a glimpse of the world outside her cell, and what she saw was not exactly appealing. Still, it was all she had to look at other than the plain, whitewashed walls of her cell and the bare stone floor. She leaned forward against the wall, closed her eyes, and rested her forehead against its coolness. She thought back to where she had left her narrative: the final battle for the Ministry of Chronic Affairs. The bombs shattering glass and destroying the delicate machinery that encased its rooms: Jim Carter flinging her through the escape hatch after Mailfist, then turning to direct fire in one last attempt at resistance.

Resistance? No, not resistance. He knew the war was lost, that the Ministry had fallen. He was simply buying her time to get away. As it turned out, his life had been worth precisely six months of liberty before the Empire caught up with her.

She was distracted from her thoughts by an itching sensation around her calves. Her veins again, no doubt. She put her hand down to scratch, and was alarmed by a sudden movement, a twitch of muscle. The feeling of soft fur. She looked down, and saw a pair of green eyes looking back up at her.

She started back, careless for a moment of what the guards might hear. The cat purred quietly and settled on its haunches, giving her time to compose herself.

'Is it you?' she whispered. She reached out to touch the cat again, expecting it to dissolve as she did so; perhaps what she was seeing was nothing more than a memory made real by the wishes of an old woman. The cat nestled into her hand, rubbing the top of its head against her and closing its eyes.

'Still no message, eh? Well, maybe next time.'

TWO

He pulled up his collar against the cold and looked around at the faces in the crowd as the fireworks exploded over Westminster Bridge and the bell of Big Ben chimed the end of the millennium. There was something hysterical about the way people were behaving this evening, he thought. Like they were all trying too hard to convince themselves that they were having fun.

The couple next to him kissed. They had, he estimated, only known each other for a few seconds. It was a tacky, drunken thing to do. Yet there was something about the way the woman's hand rested on the man's collar when they pulled back that made him feel suddenly ashamed of his uncharitable thoughts. He was, he admitted to himself, only feeling this way because he was missing Veronica. He knew how things had to be, that he would have to resign himself to long absences. Still, he wished they could have chosen somewhere else to meet: somewhere that didn't remind him quite so much of what he was missing.

He felt a tug at his sleeve and spun around. Someone took hold of him by the waist and kissed him, hard. The kiss tasted of tea and lemon cake.

'Veronica!'

She was wearing a small foil hat that fastened under her chin with an elastic band.

'What did I miss?' she asked.

'The end of the century,' he replied.

'Oh,' she said. 'Nothing special.'

She took off her hat. They kissed again.

'It's so good to see you.'

'Yes, it is, isn't it?' Veronica looked around the crowd nervously. 'I think I was followed. Through the first few timepools at least. I gave them the slip in the 12th century, though: I doubled back.'

'And here you are.'

'And here I am.'

'My Vee.'

Veronica took him by the elbow. 'Let's walk,' she said.

'Where to?'

'Away. Somewhere quieter.'

'What about safety in numbers?'

Veronica shook her head. 'I just don't like it. I don't know; it's a feeling. Come on.'

As they walked off the bridge and towards St Thomas' Hospital, Veronica feigned a little drunken stagger and slipped off the pavement. She was *good*, he thought.

They walked past the steamed-up pubs and restaurants in the Cut. Veronica suddenly stopped and turned down a narrow side alley, heaped up with rubbish. There was a skip blocking the entrance that they had to skirt around.

'Where are we going?' he asked.

Veronica stopped and turned around. Before her, crumbling and black with dirt, was a brick wall.

'Nowhere,' she said.

She kissed him. There was something urgent about the way she did it.

He pushed her away.

'I would wait forever for you,' he said.

'I know,' she replied. She leaned in again and wrapped her arms around him, tight. He felt her fingers twitch, felt something firm and cold pressing against the side of his chest.

Time stood still.

THREE

The map bubbled and churned. Occasionally, lights and buildings would take form in its turbid waters before crumbling again into shapelessness. Doyle struck the side of the tank in frustration. There was a knock at the door of the war room. He turned around, peering into the darkness. The only source of light was the map: he found that dimming all other forms of illumination helped him to make out just a little more in its depths. On the other hand, this meant that the already dark walls of the immense room vanished entirely from view. Sometimes, after long hours staring into its depths, he would look up disorientated, and imagine himself the sole living creature in the middle of an immense darkening plain. He hated this sensation: it reminded him of something he was constantly struggling to push to the back of his mind.

'Come in!' shouted Doyle.

The edge of the doorway appeared as a thin crack of light in the darkness, almost blindingly bright in contrast. A young man in a smart black uniform stepped inside.

'Close the door!' Doyle shielded his eyes. The young man obeyed, then stepped forward hesitantly into the room, arm outstretched, feeling for the wall.

'What is it?' asked Doyle impatiently.

The man produced a piece of folded paper from his pocket. Doyle marched forward and snatched it from his hands.

'Another bombing, sir. Soho, 1956.'

Doyle scanned the casualty list by the light of the map.

'Half a dozen dead. Wounded?'

'No survivors, sir.'

Doyle turned back to the map, pressing his hand against the edges of the tank. In the blue-green light, his bones showed through the skin.

'Sir?'

'Yes?'

'Brodarty, sir. One of them was Brodarty.'

'Yes. I noticed. Dismissed.'

The young man straightened up and saluted. Doyle waited until the door had closed, then moved his hands into first position on the map and started again.

It was not going to be easy. Without Brodarty — he had barely known the man, but still he felt his loss. Brodarty was the man who had — who would — who now would never win the decisive battle during London's first war of independence. Just when everything had seemed lost, he had rallied the remaining ironclads into a daring charge that had broken the enemy's lines. More than that, he had been a hero and inspiration to generations of . . .

Already the idea was dissolving at the edges, like a vivid dream that slips through one's fingers in the morning. Not that Doyle dreamed. He pressed his hands against the glass and tried to focus; tried to feel the way the sands suspended in the brackish liquid wanted to flow; tried to find where the growing fault lines were located.

The keys rattled in the lock. The old woman didn't turn around. A rare beam of sunlight had forced its way into her cell, and she stood in its glow, eyes closed, feeling herself dissolving in light and warmth. Perhaps this was how it would be when the inevitable came: she was sure it would be soon.

There was a cough, and she heard boots shuffle on the dusty floor. She knew who it was: not by name, of course–they never gave her their names. She got to know every one of her guards extremely well: their physical appearance, their habits, their little kindnesses and cruelties. This one she had nicknamed 'the Schoolboy': he didn't look a day over 12, had ruddy cheeks and a too-short haircut that emphasised the cherubic roundness of his face. He was more or less permanently unsure of himself, and tended to draw attention by coughing, sniffing, or shuffling: anything other than actually saying what he wanted.

'What is it?' she asked.

'You've got a visitor, ma'am.' *Ma'am*. She liked that. Some good old-fashioned courtesy. She wheeled around and smiled. The Schoolboy shrunk back, steadying himself in the doorframe. She winked at him.

'Don't worry,' she said. 'I'm an old woman now. My body's long gone, and my brain will be following shortly. I couldn't — *I wouldn't* — hurt a fly these days.'

'Precisely,' said another voice, loud and confident, 'an old woman.'

She barely had time to prepare herself before he was in the room. He looked just as she remembered him — a little while after the events at the Frayn Collection, she had glimpsed him leading the charge at the Ministry, the bones of his skull standing out in the flash of flames and gunfire. And then afterwards, when she had been taken prisoner — but she preferred not to think about that.

'Come, come,' said Doyle. 'Don't stand on ceremony with an old friend. I know it's been a long time.' He counted off his fingers. 'How long exactly? 20? 30? 40 years? One loses track.'

'For me.'

'Naturally. For you.'

'But not so long for you, eh?' the old woman said, trying to control her fury.

'Oh, a couple of months.'

'Really?' The old woman smiled.

'One loses track,' said Doyle, smiling.

The old woman laughed, and walked over to sit on her bed.

'I suppose one does,' she said. 'But you know, Doyle, the strange thing is that I seem to remember you saying that you had done with me. That if I wouldn't answer your questions, you would just leave me here for the rest of my life to wither away and die. Well, Doyle, my memory might not be what it was, but I remember that day vividly enough. And I'm not dead yet. Unlike you. So what brings you here?'

Doyle's smile curdled into a grimace.

'She's back, isn't she?'

'Miss Pendleton!'

'Back and causing your lot no end of trouble, I expect. Well, good for her. And very kind of you to come around and tell me. Using my name again, I note. Well, all in all it's been quite a day.' She lay back on her bed, stretched, and closed her eyes. 'Do close the door on your way out.'

'Miss Pendleton, I'm not here to dredge up the past—'

Gabrielle opened her eyes a little.

'Twice in one day. You know, during my interrogation, you never once called me by my name. It's a terrible thing to deprive a person of their name, do you know that? It's a way of wiping them out of existence. I suppose that was your intention. Perhaps you could tell me what's changed that I am afforded such courtesy now.'

'You may not agree with our methods, Miss Pendleton, but

you must agree that any form of order is better than anarchy.'

'Hm,' said Gabrielle. 'That's as maybe.'

She opened her eyes fully. Doyle stepped towards the bed: she noticed the little patch of light was still there on the floor, even though he was standing directly in the path of the beam.

'Miss Pendleton,' said Doyle, 'Veronica Britton has become the most significant threat facing the continued survival of this city.'

'Good.'

'Every day there is another bombing, another assassination. Every time we try to make good the damage, to set the timelines on their proper course again, she tears it all to pieces.'

'I don't blame her. Your Empire is hardly a model of gentility.' She closed her eyes again. 'Now leave me. I can't help you. More to the point, I don't want to.'

Doyle stayed where he was.

'Miss Pendleton,' he said, 'Veronica Britton is no longer the woman you knew. She's become something else. Her and her followers are fanatics. Most of them haven't even met her. She probably doesn't even know they exist. But they still do things in her name. Terrible things. They're ripping up time, creating paradox after paradox. We're being stretched very thin, Miss Pendleton. I don't mean the Empire. I mean the whole city. The whole world.'

Gabrielle sighed.

'And why is the city at risk, eh? The world? It's because of your Empire. Wanting to make everything fit into your little box. Nothing growing as it should. Uniform times, uniform people. Even chaos sounds better than that.'

'Do you really believe that?' asked Doyle. 'Are you sure?'

'Quite sure.'

Doyle moved over to the doorway.

'The Infinite Empire was established to serve the interests of Britain, and of the Queen—'

'Ah yes,' said Gabrielle, sitting up as if suddenly interested. 'The Queen. As I recall, she had no idea that elements in her own government and armed forces were planning to give her all of space and time as a present. Was she grateful? In fact, whatever happened to her?'

Doyle ignored her.

'You will help me, Miss Pendleton. You have no other option. Together, we will find Veronica Britton.'

Gabrielle shook her head.

'I don't think there's anything you can threaten me with anymore, Doyle. And there's nothing that I want from you. Do close the door behind you. There's a terrible draught.'

'You forget, Miss Pendleton.'

Gabrielle shrugged.

'I forget all sorts of things.'

'There is one thing I could give back to you if I chose to.'

He smiled. In the waning light of the cell, his grin extended all the way back, the skull showing through his cheeks. He didn't go into details. He didn't need to. She knew what he meant, had known he was going to offer it from the moment he walked into her cell.

Her youth.

'Leave me,' she said, suddenly.

'You need to consider my offer,' said Doyle, gently. 'I understand.'

Gabrielle looked away.

'Just leave.'

'Don't take too long, Miss Pendleton,' said Doyle. 'Time is of the essence.'

FOUR

It was the sort of shop they called a 'cat's face'. A narrow front with row upon row of stock in the window, and just enough space inside for the counter and a customer or two. The shopkeeper was a middle-aged man whose clothes were too loose for him, as if he had recently lost a lot of weight: his trousers were held in place with a safety-pin, and his jacket hung awkwardly on his shoulders, the collar and lapels worn and shiny. He peered uncertainly out of the window through cracked glasses as he wound up the last watch for the window display.

'There we are,' he said. 'Done.'

His assistant, a younger man with a pudding-basin haircut, was spreading a layer of marmalade very thinly onto a slice of toast.

'Good,' he replied. 'Now all we need are some customers. We can't live on tick for much longer.'

The shopkeeper grunted, lumbered over to the counter, lifted the hinged section that separated it from the main part of the shop, and pushed a few buttons on the till.

'I don't know why you bother winding them,' said the assistant, sadly, handing the shopkeeper the toast. 'They're purely decorative these days.'

'Standards, my boy,' said the shopkeeper. 'Standards must

be maintained.'

The assistant said nothing, but looked at one of the window panes that had a peeling strip of brown paper pasted over a large crack. The shopkeeper pulled a single sheet of grey, pulpy newspaper from his pocket and spread it on the counter.

He started with a story from abroad: something about the latest rocket launches in the Australian outback — another attempt to re-establish contact with the Martian colonies. He was distracted by a faint chiming, like a fork being tapped limply against the side of a glass.

'Sir?' said the assistant.

'Mm?'

'A customer.'

The shopkeeper looked up to see a woman in a hooded cloak standing next to the window display. She had her back turned to him.

'I say,' he gasped. 'I — we — that is, are you after something? Can we sell you something? I mean, can we help you?'

The woman pointed a velvet-gloved hand at one of the items on the shelf. The shopkeeper let himself out from behind the counter, dismissing his assistant with a wave, and moved over to the cabinet. He took a collection of keys from his pocket, selected one, and unlocked the cabinet.

'An excellent choice,' he babbled. 'Quite a rare item.'

He lifted the device out and held it up in the dusty light.

'You see, it's a rather unusual sort of a pocket watch. The mechanism is housed in an enamelled box. The face is here. The clever thing is that as you open and close it, you're also winding it. So if you check the time every now and again, the winding takes care of itself.'

The customer didn't reply. The shopkeeper replaced the item in the cabinet and picked out a wristwatch with a pale leather strap.

'Perhaps something more conservative? This, too, is a lovely piece. The spring, you see, runs the entire diameter of the case. So it can go for a whole week on a single wind. Would you care to have a closer look, ma'am? Oh my God, it's you! I thought you were dead! What do you think you're doing here, in broad daylight?'

'Do go on, Mailfist,' said J. 'I was enjoying that.'

Mailfist spun around in panic to see his assistant was already outside pulling the shutters down. The assistant re-entered the shop, locked the door behind him top, middle, and bottom, and pulled the curtain over the entrance. The three of them stood in the gloomy interior in silence.

'Don't use that name,' said Mailfist after a few minutes. 'I'm trying to keep a low profile.'

J looked around.

'You're succeeding.'

She wound the watch Mailfist had given her, and held it to her ear.

'It doesn't even go.'

'No, no.'

Mailfist took the watch from her irritably, and gently completed the wind.

'There, you see,' he handed it back to her. 'You just need to treat it with a bit of love.'

J slipped the watch onto her wrist, buckling it neatly with her nimble thief's fingers. She stepped over to the till and hit a few keys: it opened with a jarring ring.

'Business isn't exactly booming, I see.' She ran her gloved finger around the interior, picking up dust. Mailfist noticed that she was busy slipping what coins there were into her pocket with her other hand, but he was too polite to say anything.

'Look, J,' he said. 'We're on our uppers. That's the way things are. We had to abandon the Ministry without so much as a penny to our name. We've been hunted ever since. Luckily we always had this shop on the go. A safe house and a potential source of revenue; I can't say that any other government agency has ever managed to keep costs down quite so efficiently. Even so, we have to change the time zone that we're in every so often just to make sure. So our opening hours are rather irregular.'

'I'm just getting a feel for things,' said J, fishing underneath the counter and pulling out the revolver and rapier concealed there. 'Finding out what we have to work with.'

'The Ministry is out of our reach, as you know,' said the assistant, stepping back as J took a few experimental swipes with the sword. 'Our timepools, too, are no longer under our control. The majority of my brothers—'

J looked at him carefully.

'Oh yes. It's you. You were the Roman one.'

The assistant nodded curtly.

'Do you have a name these days?'

'I have an alias.'

'Do tell.'

The assistant looked embarrassed. 'Babbage.'

'Perfect. Anyway, you were about to get to the important bit. Equipment we can rebuild or steal. Preferably steal, it's quicker. But people . . . Rather harder to replace. How many more clerks? How many porters, how many agents?'

Mailfist cleared his throat.

'There's the resistance, of course, but they're a wild bunch. Diffuse, no leader, they just seem to act randomly. We can't work with them. You might as well try to work with a whirlwind. Planting bombs, surprise attacks, ambushes, that sort of thing. They do it in the name of Veronica Britton, though none of them have ever met her. They don't even know very much about her. They say she comes to them in dreams.'

'Veronica Britton is nothing but a name now,' said Babbage.

'And probably better off for it,' said J, cocking the pistol and sighting it. 'Still, you haven't answered my question. How many of us are there?'

'Well,' said Mailfist, 'at this very moment there's just . . .'

'Just us,' said Babbage. 'Mailfist and I.'

'And you,' said Mailfist, with forced cheerfulness. 'Assuming you're here to join us.'

'Ah,' J replied.

She leapt forward just as Babbage squeezed the trigger of the pistol that he had pulled from the drawer in front of him, and knocked the gun cleanly out of his hand. The weapon — a flintlock that bore the scars of heavy use and frequent mending — went off, sending a discharge of soot out along with the ball. It hit the ceiling, dislodging a shower of plaster and dust. J slid over the counter and pointed the revolver at him: he grabbed the barrel, pulled it out of her hands, and struck her across the temple with it. She reeled backwards as he twirled the gun around and pointed it at her.

'Babbage!' shouted Mailfist. 'What the devil do you think you're doing?'

J looked straight ahead at the gun, weighing up her chances, shifting her weight from foot to foot.

'We can't trust her, sir,' Babbage replied.

'Of course we can! J is one of my most loyal — '

'She was last seen being dragged away by Empire troops, sir. So how did she get away? What was the price they asked for her freedom? Maybe it was tracking us down. You know, I think the Empire are already on their way.'

'Now, now,' said Mailfist, looking nervously at the shutters. 'You know as well as I do that J could get out of a locked safe if she had to.'

'I did once, actually,' J interjected. 'Get out of a locked safe, that is.'

'That's enough,' Babbage hissed. 'We can't take any chances. Once the Empire has taken someone, they're dead or a collaborator. We know that. And once we're dead, the Ministry's gone. Finished. Just a name, like Veronica.'

'We'll just have to take that chance,' Mailfist replied. 'Put the gun down, my boy. That's an order!'

Babbage paused for a moment, the gun perfectly balanced, J precisely in his sights. He was looking at her, Mailfist thought, as if he were planning not just the shot, but also the process of cleaning up afterwards and disposing of the body. Then he relaxed his grip, uncocked the hammer, and placed it in his jacket pocket.

'Thank you,' said J.

'Say what you like,' said Babbage. 'There's no way she escaped on her own.'

J dabbed at the cut on her head and winced.

'I didn't,' she said. 'I was set free for a reason.'

Babbage whipped the pistol back out in a flash.

'Whoa!' shouted Mailfist.

'Sorry! Bad choice of words!' J held up her hands. 'I was broken out of a transport.'

'Who by?' Babbage demanded.

'The Nameless.'

FIVE

They had patched her up physically, and assumed that her
memory would return as she moved further away in time
from whatever traumatic event had obviously happened. Yet
here she was, two weeks on, and still nothing.

The trouble was, she felt, that they assumed that the disaster that had landed her here was over, and receding into
the distance. Yet she had the nagging feeling that it was still
going on *right now*.

An old lady from the hospital's League of Friends had sup-
plied her with some clothes that were about the right size:
black Capri pants, a pullover, and a pair of slip-on shoes.
She took them from the chair, got dressed, and walked out
of her room.

The corridor outside was silent; the ward rounds were over
for the day, and the nurses were busy with the other patients.
She walked up to the nurses' station purposefully—she liked
having a task, however minor, as it made her feel much more
like herself. Whoever she might be.

'I'm just going downstairs for a bit,' she told the nurse at
the desk.

The nurse, a young man with crew-cut dark hair, nodded
and smiled. 'Don't be too long,' he said.

The atrium, a huge open space with a long rectangular reception desk, was relatively quiet. Clinics and visiting hours were over: the daytime staff had gone home. A few figures in dressing gowns were smoking cigarettes outside in the courtyard on one side; on the other, a traffic jam had snarled up the Euston Road. Horns blared, muffled by the thick glass of the doors.

She walked over to the small shop, to pick up a couple of newspapers. She spent every evening scouring national and local papers to see if they carried any story that might be vaguely related to her. Of course, the police were making inquiries, but she wanted to feel as if she was doing something, however minor, to contribute.

The middle-aged man at the counter didn't look up as she placed the papers in front of him.

'Excuse me?'

The man looked up from his mobile phone.

'I can't get a signal,' he explained. 'It's not working.'

He pointed at the screen.

'My son called me,' he said. 'He got cut off.'

'Was something wrong?'

'He said something about the news. Tanks in Trafalgar Square.'

'What?'

The ground began to rumble. She turned and ran back into the atrium, ignoring the pain in her side, and out, down the front steps to the Euston Road. The traffic was still stationary, but the drivers were now getting out of their cars, abandoning them and fleeing on foot. Only they didn't seem to know what direction to flee in; the pavements were crowded with bodies, pushing and shoving and trying to escape. She picked her way through the crowd and stood in the middle of the road. The rumbling had become a roar. Approaching from both directions were two groups of dark, heavy machines that blocked both road and pavement, sweeping the crowd before them. They were like giant black woodlice, crawling slowly but inexorably towards her.

The cars had been pushed forward by the ironclads so that they were crushed together, side-on and end-to-end, blocking the road. Some of the ironclads — yes, that was their name, ironclads — were beginning to drive up over the vehicles, metal crumpling and glass shattering under their weight as the occupants tried to flee. The people were in a state of panic: the ironclads obviously wanted them to move, but where? In every direction, they were driven back into the crowd. She climbed on top of one of the stationary cars, right in the middle of the Euston Road, trying to get a better view.

One of the vehicles was outstripping its companions. It snorted and roared and it tore its way along the stacked cars towards her. At one point it entered a dip, and seemed to get stuck behind an awkwardly-angled car: for a few seconds it ground its gears, with a sound like a caged animal gnashing its teeth. Then a bolt of lightning burst from the cannon at the front, blowing the obstruction out of the way. As it regained the high ground, it accelerated. The lamps at the front turned and focused on her. The ironclad picked up more and more speed. She stood directly in its path, studying it carefully. A few of the hemmed-in crowd spotted her: she was dimly aware of their cries in the background, some screaming for her to run, others cheering on what they thought was a heroic act of defiance.

The machine came to a sudden halt a couple of inches in front of her. The lights swivelled, running up and down her body as if trying to place her. She, too, examined the iron-clad. After weeks of not knowing where or who she was, of grasping onto slender threads of identity that fell apart in her hands, the sheer physical presence of this thing suddenly clicked into place with a familiarity that was almost reassuring. It brought something to the surface in her memory. She saw a landscape: a dead world of dust and white rocks, and, coming over the horizon like a herd of prehistoric monsters, a group of these machines.

The ironclad whirred. A hatch slid open, and a constellation of bronze rods slid out. They ran along her face, brushing gently against the skin. Then they withdrew an inch or so: at the ends, she saw, were small black glass beads, like the eyes of an insect. The bronze rods snapped back. Without warning, a thicker metal tentacle shot out from the rear of the machine, wrapped itself around her, and started to pull. She tried to shrug it off, and it delivered a sharp electric sting that made her limbs contract painfully. The ironclad turned around and trundled off slowly, dragging Veronica along after it like a reluctant pet.

Gabrielle was woken by a scratching sound. It had slipped into her dreams, leaving images of fur and claws, sharp teeth and tails. The images persisted as she opened her eyes: she thought she saw a lithe shadow slipping out of the window of her cell. Slowly she sat up and rubbed her eyes. It had been many years since the cat had last visited her: that day Doyle turned up and demanded she work with him. She had thought of the cat often, as if imagining it could summon it into being.

She put her hand out to the small side table with its stub of a candle in a cheap tin holder. Her fingers felt around for the matches, but came across something quite different: a crumpled piece of paper. She lifted it to inspect more carefully, running her fingertips over the surface. It was pitted as if it had been carried in an animal's mouth, one with a sharp set of fangs. Next to it was a smooth, pebble-sized object.

Gabrielle forced herself to put the stone down slowly. She didn't want to get too excited; she couldn't risk getting clumsy. She found the matchbox—two matches left—struck one, and lit the candle. As the flame rose, she saw that the stone was a sapphire, so clear that it looked like an outsized drop of perfect blue water. She put it down, picked up the paper again, and examined it. The side facing her was blank: she turned it over and saw a word and two letters written in a neat copperplate hand that she knew extremely well.

SWITCH!
VB

She heard footsteps along the corridor. Quickly, she blew out the candle and wafted away the smoke and the smell of wax. She turned and felt for the narrow crack in the wall next to her bed: she tucked the paper and the stone in carefully, then lay down, pulled the thin grey blanket across herself, and feigned sleep.

The door opened, and a light snapped on.

'Have you had time to consider my offer?' said a voice.

Gabrielle opened her eyes.

'A little,' she replied. 'How many years has it been since we last spoke?'

'Five or ten,' said Doyle, 'give or take.'

'For me, of course. I suppose you've just been away for a couple of minutes?'

'Naturally.'

Gabrielle stretched and sat up.

'Maybe we can come to some arrangement.'

Doyle's face betrayed no emotion. As she looked at him, Gabrielle fancied she could see through him to the cables and stones of the corridor behind, as if he were a ghost.'Shall we go for a walk?' she suggested. 'Not the courtyard. I'm sick of that. A proper walk, that's what I need. Take a look at the old city, you know.'

Doyle hesitated.

'Come on, Doyle,' said Gabrielle. 'I'm hardly likely to over-power you, am I? I'm practically falling to pieces as it is.'

'Very well,' said Doyle. 'Can you be ready in 15 minutes?'

'Provided you give me some proper outdoor clothes,' said Gabrielle. 'Nothing fancy, just whatever people are wearing these days.'

'I never imagined,' Gabrielle whispered. 'I simply never imagined.'

She shielded her eyes and braced against the biting wind that blew across the red sludge of the Thames, stinging her eyes and bringing with it a corrosive smell that made her wince. Tower Bridge was barely recognisable: the stone towers either side had crumbled, exposing rusting steelwork. The bridge itself had long since collapsed, and its remnants were presumably resting at the bottom of the river. Potter's Field, opposite, was covered in discoloured, cracked cement. Shad Thames, which should have been just across the water to her left, was a heap of rubble: a charred bunker was the only structure that looked even vaguely sturdy. Armed guards stood sentry outside, and Gabrielle assumed that this was now the entrance to the Ministry. She felt unexpectedly nostalgic for the thick fogs, darkened streets, and sinister echoes of the old set-up, the wooden door with the tarnished panel.

The sky was roughly the same colour as the water. It was hardly the sunrise she had promised herself she would enjoy if and when she ever escaped from her cell. There was a clank and a sloshing sound from the opposite bank. An ironclad surfaced and crawled out of the water onto the cement. It was moving awkwardly, as if wounded: its belly scraped against the ground.

Gabrielle had seen enough. She turned to Doyle and raised her hand to strike him.

'You did this!' she shouted.

'Don't be a fool,' said Doyle, grabbing her wrist. He nodded up at the Tower wall. 'There's a man up there with a rifle. If you try anything, anything at all other than polite conversation, he'll shoot you. Do you understand?'

Gabrielle glared up at the location of the sniper, hoping the anger in her gaze would shock him into falling off his perch. Some hope. Doyle let go of her wrist and she lowered it.

'So this is what you fought for,' she said, shaking her head. 'I hope you're satisfied.'

'It wasn't supposed to be this way,' Doyle replied. It was not an admission of guilt. 'It was supposed to be *safe*. Security for Britain, and for the world.'

Gabrielle rolled her eyes.

'I didn't think you'd understand,' said Doyle.

'All you know how to do is destroy,' said Gabrielle. 'Can't you see it was bound to turn out this way?'

'And how much of the future *did* Veronica show you?' Doyle asked. 'Did you see what would happen to this country?'

'I saw enough,' Gabrielle replied abruptly.

'I doubt it,' said Doyle.

He pointed upriver, where cranes dotted the skyline.

'I know what it looks like,' he said, 'but we're rebuilding. There was something rotten at the heart of this city, something that would have spread right the way across the British Empire if we'd let it. A softness, harmless at first, but—well, we would now be in the aftermath of two world wars. In the first I believe we would have picked the wrong side, and its conclusion would have made the second war necessary. The second one would have bankrupted the country and dissolved the colonies for good. It's a disease, you see, a serious one that we simply had to deal with. Of course the consequences aren't pretty—the aftermath of surgery never is.'

Gabrielle had stood uncomfortably through Doyle's speech, feeling the collar of her tweed jacket itching against her skin. She ran her finger along it: she tried not to think about where it might have come from. Another prisoner, perhaps, one who hadn't made it out of the Tower. There was the sound of an explosion in the distance.

'You'll never tame this city, Doyle. Never.'

Doyle pointed across the river to the black bunker. 'The Ministry has just begun to yield its secrets, Miss Pendleton. We can get this city back on track.'

'I'm only ashamed we let you get the upper hand. What a collection of blunderers you are.'

'The situation got out of control, Miss Pendleton. I'm the first to admit that. We were naïve: we didn't know quite what we were taking on. But Veronica Britton is a far greater threat now than we ever were.'

'How so?'

'Something in her changed. After the events at the Frayn Collection. Yes, yes, she survived. But she came back . . . altered, somehow. She's out of control, Miss Pendleton. Her followers strike indiscriminately, soldiers, civilians, it's all the same to them. We tried using some of them to trace her, but it was no good: she has no more connection with them than God has with his worshippers. They think they meet up with her in dreamland, if you can believe that. As for what we can pin on her: well, she's playing an even more dangerous game.'

'And what's that?'

After she said it, she knew she had spoken too quickly. It seemed the patience she had learned in prison was quickly forgotten, after all. Doyle smiled, and walked over to the group of ironclads stationed outside the Tower. His shadow was thin and indistinct on the concrete.

'Come with me, Miss Pendleton,' he shouted over his shoulder. 'I'll show you.'

Veronica passed out several times during the long march south through the city. On each occasion, an electrical jolt from the tentacle had brought her painfully back into consciousness. She had a vague set of impressions: rubble lining the roads; ironclads crawling along streets with their sides scraping against the bricks of buildings; cars on fire; bullet holes in the walls. At one point, she slid her fingers gently underneath the tentacle to probe it for any points of weakness: it sensed her intentions, and tightened its grip.

The fighting continued to rage around her. She was dimly aware of a group of men in green uniforms charging on the ironclad in a wave: she tried to shout out to them, to warn them to keep away, but the machine squeezed her tighter. The ironclad's heat cannon made short work of her would-be rescuers. As the machine trundled closer to the river, the ground shook with the force of a nearby explosion and the wall of adjacent building collapsed onto the pavement next to her, forcing her to take refuge behind the ironclad: it began to climb over the rubble, dragging her remorselessly though the dust burned her throat and stung her eyes.

After Whitechapel, they turned towards the Tower of London. She saw fire leaping from the windows: there were figures on the roof, trying to get to safety. The ironclads were congregating around the walls; one, with an attachment at the front that looked like a battering ram, was engaged in breaking through. Her legs gave way, and she felt herself slip to the ground. She was convinced, as she passed out, that she heard a voice. 'Be strong,' it whispered, 'this part you survive.'

SIX

They passed along a narrow street that had long been abandoned to its fate. Everything was coated with grey ash: it had the stillness the city used to have in the small hours after a heavy snowfall. The thoroughfare was clogged with skeletal, box-like structures: they had been burned and then spent what might have been decades gradually decaying until one could no longer tell whether they had been automobiles or horse-drawn carriages. They had to pick their way around them, and over some strange dusty mounds on the surface of the street itself that Mailfist didn't care to look at too closely. Babbage and J were ahead of him; his clerk was sticking to her closely, watching her every move suspiciously. If he didn't get a move on, he'd have fallen behind before they noticed. He sensed that they were heading east. He pulled up his threadbare collar and shivered. East meant danger, and he had to keep his wits about him.

'How much further?' he heard Babbage ask J.

J stopped and bowed her head, as if in silent prayer. 'Not much further at all,' she replied.

She turned the corner into what must have once been a coaching-yard. Rotting remnants of wooden picnic tables littered the ground, and the windows of what had presumably been the old inn were covered in rusted sheets of corrugated iron. Someone had been here recently, Mailfist noticed: the

Britton fanatics, by the look of things. An elaborate 'VB' in swirling letters had been sprayed across the metal.

J walked up to the metal panel covering the door of the inn, put her shoulder against it, and pushed. It scraped open slowly, leaving a deposit of rust on her jacket. She glanced inside and then slipped through. Babbage followed, and then Mailfist. He had to breathe in and strain in order to edge his way through the narrow gap.

The pub had been grand in its day, as such places go. The skeleton of a chandelier hung from the ceiling: there were even a few pieces of its crystal still intact. The wood from the bar was warped and rotting, and the glasses and bottles that used to stand behind from floor to ceiling were long gone; only a tarnished mirror remained.

Mailfist walked over to join Babbage and J, who were standing at the entrance to one of the snugs. J seemed relieved; Babbage was uncertain, looking as if he was considering making a run for it. It was only when he stood closer that Mailfist realised his clerk was shaking with fear.

There was a hiss and a rattle from the snug, and the slightest twitch of movement. It was as if a sleeping snake had been roused. Mailfist saw it then, the figure sitting in the corner, as it turned its head to face them. It was wearing a black Homburg and a matching Astrakhan overcoat; its gloved hands were resting on the surface of the table.

'Good God,' Mailfist whispered involuntarily. The Nameless cocked its head and half-rose from its seat.

'What does it want?' asked Babbage.

'Shh,' J replied.

Mailfist stepped forward and offered his hand.

'Mailfist,' he said. 'Ministry of Chronic Affairs. You might have heard of our organisation. It's an honour to meet you, sir.'

He kept his hand there for a moment as the Nameless shifted a little closer, and ran its blank face closely across his palm as if taking his scent. Then the creature stood upright abruptly, and pushed its way out. It strode over to the bar, knelt down behind it, opened a trapdoor, and began to descend into the cellar. It stopped halfway down and gestured for them to follow.

'Far to go,' said J. Her voice sounded different: dry, like dead leaves.

'I think we should turn back,' said Babbage. 'There might be thousands of them down there.'

'There probably are,' said Mailfist. 'But if they meant us any harm, it would only take one. We don't have a choice, Babbage. There's nothing left for us above ground.'

He walked over to the trapdoor, and followed the Nameless down.

Veronica was led from the ironclad towards a group of other prisoners. They, too, showed the tell-tale welts and bruises of the machines' tentacles. They were being mustered next to a gateway leading into the Tower. Veronica assumed that this was where they were going to be held until someone in charge decided what to do with them. She could hear chatter over the soldiers' radios. The ironclads formed a protective circle around them. Troops with guns were perched on the turrets, watching.

'It's her.'

She couldn't work out who it was in the crowd that said it, who had recognised her — she, the woman who didn't even recognise herself — but in an instant it was spreading through the crowd. People were staring at her, nudging each other: some looking as if deliverance had arrived, others arguing the point. *It must be her. It can't be. I saw her in a dream. It's her. It's* her. One of them reached out to touch her arm—an elderly man, the side of his face grazed and swollen. 'I kept faith with you,' he pleaded. 'All these years, I kept faith.'

'Get your hands off her!' shouted a soldier, wading into the group and striking the man with the butt of his gun. He prepared to take a second blow: Veronica reached out and grabbed him. She was surprised by her own strength. In an instant, he was on the ground, flailing on his back. He pointed the gun at her and fumbled with the trigger. The weapon discharged: she ducked instinctively. The crowd panicked and surged out towards the ironclads. Suddenly, more soldiers started firing. Loudspeakers began to bark contradictory instructions. She began to run. She didn't care where. A soldier stood in her way, brandishing what looked like a length of rope that glistened. He flung it towards her: she flipped it back with a flick of her wrist, and it wrapped itself around him, delivering a shock and then tightening until his face went red and his eyes bulged. She continued to run, up a flight of stone steps and onto the bridge.

'Stop there.'

The voice echoed across the water.

'The bridge is blocked both sides. The water is cold and deep. The undercurrents will drag you to the bottom in an instant.'

She paused. It seemed familiar, but somehow scrambled, like the elements of a dream. And, as one would in a dream, she acted with a volition that was not entirely her own.

Veronica looked either side of the bridge: it was true. She was surrounded. A line of troops stood on the north side, and on the south she could see a group of ironclads. Quite calmly, she began to walk across.

'Stop!'

She didn't flinch as the warning shot was fired above her

head. When she was precisely halfway, she stepped up onto the iron siding, balancing her weight carefully, and looking into the turbid waters below.

'Fire!'

SEVEN

Blood and scorched metal. That was it, thought Gabrielle: the smell that permeated the whole of the basement. From behind the solid oak door, she could hear sounds of conflict: clashing, hacking, screams: and above it all, cheering.

The journey from the Tower had taken far longer than it should have: they had hardly moved a great distance along the river, just as far as the old city Guildhall. At one point, as the ironclad jostled through a narrow side-street, and the clatter of stones thrown by unseen hands sounded from the roof, she had turned to Doyle and said, 'We could have walked, you know. The weather's not too bad, considering. And I was looking forward to stretching my legs a little.'

'It's safer this way,' Doyle had replied. There was a deafening sound of gunfire from the front of the vehicle. 'That's it,' Doyle had shouted. 'Clear the way!' He turned to the driver, sitting side-on from them. 'Any more obstructions up ahead?' he asked. The man had glanced around and pushed up his goggles. 'No, sir. Plain sailing from now on.'

'Keep an eye out,' said Doyle. 'Any more trouble, and we'll have to think about returning to base.'

The driver nodded, pulled his goggles back down, and returned his attention to the road ahead. He had been right: the rest of the journey was peaceful. 'Too quiet,' Gabrielle had heard Doyle mutter to himself at one point, shaking his head. 'Too quiet.'

They had pulled up in what had once been a courtyard: rubble defined three sides, and the building on the fourth — the Guildhall — was riddled with holes and barely standing. As Gabrielle got out of the ironclad, she saw that a perimeter fence of barbed wire surrounded the area, with guards posted at regular intervals.

Doyle was standing next to the ironclad, examining its hull.

'I wonder,' said Doyle. 'However did they do that?'

The letters 'VB' had been stencilled on the side in bright red paint. Doyle was standing in front of them, but Gabrielle could make them out as if she were looking through a pane of frosted glass.

Doyle had led Gabrielle through the gate and up to the main door of the Guildhall. The last time she had been here — in the early 21st century — it had been made of glass. Now it was an iron door, with a small slit at eye-level. Doyle knocked twice, and the slit opened. A pair of dark eyes regarded them suspiciously.

'You've had a good enough look,' said Doyle. 'Open up.'

There was a rasping noise, a click, and the door swung open. Once inside, three guards greeted them.

'You stay here,' Doyle said to two of them. He turned to the third, a middle-aged man who looked like he hadn't slept in a fortnight. 'You, with us. No, no, not inside. Just stand guard outside the door, and be prepared. Come on.'

The Nameless scampered ahead down the sewer tunnel, its shadow jagged in the pale green phosphorescence of the walls. J followed close behind: she mimicked the movements of the creature, gripping the brickwork with her hands and feet to propel herself along. Mailfist wondered, as he stumbled and sloshed through the filthy, sweet-smelling foam, exactly how long she had been living with the Nameless. Babbage walked just ahead of him with a slow, even tread, holding his handkerchief close against his nose.

'I say!' shouted Mailfist. His voice reverberated in the enclosed space. The Nameless kept going. He tried again. 'I say!' This time, the Nameless paused, crouched halfway up the wall like an enormous spider. J and Babbage stopped in their turn.

'I say, is it much further?' Mailfist asked.

'Far to go.' The whisper could have come from either J or the creature; he wasn't sure. 'Very far.'

'Well that's my point, really,' Mailfist replied, trying not to sound nervous. 'Very far, but where to, eh?'

The Nameless descended from the wall and faced him. The creature put its hand on J's shoulder and turned her around, too.

'Where have you been?'

There was no mistaking it. Somehow the Nameless was controlling J, using her to provide it with a voice.

'It's okay,' she said, herself again. 'Don't look so worried. It doesn't hurt.' Her eyes clouded over and she spoke in the dry voice of the Nameless. 'Where have you been?'

'What sort of a question is that?' said Babbage, indignantly. 'Where have we been? We've been holding the fort. Keeping our end up. The question is, where were you, eh? Both of you? You in particular,' he addressed the Nameless. 'You vanished without a trace. One minute you're a thorn in the Empire's side, and the next you lose all stomach for the fight. Where were you when they brought down the Ministry, eh? When they were rounding people up with the ironclads, executions every morning at the Tower—'

'Babbage,' Mailfist interjected.

'You might not care,' Babbage continued, 'but that place was my life.'

'That place,' said the Nameless through J, 'was the beginning.'

'The beginning? The beginning of what?' Mailfist asked.

'Far to go,' the Nameless repeated. 'Very far. Where have you been?' It sloshed around and scuttled back up onto the wall.

'Pussycat,' said Mailfist, as they moved off again.

'Eh?'

'Pussycat, pussycat, where have you been? Oh don't look so mystified, Babbage. It's a rhyme. A children's rhyme.'

'I see, sir. And where had the pussycat been?'

'Why, to London,' said Mailfist. 'To see the queen.'

Doyle and Gabrielle descended a broad metal staircase into the basement of the Guildhall; the guard accompanying them lit the way with a torch. They came to a door; the guard unlocked it in two places with a set of keys roped to his belt, and led them onwards. They went through two similar sets of doors, the smell of war, of death, and the sound of the crowd getting louder and louder as they went.

The final door looked older than the rest: it had a single large lock, and bolts top and bottom. The guard took a key from his pocket and unlocked it, then slid the bolts. Doyle rested his palm on the handle.

'If you hear anything,' Doyle said to the guard, 'anything at all . . .'

The guard nodded and unholstered his gun. Doyle turned the handle, and stepped into the darkness.

The water lapped gently at the stone steps, buoying up the

weed that grew there. Veronica watched it for a while as it swayed in the ebb and flow of the tide, feeling her own body tugged gently by the currents. She sensed herself being pulled a little further out each time; she wondered how long it would take before she was back in the river, floating out of London, through the marshes of the east and into the sea.

She closed her eyes and imagined sinking finally into the depths, down into the mud where she would dissolve. The Thames had been freezing cold at first, but now she felt enveloped by a comfortable haze, one that took away all of the pain.

There was a chattering sound from her left, a rustle, and a click. Vague memories intruded into her consciousness, of blank faces, thin hands grasping at her. She shook her head from side to side as she tried to clear her mind. There was a sudden *crack*, and a stick hit the ground immediately in front of her, making her flinch. She was aware of scratching, a flash of dark wet fur and stringy tails as a pack of rats scattered and vanished into the cracks in the stonework.

'Go on! Get lost!' shouted a hoarse voice.

Veronica felt warm breath on the side of her face, and smelled gin and cigarette smoke.

'Poor thing. Pretty thing. I thought you was dead. Was going to put you back in the water. Ain't no one to bury you, and a shame to have you all chewed up by them rats.'

A hand stroked the hair back from her face.

'There. Peg's here. Can you talk?'

Veronica opened her mouth and tried to force the words out.

'I—I—I—'

'Don't worry, love. You're cold as them stones. I know somewhere. Somewhere warm, somewhere no one will bother us. I'm going to sit you up, sweetheart.'

Veronica felt hands around her shoulders, surprisingly gentle hands, easing her upright. 'Hold on a minute, darling. Stay there.' Something warm and heavy was thrown around her shoulders. 'That's me coat, love. Don't worry about getting it wet. We can dry it by the fire later. Oh yes, a fire! And something hot to eat, eh? How d'you like that?'

The woman, Veronica realised, was trying to get her to talk, forcing her to stay conscious. Her jaw juddered almost uncontrollably when she spoke: 'Thank you.'

'No need to thank me,' said the woman, Peg, 'the Angel blesses those who help a stranger, don't you know that? Now come on, see if you can walk a little. That'll get the blood going. And anyway, you're too big to carry.'

The floor was uneven, and sloped on both sides towards what Gabrielle assumed was the centre. There was a deep rut or groove where the two halves met. It was perfectly quiet for now; the noises she had heard seemed to have stopped the instant the door closed behind them.

'Where are we?' she asked Doyle. 'What is this place?'

A cold wind blew around them, bringing again the unpleasant scent that had filled the basement of the building. She squinted and tried to see where it was coming from: a fan, some sort of vent, possibly? As she did so, she noticed something strange. The wind seemed not only to be stirring up the dust and grit around her, but also physically driving away the darkness. In a matter of moments, they were standing in broad daylight. The roar of the crowd returned; it got louder and louder until the ground shook and her ears rang. She felt displaced, as if she were standing on a rolling deck. Then came the nausea and the light-headedness. They were travelling through time: or rather, time was rushing past them. It was horribly disorientating: like sitting on a train pulling out of a station, when you get the notion that you're staying still, and the whole world is slipping away from you.

'Get back!' Doyle shouted, and grabbed hold of her arm.

A man in a dented helmet, wearing armour over one shoulder and gauntlets, crashed to the ground next to her, snared in a net. He gripped his sword tightly with grazed hands, trying to work it against the mesh and cut himself free.

'What's going on?' she shouted.

'The kill!' Doyle replied, and as he said it the lighting dimmed, the roar of the crowd faded and became distant, and the figures before her — of the felled gladiator and the man standing over him with the net and trident — froze. They flattened and turned into what looked like luminous green line drawings on dark glass. The crowd continued to scream, but the sound was tinny, artificial: rather than surrounding her, it was coming from a single point on her left. Loudspeakers, she thought to herself. She looked up. The sky had gone: there was now a roof over their heads.

'Doyle?'

'Wait.'

The voices of the crowd increased in volume again, and the room brightened, only it wasn't daylight now — it was the white glare of arc lights. She heard scraping, whirrs, ticks, the hiss of operating pistons. Damaged machinery shrieked, and there was the rattle of broken clockwork.

Ahead of her, the fighters in the arena had taken solid form once more; but now their movements were jerky and irregular, and as the trident glanced off the gladiator's shoulder, she saw a blue flash of electricity. They had gone from men, to museum exhibits, to machines: and all before her eyes in less than 60 seconds.

'Them things,' said Peg, 'I've seen them crawl in and out of the river like it was nothing. Go through walls like they was paper. All my life I've been afraid of them. When I was in the hospital we used to see people all the time who'd been caught by them. Horrible.'

'The hospital?' Veronica whispered, as the ironclad rounded the corner and trundled away down the main road. They waited a moment, then stepped out of the doorway.

'Field hospital. I was with the Vee Bees back in the day.'

'The Vee Bees?'

'You don't know much, do you, love?'

Veronica thought back as far as she could remember coherently. The hospital: that was all she had known. But even there, cooped up on the ward, surely she would have heard about a civil war.

'Love?'

Veronica shook her head.

'I can't remember.'

'Can't remember what?'

'I can't remember.'

Peg cackled. 'Confused, eh? Look, you probably gave yourself a shock when you went into the river. It's natural to forget things after a fright like that. Come on, home's just round the corner.' She stopped and pointed into another derelict doorway. A lithe ginger cat stood there, its front paw on the freshly-broken neck of a rat. 'She's got the right idea, eh?'

The metal gladiator tried to raise itself on its elbows; its opponent struck out fiercely and knocked one arm clean off. It turned to the imperial box for approval. A bank of cathode-ray screens high above the seats showed a close-up of a hand. It wavered for a moment, before turning down with a stabbing gesture. The victor acknowledged the signal; Gabrielle now saw that what had looked like rippling muscles were in fact hundreds of tiny brass cogs; that its eyes were dark lenses; that the rest of its face was quite blank. The machine stretched back and raised its trident, positioned itself perfectly for the kill—

And froze.

Gabrielle turned to Doyle. She couldn't find him at first: he was only a little way away from her, but almost completely transparent.

'Doyle, you've made your point. Whatever it is, we need to leave. I can't believe they haven't noticed us yet.'

'They won't,' Doyle said. It sounded like he was shouting at her from behind a pane of glass. 'We're out of phase.'

Gabrielle looked again at the frozen warrior: the crowd was booing as a pair of technicians inserted a key into its side and began to wind frantically.

'I've never been here,' she said. 'What time is this?'

'The fourth Roman Empire,' said Doyle. 'It didn't used to exist.'

Peg sifted carefully through an apparently random scattering of boxes, crates, and sheets of plastic to retrieve a shopping basket full of tins. A can opener was attached to one of the handles with a long piece of twine.

'Let's see what we have here, then,' she muttered. 'Fancy some beans? Some nice steak and kidney pudding?'

'Anything,' Veronica replied. 'Anything at all.' She wrapped the blanket closer around herself: her clothes, and Peg's coat, were propped up on an old office chair, drying by the fire. The fireplace was contained by a semicircle of bricks next to the wall: a makeshift flue had been constructed out of sheets of scrap metal, directing the smoke outside via a broken window. Peg ambled over and put the open can of beans on the hot coals, along with a metal billy in which floated the pudding. She took a pocket watch from the folds of her many layers of clothing and checked it.

'Time of day doesn't mean much,' she said. 'Only time that matters is the time it takes to boil up a cup of tea, eh?'

She took a flask from the satchel she carried around her shoulders, twisted off the plastic mug at the top, undid the cap, and poured a cup of tea for Veronica.

'I didn't know you was showing up,' she said. 'So it's made the way I like it. Strong and sweet.'

'Thank you,' said Veronica, taking it. 'It's just what I need.' She sipped at it. The flavour — slightly stewed beneath the creamy taste of condensed milk and sweetness of too many sugars — seemed to remind her of something, though she couldn't quite pin it down. She had the image in her mind's eye of a cavern: there was a metal pot boiling over a fire, rather like this one, and in it a bunch of leaves darting around in the water. There was somebody with her, somebody she felt was so familiar as to almost be a part of herself.

'All right, love?'

'Yes,' Veronica murmured, suddenly back in the room again.

'Time travelling, eh?'

Veronica started. 'What?'

'It's what I call it. Looking into the fire. Letting your mind drift. Time travelling.' Peg waved her arm to indicate the world outside. 'They can do it in their machines. Trample all over time. Only they can't control what's in your head. Your memories. You can pick one and go through it — every little detail you remember. Spend all day there, if you want. They can't do nothing about it.'

'But what if they change the past?' said Veronica. 'Don't

your memories change, too?'

'You know,' said Peg. 'You just *know* the way things should be.'

'Well, you must know *something* about their queen,' said Mailfist. 'Haven't they dropped any hints?'

J looked over at the Nameless. It stood hugging the wall, what would have been its ear pressed firmly against the bricks.

'They don't drop hints. It's more like they show you things. Even then, it's not straightforward. They speak in stories. Their own mythology. It's all very metaphorical.'

'Sir,' said Babbage. Mailfist turned to face him. He was staring at his fingers, studying them in the faint light from the walls.

'In a minute,' said Mailfist. 'So you haven't met her? They're keeping her safe, but she's under wraps, is that it?'

'They've kept me on the move the whole time. All three of us had to be present before a meeting could be arranged. She insisted on it.'

Mailfist mulled this over. 'Hmm. And what do *they* make of her?'

'She's always in their thoughts,' said J. 'But they never see her clearly. She's out of focus, or you sense that she's there but just outside the frame.'

'You mean they're hiding her from you?'

'No. It's more like they're afraid of her. As if it's the name of God, some sort of taboo. They're not allowed to see her clearly.'

'Evidently she's made quite an impression,' said Mailfist. 'Sir?'

'Oh, what is it, Babbage?'

Babbage held up his hands, fingers outstretched.

'It's my fingerprints, sir. I think they're vanishing.'

Before Mailfist could reply, J swung around and put her fingers to her lips.

'Shh!'

Behind her, the Nameless was performing the same gesture. Mailfist listened. He could hear a distant rumble of rushing water, and the constant *drip-drip* of fluid from the walls.

'What is it?' he whispered.

'Shh!'

There was a splashing noise, as if someone were skimming stones across the surface of the water. It multiplied rapidly, becoming louder, getting closer. Then they saw it, bounding around the corner into their section of the tunnel: a large rat. The Nameless picked it up and held it close to its head, as if trying to hear what it had to say. It squeaked in protest.

'My God,' murmured Babbage. 'What a brute! I've never seen one that size.'

Another couple of rats, bigger than the first, ran into view; then another pair, and another. In a couple of seconds, the entire floor of the sewer was filled with wet fur and huddled bodies, crawling over each other, fleeing desperately for their lives. The splashing mounted to a roar, and the water at their feet frothed and bubbled. The rats fanned out, and began to mount the walls in their attempt to escape.

'What are they running from?' asked Mailfist.

The bellow of an ironclad echoed down the tunnel towards them.

In the courtyard, Gabrielle leaned back against the wall of the ironclad. It felt cold, its edges sharp through her clothes. Her hip ached, and she was feeling decidedly out of breath.

'Tell me when you're ready to move on,' said Doyle. He sounded almost sympathetic. Gabrielle rubbed her eyes with the back of her hands: they stung with the sand and fumes of the arena.

'There was no way you'd have believed me,' said Doyle. 'You had to see for yourself.'

'What's going on down there, Doyle? It looked like the same event was being stretched across centuries.'

Doyle started as he heard a small fall of rubble from one of the buildings nearby. He looked over his shoulder to check, then turned back to Gabrielle.

'What you just saw is what will happen to the whole of London — to the whole world — unless we find Veronica Britton.'

'That's convenient.'

'It's also true. That area under the Guildhall was the arena when London was a Roman city. It was lost for centuries before being excavated and opened as a tourist attraction in several versions of the 20th century. When the Roman Empire is reborn — many centuries from now — it reverts to its previous use. Only they abolish flesh-and-blood games in favour of machines.'

'They were changing,' said Gabrielle. 'Changing so quickly, as if the years in between were nothing. Just the blink of an eye.'

'Exactly. It's all collapsing, Miss Pendleton. Time folding in on itself. Over there —' he indicated west, '— do you know what they've found? Dinosaur bones inside a tube carriage. All because of Veronica Britton.'

Gabrielle laughed sharply. 'Impossible.'

Doyle knelt down and swept away a patch of rubble at their feet.

'It shouldn't be too hard to find one,' he said. 'They're cropping up everywhere.'

'What?'

Doyle ignored her. He had found something: the curl of what looked like a stylised piece of writing carved into the asphalt. He dusted further with his sleeve, following the lines.

'There,' he said, and stood up. Gabrielle crouched down to read. She traced the lettering with her finger.

VB

'Vee Bee fanatics are out of control,' said Doyle. 'They're communicating through time, trying to stop us at every turn. But it's like cutting off the head of a hydra. The more they interfere, the more problems they create. To put it quite simply, they're tearing holes in the texture of time. We need to find her, and get her to put a stop to this.'

EIGHT

'Time to rest now, my dear.'

Peg was busy arranging two nests of cardboard and blankets. She patted one of them, as if she were summoning a cat.

'Nice and warm. A sleep will do you the world of good.'

'Cats,' said Veronica.

'Eh?'

'There was something about a cat. An important cat.'

'I dare say there was, love. All cats think they're important.'

Peg shifted over to the space between the beds, picked up a dustpan and brush from its spot next to the fire, and began to sweep.

'Just one more thing before bed. We need to thank the Angel. You, especially. Angel's good to me. Keeps me warm, keeps me fed. I spent my life in the service of the Angel. Sometimes I wish I wasn't so old, so I could be out there with the young ones doing my bit. Deep underground, they are now. Probably beneath us right now, they are.'

She fumbled in the pockets of her greatcoat, and pulled out a set of stubby chalks.

'Probably daft, this. But it makes me feel she's watching over me.'

Veronica watched as she drew two letters on the floor with a flourish.

VB

The tunnel shook as the ironclad advanced at full speed. Mailfist saw that its design had been modified for the sewers: if the land ironclads were like metal woodlice, this was like an articulated metal worm, with treads latching onto the sewer wall around its body. It pointed its lamp at them, silhouetting the Nameless.

'Stay where you are.'

The front of the machine opened up, and a cluster of tentacles slid out, snaking through the water towards them. The Nameless turned to face them. Or rather, Mailfist noticed, it turned to face one of them in particular: Babbage.

'Run,' he said.

The Nameless turned back to the machine, leaned forward, and began to grab at the tentacles, plucking them out one by one. They writhed and crackled with electricity; its body convulsed with the shock, but it kept going.

'One man can't face down that brute!' shouted Mailfist.

Babbage was regarding the Nameless with an expression of pity.

'That's not a man,' he said.

Babbage turned and ran away down the tunnel, followed by J and Mailfist. The roar of the ironclad followed them. There was a flash of lightning and a rumble.

'The tunnel's collapsing!' yelled J. She leapt forward and barrelled into Mailfist; he was thrown forwards and landed on Babbage. The three of them went down in a heap in the foul water of the sewer as the arch of the tunnel above their heads gave way. Mailfist felt hands plucking at his sleeve, and then a sharp tug of his whole body: the sort that comes when one wakes from a dream.

The tea was wretched. It had probably been recycled a good number of times. Gabrielle sat in an old leather armchair in one of the larger rooms of the Tower—probably where they used to display armour, she thought—as Doyle fiddled with what looked like a large tank full of murky water mounted on a dais. She glanced out of the window at the city; the skyline shimmered and undulated. It made her feel rather ill. Doyle adjusted a brass panel fixed to the side of the tank, and lightning flickered within.

'Miss Pendleton,' he said. 'Would you draw the curtains, and come over here?'

He turned a lever, and the tank began to sink into its base, so that by the time she reached it they were looking into its depths. There was a hazy glow around it, of a distinct colour and feel that Gabrielle knew very well.

'A four-dimensional map,' she said.

'Quite.' Doyle passed his hand over it. The surface rippled, and vague structures began to take shape.

'What year are we looking at?'

'Present day.'

'Which is? I've rather lost track.'

'1953.'

'Goodness me. So I'm pushing 100. I think I've done rather well, considering.'

'That's what passing through the timepools does for you.'

'Yes. Veronica told me it makes one wear the years rather lightly. Though I sometimes wonder about the long-term effects.'

She looked at her reflection in the water.

'Mind you, I don't know why I'm so proud of myself. I'm just rather old. You're dead.'

She gazed further into the tank. London, as far as she could make out through the grit, largely consisted of rubble and walls pockmarked with bomb damage and bullet holes.

'Oh dear. You know this was supposed to be a coronation year? Never mind.'

Doyle was fiddling with a brass dial at one end of the dais.

'I need you to look very carefully at this,' he said. 'You're very time-sensitive. As Veronica's at the centre of all of this disruption, the motivating force behind it, she should be shining like a beacon. There, we'll go as far back as we can.'

The image broke up and reformed as a hilly landscape: dead trees and craters were dotted around. The Thames looked stale and polluted. The picture held for just a moment, then dissolved again. It was like looking into a blizzard.

'This is hopeless, Doyle.'

'It's all we have, Miss Pendleton.'

'No it isn't.'

'What do you suggest?'

'I think it's time to go back to the source.'

The creature with no face was reaching out to her, its hand spread, its fingertips resting lightly around her face. It was as if a giant insect were resting there.

She tried to shake it off, but the creature maintained its grip. She raised her hand to pull it away, but it held firm.

'Only this is real,' she heard a voice say: it took her a moment to realise that she was talking to herself. She became gradually aware of her surroundings; the recollection of how she had got there took a moment longer. Her longer history was still a blank, but she felt its presence there in the darkness, just outside the glow of the dying fire.

Veronica sat up slowly and looked at Peg. She was wrapped up tight; only a small area of her greying hair showed through the rolls of blanket. Veronica slipped herself all the way out of bed, then took her clothes from the chair. They were stiff and smelled of the river, but at least they were dry. She dressed silently, put her shoes on, and leaned over Peg.

'Thank you,' she whispered, and planted a single kiss on her head. Then she walked out of the warehouse, and into the streets. There was a gunmetal tint to the sky, which she took to mean it was dawn.

Doyle rapped on the door. His eyes were so deep in their sockets that they were barely visible; the skin on his face was virtually transparent. He seemed to be permanently on edge, all of his old arrogance rapidly diminishing. It was as if he were a criminal living in permanent fear of arrest. The door was opened by one of the troops, who saluted as they went inside and began to descend the spiral staircase that led to the Ministry.

The first thing Gabrielle noticed was the harshness of the light. Whereas the stairs had previously been softly lit by oil lamps placed in the alcoves, the Empire had rigged up a set of electric bulbs to guide their way. It made the place look shabby; it was like seeing behind a stage set. They emerged into what had previously been the front office. The books that Gabrielle remembered were still on the shelves, but the high desk and chair had been replaced by a simple trestle table at which another of the troops sat. He had a sign-in book open in front of him, and a register next to it. He checked Doyle off as he wrote in the book, whilst Gabrielle stepped over to the nearest shelf and took one of the volumes down. The binding was, as before, of thick dark leather. But all the pages were blank. She replaced it and examined another. The same.

'Miss Pendleton?'

She closed the book. 'No time to lose, eh?'

Doyle nodded, and made to take her arm. She shrugged him off. They walked past the guard post and into the tunnel that led down beneath the river. That, too, had been helpfully lit; the metal struts and arches that held it up were clearly visible; they were so furred with rust that Gabrielle wouldn't have been surprised if the whole lot were to fall in. The earth vibrated; she heard a rumble overhead that she took to be an ironclad or two patrolling the river.

They emerged into the main chamber of the Ministry. It was barely recognisable. The clerks, of course, had gone; their desks, too, had been cleared away. It was so dark that even the Empire's lights couldn't penetrate the gloom. The walls, which had once rippled and glowed with the movement of the machinery within, were now covered in mildew; the cogs visible beneath were coated with verdigris. The whole place was silent; the mechanism had stopped.

'It's dead,' she whispered. 'You've killed it.'

Veronica stuck to the side streets as she made her way west. The landscape shifted around her as she went; she would turn back from time to time and find the streets had changed configuration behind her. Her journey had the disjointedness of a dream; she was only able to navigate by sticking close to the river. At Waterloo, she crossed over a rickety bridge, and went north across the Strand and towards Covent Garden.

She passed few other people, and those she met cast their eyes down, hurrying up their pace. They were dressed in a strange mixture of clothes, shapeless robes mixed with finely-tailored jackets with shining buttons, or woollen greatcoats, or even, in some cases, patches of metal armour. She heard the occasional rattle of gunfire, the odd explosion; some streets were covered in a pall of smoke.

Eventually, she rounded the corner of the old opera house — every window had been broken, leaving a white skeletal frame — and looked cautiously into the main piazza. She darted back: standing at the centre, amidst a pile of rubble and a large square crater, was an ironclad.

Veronica gave it a moment, and then looked again. The machine was quite still; this, she knew, was unusual. All the ones she had seen the previous day were constantly shifting on their treads, twitching, swivelling around as if they were alive. She crept forward across the square, moving fast, keeping low, and examined the ironclad.

The lamps at the front were shattered; there were a few stubby lengths of brass where the tentacles had been severed. She looked up to examine the top; the entrance to the hatch wasn't shut properly. It sat at an odd angle, as if it had been forced. Veronica found a handhold and climbed up. She lifted the hatch completely open — the black metal had actually been torn through — and descended the rungs into the main body of the machine.

It was dark inside; thin shafts of light penetrated from holes in the machine's armour. She could make out a tangle of wires, cogs, fragments of wood, and scraps of torn leather. From one of the wall panels, dented as if someone had beaten it in with an axe, hung a scrap of cloth. She picked it up and examined it in the light of the open hatch: it was part of a uniform, with a patch sewn onto it. The patch depicted a lion with its mouth open displaying a jagged set of teeth. Its front paw rested on a globe and a clock face, intertwined.

Was this it? Was this what she was supposed to find? She had woken with the irresistible sense that she had to get moving again. She had come here by instinct, letting her feet guide her as if retracing her steps. Going back to the beginning, starting again to try and recover what she had lost. It was all she had to go on; but at the moment, it seemed like very little indeed in comparison with a warm bed. She made her way back up the ladder and through the hatch. Her first thought, on emerging from the ironclad, was that a forest of trees had suddenly sprung up around the machine. Then she looked again.

They surrounded her on all sides, all perfectly still, all in the same pose: arms at their sides, heads tilted, watching the ironclad for signs of life. Thin figures with blank faces, like the one she had seen in her dream. They were all dressed in black outfits of one sort or another. They made a chattering noise as they caught sight of her: those closest to her began to tremble. They put their arms up in the air, and, as she descended from the ironclad's turret into the piazza, knelt down as one before her.

Gabrielle pointed to the ceiling.

'You took that to bits, too, I suppose. To construct that murky fish tank you showed me back at the Tower.'

'It was re-fitted exactly as we found it,' said Doyle.

Gabrielle shone her torch up.

'That great big crack across it,' she said. 'I suppose that was exactly as you found it, too, eh?'

She examined the various dials positioned in the brass enclosure at the centre of the monitoring room. All had stopped.

'If there's nothing you can do . . .' Doyle said.

'I didn't say that,' Gabrielle replied. 'I didn't say that at all.'

She ran her finger along the dial nearest to her: it was that of a wristwatch, depicting a cartoon mouse. The creature's arms made up the hour and minute hands.

'You know, Doyle, I always felt invigorated by my visits to the Ministry. Like a champagne breakfast — not that I imagine you've ever allowed yourself such a pleasure. Maybe all I need to do is give a little bit back.'

Gabrielle held her palm over the dial; in the gloom, a faint glow came from it. She removed her hand. The movement stayed frozen.

'It's not enough,' said Doyle.

'Shh.'

In the darkness, a barely perceptible ticking began. Gabrielle knelt down slowly to examine the dial: the mouse's eyes were moving back and forth, keeping time with the passing seconds.

'Who are you?' Veronica asked. They did not reply. 'What are you?' The chattering noise rippled through the crowd again, but died down swiftly. She wondered if the best move would be simply to make a run for it, but rejected the idea reluctantly. She knew, just as she had known the way here, that these creatures — whatever they were — were the reason she had come. She walked over to the nearest one and tugged at its shoulder, trying to pull it up to face her.

'What do you want? I'm talking to you!'

With one fluid movement, the creature stood up, stretched out its hand, and clasped it lightly yet firmly around her face.

She was both there in the moment, and looking back on it as an adult. It was a perfect summer's day, the sort that only occur in childhood. She was on a swing in the back garden of a house somewhere in North London. As she thought about it, time filled itself out into the past and the future: she saw the street, with its row of imposing new houses; their bay windows, railings, and steps down to their basements. She saw the dark wooden furniture of her parents' dining room, the gleaming silver, and the white plates with the blue Chinese decoration. Then the drawing room, smaller, cosier: the armchair covered in green velvet that her father sat in with his newspaper. One of the arms, she remembered, was burned from the time he had absent-mindedly rested his pipe there and forgotten about it.

For now, though, it was summer. There were bees in the lavender behind the swing: she could hear them buzzing. And on the fence, looking down at her, was a small ginger cat. It swiped at a butterfly swooping past.

NINE

Flickering candlelight illuminated the row of statues that lined the wall: as far as Mailfist could tell, the recurrent theme was a man slashing a bull's throat. Before them was an altar draped in red velvet. A hooded Nameless knelt in front of it, muttering and shaking in prayer.

'Probably a Mithraic temple,' said J. 'The Romans used to love places like this. Secret passageways, passwords, animal masks. Couldn't get enough of it.'

Babbage had stopped worrying at his fingertips, which was, thought Mailfist, a welcome relief. Unfortunately, he now seemed to have become obsessed with the size of his nose.

'For goodness' sake,' he whispered. 'Could you stop fidgeting for one moment? We're about to meet the person who's at the bottom of all of this.'

Babbage looked back at him.

'Tell me,' he said. 'Do you think it's getting smaller?'

Mailfist was thinking up a suitably cutting reply when the chattering prayer of the worshipping Nameless was taken up by the trio who had rescued them from the tunnel and guided them here; it was echoed from the shadows, getting louder and louder, like a wind picking up and rustling through the trees. It came from the ceiling, from the floor; the Nameless, Mailfist realised, must be packed around them unseen in their dozens. He looked closely at the altar: a large piece of a black, gauzy material was hanging in front of it. As he watched, it seemed to grow more solid, to take on the shape and proportion of a human body. The candles in the temple flared up, as the Nameless grew more and more agitated; they were working themselves into a frenzy. Mailfist could see a shape curled around the shoulders of the person who was gradually phasing into existence in front of him: it was a small creature with a reddish tinge, and gleaming ivory teeth in a mouth that yawned wide. There was a sound like a heavy door slamming, and a shockwave that sent Mailfist, J, and Babbage reeling. The Nameless fell silent.

The woman who stood in front of them wore a black dress patched from countless different materials: wool, cloth, leather, lace, plastic, and more. Around her neck, she wore a necklace of brilliant sapphires. Her dark hair was piled in an elaborate tangle; feathers, clips, and dark jewels were scattered here and there. Her face was pale, the pupils of her eyes almost black. She reached up and stroked the cat that rested on her shoulders, pawing at a loose strand of her hair. It rubbed its chin against her fingers affectionately, eyeing the newcomers with suspicion all the while. She extended her other hand towards them, silver rings clicking against one another as she gestured for them to come closer.

'You're here. Good. Then we can begin.'

'Veronica Britton!' cried Mailfist. He hurried towards her and took her hand; her grip was warm and firm. 'How did you—I mean, I had no idea—I didn't dare to hope—you're alive!'

'Possibly,' said Veronica. 'Possibly.'

'What do you mean, 'possibly'?' J cut in.

Veronica shrugged and gave them an apologetic grin.

'Look, I'm sorry, but there's no easy way to tell you this. I'm currently at the point of death at some moment in the future. You're all figments of my imagination, or rather, people I remember who play a really important part in all of this. You're being reconstructed as we speak, as if I'm writing all of this down in a book. I might have succeeded, in which case I'm in the same state as I was once before, when the Nameless picked me up in Covent Garden. I was badly injured: they made me whole again, gave me back my memories from day one. It was very strange living my life all over again, looking back but at the same time not knowing what was coming next. They brought me here afterwards, and turned me into a god. They gave me presents and everything.

'The other possibility is that I've failed, it's the end of the world, and my life is flashing before my eyes like some sort of consolation prize.'

She — I — stopped and petted the cat. She had grown restive. She was standing up and circling back and forth on my shoulders.

'Calm now, Hodge,' I said. I returned my attention to my guests. 'Right. Before we go any further, are there any questions?'

TEN

We sat in the cafe next to one of the larger potted palms. It was at least a token effort at concealment.

'So what did you think?' asked Doyle, once the waitress was out of earshot.

'What did I think of what?' I knew of course.

'You know. Just now.' He was looking around nervously, checking out the other customers in the mirror on the wall behind me.

'Oh,' I said. 'That.' I reached down the front of my dress, and fished out the pendant I had bought at one of the stalls off Carnaby Street: it was a circle, with a cross at the centre, its horizontal arms sloping symmetrically downwards.

'Vee! Put that away!' Doyle whispered, as the waitress returned with a silver tray and started putting the tea, cakes, and sandwiches on the table. I continued to toy with it: she glanced up once, but didn't say anything, and why should she? It meant nothing to her. Doyle was always convinced that some trivial slip like that was going to change the course of history. History is actually pretty robust. Well, that's what I thought back then, anyway.

'If you must know,' I said after the waitress left us, 'I thought it was quite indecent. One thinks of so many ways the world could be in 100 years, but the 1960s are nothing like *the future*. Much more like the Regency period than anything else.'

'Is that what you think?'

'Mm, yes.' I lifted the lid of my teapot and gave the leaves a stir. 'Such language. Such parties. And the way a young lady was expected to dress.'

'I rather thought you looked like you were enjoying yourself.'

'Oh I was, my darling. Much too much.'

The forest was dark even in the daytime. At night, you could barely see your hand in front of your face.

'Do you have it?' Doyle panted, as we rested for a moment. The cries of the villagers and the howls of their dogs sounded through the wood. I fumbled in one of the pockets of my belt.

'Yes,' I said. I pulled out the revolver to show him. 'Not very impressive, is it?' I added. And it wasn't: just a rusty old service revolver, the kind old soldiers keep in a tin box in the attic.

'It's enough,' he replied. And indeed it was. Enough for one man to take back to the past and set up his own private kingdom with. I had been following him for a set of minor thefts, whilst Doyle had been on his trail for the rather more serious crime of altering the timeline so that the armies of Julius Caesar would, in due course, be met by a force of Britons in full fighting frenzy armed with guns. Anyway, he was dead now: killed with his own weapon.

'How much further to the timepool?' I asked.

Doyle consulted his wristwatch. It was a skeleton watch, the type with a glass face so you can see the insides working. I could see the machinery inside glowing very faintly in the blackness of the forest.

'Not far at all,' he replied. 'You see where the ground rises? Just over the ridge.'

We listened for a moment. The villagers were moving away from us. We heard a hunting horn blow, summoning them.

'Now's our chance!' I said, and began to make my way up the slope. Doyle didn't move. He just stood there, sniffing the air.

'Vee,' he said.

'What?'

'Do you smell burning?'

'Yes. There's definitely something burning.'

'Run!' shouted Doyle, pushing me ahead of him as a wave of orange flames roared out of the darkness. 'They're burning us out!'

'That's what you get for killing a god!'

We fled through the fire and towards the timepool. The conflagration had, at least, made it clear: an inviting dark archway outlined against a roaring backdrop of flames. I ran as fast as I could towards it, gulping for air amidst the scorching heat, and leapt through into the delicious coolness, Doyle following close behind. I reached out for his hand as we whirled through the darkness.

'What is this place?' asked J, curling a strand of red hair around her finger.

'This place?' I answered.

'You looked like you were somewhere else for a moment,' she said, impatiently.

'I was,' I said. I wondered if she really was as annoying as I remembered her being.

'Well, where are we now?' she demanded. Mailfist, standing next to her, looked apologetic. His companion, the clerk they were calling Babbage, had got hold of a pocket mirror from somewhere and appeared to be studying the size of his eyes.

'Light,' I commanded. The Nameless who had come with us knelt down, rolled up his sleeves, and plunged his hands into the water of the pool that filled most of the room. It lit up; the colour of old, dusty gold. The particles inside began to whirr and forms shapes.

'Good Lord,' said Mailfist. 'They did this all for you?'

'This was here long before I arrived. Mailfist, have you not worked it out yet?'

'What?'

'This is the original Ministry.'

'Oh.'

J knelt next to the pool, and watched it as the city began to form within.

'When is this?' she asked.

'Present day.'

She wrinkled her nose. 'Something's wrong,' she said. 'Look, there's a Roman encampment there. And a Bronze Age village next to it. And half a mile down the road, a shopping mall. Can you move it on a hundred years or so?'

The Nameless crouching by the water angled his face towards mine: I nodded, and he began to wriggle his fingers underneath the surface. J watched and waited. Babbage came over to join her, momentarily distracted.

'It's not working,' said J. Babbage turned pale.

'It *is* working,' he said. 'Oh dear. Oh no, no, no.'

'Eh?'

'It isn't changing,' he said. 'Time is collapsing.' He began to scour the map carefully. 'We must find the epicentre.'

It was one of those wild nights between the wars. The late

1920s, I think: Piccadilly Circus blazing with electric lights, motorcars driving back and forth along the banks of the Thames all night, taking young people to and from parties. We stood next to Cleopatra's Needle, an Egyptian obelisk that stood on the north bank of the river in those days. We were looking at a barge that was filled with men in dinner suits and women in cocktail dresses dancing to a jazz band.

As the boat sailed away in the direction of the Houses of Parliament, Doyle pointed to the base of the Needle. 'I was here when they put this thing up,' he said. 'They put a box underneath it. A time capsule. It was full of all sorts of things. Pictures of fashionable women, a razor, copies of the Bible and Bradshaw's. I always wanted to come back here when they open it up again. See what they make of it.'

'And when is that?' I asked, tapping the obelisk with the tip of my umbrella.

'Another two centuries,' Doyle replied. 'During Darby's London war of independence, this place will take a direct hit.'

I took his hand.

'Doyle?' I said.

'Do you know,' he replied, 'you're the only person who calls me by my proper name?'

'Why have you brought me here?' I asked.

Doyle sighed, and walked over to the wall of the embankment. He looked at the lights dancing in the water. I went over to join him. I thought of the time we had been to one of the frost fairs together, when the surface had frozen over, thick and cold as iron.

'Mailfist called me into his office,' he said.

'Really?' I said. 'Where are you off to now?' I knew, of course: my question was just a way of postponing the inevitable.

'He wasn't himself,' Doyle replied. 'None of the usual chatter. He didn't even have his breakfast things out. He just looked me in the eye and said . . .'

He stopped and bowed his head. I took his hand: it was like ice.

'He said, "It's almost time."'

I pulled Doyle around and held him close. A group of young men walking past cheered. I envied them their innocence; they couldn't imagine that two people could embrace with anything other than complete happiness. This was why Doyle had brought me here to tell me his news, after all: it was one of my favourite times, a brief bubble during which everyone believed, or wanted to believe, that the worst was over. Soon enough, these young men, too, would know what it was like to hold the person you loved for the very last time. They would know how it felt: like the last breath of air before the undercurrents drag you beneath the water.

'I'm so sorry,' Doyle whispered. 'I should never have got involved with you, Vee. I knew from the first day I was recruited into the Ministry that it would end this way.'

'Hush,' I replied. 'Mailfist's wrong! He's got things mixed up. You know how he is. He needs the clerks to tell him everything.'

'Don't pretend you're taken in by his act like everyone else.'

'Why didn't he let you know sooner? You have a right to know.'

'Rights? I have as many rights as Mailfist allows me. No more, no less.'

'I don't believe that. I don't believe you have to die at all.'

Doyle took my arm. 'Let's walk,' he said. 'It always helps me to think.'

We strolled in the direction of Westminster Bridge. I felt

tired all of sudden, infinitely tired.

'All Ministry agents' deaths are fixed,' said Doyle. 'They have to happen.'

'Nothing *has* to happen.'

Doyle shook his head. I couldn't believe he could be so fatalistic about what was going to happen to us. It never occurred to me that there could be anything worse.

'So where does it happen?' I asked, forcing the words out. 'Has he told you that, at least?'

He pointed across the river.

'In the Cut,' he said, 'at midnight. Though he didn't tell me any more than that.'

We stopped and looked at the bridge as Big Ben struck.

Babbage had pushed J out of the way, and was leaning over the pool so close that his face was virtually touching the water. He had dipped his hands in, and was shifting and focusing the image in concert with the Nameless.

'Nearly,' he said. 'Nearly. Just here. By the river. You see that fluctuation? Freeze that. Expand.'

Mailfist tapped me on the shoulder.

'Did you bring him here to do this?' he asked.

'The Nameless asked for him,' I replied. 'All the other clerks are locked up, so he seemed the easiest to get hold of.'

'I say,' said Mailfist, addressing his clerk, 'have you done this before?'

'I don't know, sir. Shh.'

'Why couldn't they do it themselves?' asked J.

'I don't know,' I said. 'But I think Babbage has some skill they've forgotten.'

'Forgotten?' said Mailfist.

'Don't tell me you hadn't seen the resemblance, Mailfist. One becomes the other.'

'One becomes the . . . Oh my word.'

Mailfist looked back at the Nameless and Babbage, working in harmony.

'Look,' said Mailfist. 'He's got it. By Jove!'

The pool was now glowing like molten metal. The fluid churned around and around.

'I can't see anything,' J complained.

Babbage looked up at the Nameless and nodded. A picture began to resolve out of the chaos, little glimpses flickering like an image caught through the slits of a zoetrope. I could see the ridged walls of the Houses of Parliament, the tower and the clock face, a crowd on the bridge; there were little bursts of fire in the sky overhead. And there, a little way south of the river, in a narrow alley off the Cut, were two figures locked in an embrace.

'It's a man and a woman,' said Mailfist. 'Wait a minute, one of them is — is you!'

I nodded and kept my eyes on the pool. 'Hold that image,' I said to Babbage.

'There's a mistake!' he exclaimed. 'Look!'

'Hold it!' I shouted. 'Hold it steady'

'I'm trying!' he replied, immersing himself in the pool along with the Nameless. The image sharpened for one fraction of a second before exploding into thousands of fragments. The surface of the water settled again; but the picture had gone. J and Mailfist pulled the clerk out; the Nameless hauled itself from the pool and lay exhausted as the light died away.

'Did you see it?' asked Mailfist.

'Yes,' I replied. 'I saw.'

'Veronica Britton,' said Carter, kicking the chair out from under his desk. 'Take a seat.'

I stayed standing. He looked me in the eye, his face growing red.

'You'll sit when I tell you to sit, damn you!' he snapped.

I sat.

'Miss Britton,' said a voice behind me, 'you've been elusive of late.'

'Cut it out, K,' said Carter. 'There'll be no cat and mouse in my office.'

K slunk out from his spot behind me, and perched on the edge of Carter's desk.

'You've brought a whole heap of trouble down on me, Miss Britton,' said Carter.

'I don't know what you're talking about,' I replied.

Carter sighed and closed his eyes. His anger was dissipating: he just looked very, very tired.

'Miss Britton,' said K, taking a dagger from his belt and polishing the blade on his cloak, 'where is agent D?'

'Dead,' I replied.

'*Wrong.*'

Carter opened his eyes. 'The Ministry sent people round to my house last night, Miss Britton. To my *house*.'

K fumbled around his collar. He took off a pendant and handed it to me, closing my fingers around it. Its clockwork twitched in my hand like it was a living thing.

'D's is still going,' said K. 'And time is running out. If he's not where he's supposed to be when it stops, then everything — all of this — begins to fall apart. London time is built that way, Miss Britton. Just one little flaw, one tiny weakness, and the whole thing collapses. Not an alternative future, Miss Britton. No future at all. Do you understand that?'

'I don't believe that. I can't!'

'I don't care whether you believe it or not!'

'What about you, K? What would you do?'

K took the pendant from my hand, and put it back around his neck.

'Don't presume that you know what I would or would not do.'

'Veronica!'

Carter brushed K to one side and took my hand.

'We've all made sacrifices,' he said.

'Is that supposed to make me feel better?'

'No. No it isn't. Nothing can. But Veronica, come and see this.'

He led me over to the window. We looked out at the Strand.

'What am I supposed to be seeing?' I asked him.

'Normal people,' he said, 'normal lives. All of them depend on you, Veronica. We can't have lives like theirs. But we can't be angry with them because of it.'

I leaned against the window pane and closed my eyes.

'Doyle may survive, Veronica — but everything good about him will die. You'll still lose him, only it'll be worse. Because even your memory of him will be tainted by what he'll become.'

'I've seen them before,' said K. 'The undead. If death is cheated, the man becomes nothing but the embodiment of the most terrible hunger that can never be sated. If you truly love him . . .'

He came over the window and put his arm around my shoulder. I shrugged him off.

'K,' I said. 'Just leave me alone.'

'I'm afraid that won't be possible, Miss Britton. You see, Mailfist has been working around the clock with the Ministry clerks to find D. It's been more difficult than he thought. He knows D's days are almost done, he knows that his last moment occurs somewhere near Waterloo, but beyond that, nothing. I have an intuition, though, Miss Britton, of the way things are meant to happen. I wish I was wrong. But I don't think I am.'

He knelt at my feet, took something from his belt, and placed it in my hand. It was a revolver. I hesitated for a moment, then gripped it so tightly that the metal dug into my palm.

'I don't think D is missing at all, Miss Britton. He's precisely where he's supposed to be. You're the person that saves him from the only thing worse than death.'

This is where it gets strange. What I remember and what I saw in the pool were two different things.

In the pool, I saw myself and Doyle embracing. I saw my finger on the trigger, the barrel of the gun about to discharge its bullet. This was as it had been. But there was something else.

At the end of the alley were two figures: one thin and faint, almost like the figure of a man made from wire: just a skeleton, nerves, and blood vessels, nothing more. On one arm, he wore what looked like a gauntlet. An amber crystal gleamed from the back of the hand, which was outstretched towards Doyle and me.

The other figure was an old woman. She was dressed plainly, in a white blouse, dark trousers, and an overcoat cut in a military style. Her long white hair was tied back. I recognised her straight away.

Gabrielle Pendleton.

'I wondered how he survived,' said Mailfist as we left the pool.

'That gauntlet he was wearing,' I said, 'what was it?'

'Something we developed for stealth operations,' Babbage chipped in. 'It allows one to manipulate time. Over a limited range, and for a short period. But the effects can be quite dramatic. It effectively freezes the victim in a very short-lived time bubble. From their point of view, no time passes at all.'

'It's good for cheating at cards,' said J.

'Babbage, does that device have any weak points?'

'The amber crystal,' he said. 'That's the weak point. It's the oscillator. Only it burns out very quickly, so we made sure it was easy to access and replace. It's on the dorsal surface of the hand. If you knock that out, the whole thing stops working.'

'Could be useful,' I said. We had come to a door. It was covered with rust and flaking green paint. There was a large circular handle to one side.

'I'm sorry,' I said. 'I have no idea what I've brought you here for. I have no idea what happens next.'

'Perfect,' said J. 'Just perfect. How are we supposed to do anything—'

'Give me a moment,' I said. 'It'll come back to me.'

Everything fell silent. Mailfist, J, and Babbage froze exactly as they were. I felt as I sometimes did when I walked through London at night, when one of the streetlamps along a road had failed and I found myself, briefly, standing in the darkness between two pools of light. There was a tug at the hem of my dress, and I looked down.

There were two Hodges there, an old cat and a kitten. The kitten appeared to be trying to climb up on me, whilst the older one looked on disapprovingly.

'Ah,' I said. 'Yes, of course.'

I took a piece of paper from my pocket, and a pencil. I wrote a brief message, then forced the largest jewel from my necklace—the Constellation of the East—out of its housing. I folded it carefully into the paper and gave it to the older cat, who took it in her mouth.

'Find her,' I said.

The older Hodge narrowed her eyes, then turned tail and padded away, followed by the kitten, bounding and frisking down the tunnel.

I put my palm on the door handle, and turned.

'— if you can't even remember us properly,' said J. She stopped. 'The door's open,' she said. 'When did the door open?'

I ignored her and walked through. The room was a vast circular space: water trickled down the black stone walls and gathered in a gutter from around the perimeter. At the centre was a thick copper tube that ran floor to ceiling; it had been polished, and a soft light pulsated from its surface. There was a curved console at its base, as well as a large circular doorway. There was a mewing from the hallway outside. Hodge, in kitten form, scampered into the room towards me. I picked her up.

'Did you deliver it?' I asked. She purred.

'Good girl,' I said. 'Good girl.'

One of the Nameless came over, and pulled a clear plastic bag from his pocket. He took a handful of wet, flaky tuna from it, and held his palm out to the cat. She began to tuck in with little snorts and whimpers of delight.

'Sheesh,' said J. 'What's wrong with a bowl?'

'She deserves her treats,' I told her. 'She runs messages, keeps an eye on things, catches mice. She was a gift from Frayn.'

J walked over to the console, which two of the Nameless were operating together; turning dials, pressing buttons, pushing switches, winding the springs to keep the machine running smoothly.

'What is this?' she said.

'It's a timepool,' Babbage answered, and looked astonished at the sound of his own voice.

'Quite,' I replied. 'Only it's not just any timepool. This is the original.'

'I never knew about this,' said Mailfist.

'It was the prototype,' I explained. 'The Nameless built it long before the others. So it has a few special features.'

'Such as?' J raised an eyebrow.

Babbage walked over to the console, and observed the Nameless working.

'It's not static,' he said. 'Not like the ones I looked after. This one can open at any point in time we choose.'

'We?' said Mailfist. 'We?'

'Where does it open in space?' asked J.

Babbage squinted at one of the dials.

'That, too, is variable,' he said. 'You can select any location within the city. Within — ah.' He looked again at one of the readouts, which showed a wildly fluctuating line. 'Within a reasonable margin of error, it seems. Who would have thought that space would be more difficult to navigate than time?'

'I see.' Mailfist turned to face me. 'So, when do we leave?'

'Mailfist,' I said. 'I'm going alone.'

'Eh?' He blinked.

'I need you to wait here. If I fail, there may just be another chance. Don't worry,' I said. 'I'll have help.'

'What do you mean?'

Hodge miaowed, licking her lips.

'She's a very fine cat,' I said. 'A very fine cat indeed.'

I stepped into the cylinder.

'Close the door!' shouted Babbage.

The door slammed shut, the whole tube vibrating with the force. I could hear voices shouting outside, and a groaning noise like the opening of a sluice. I closed my eyes and waited for time to flow over me. It came as a trickle at first, accumulating at my feet; then it began to grow stronger, seething and babbling around me like a million voices, buoying me up, the walls of the cylinder rushing past as if the ground had dropped away beneath me. I felt the currents pick me up and spin me around in a circle and head over heels; my limbs felt stiff and heavy, and I gasped for breath. I inhaled a mouthful of suffocating, dirty water. I opened my eyes to try to get some sense of my bearings, to swim towards the light and the surface of the Thames — I knew now that the timepool had thrown me out off course, and into the river — but I couldn't see anything. I thrashed around, but the cold grabbed hold of me and dragged me down. Lights danced in front of my eyes, and I thought for one irrational moment that they were the souls of others who had drowned; then the lights died, and I knew I was losing consciousness.

It was at that point that I felt arms take hold of me and haul my body upwards, fighting with the currents to pull me from the water. Once, twice, I was dragged back down, but my rescuer had a firm grip and was not going to give up easily. Finally I broke the surface — it felt like I was being flung through a plate-glass window — and took a deep lungful of air. I choked, swung round and gripped the side of a small rowing-boat. My hands were cramped and numb, and I found it almost impossible to maintain my hold. The boat rocked violently.

'Easy,' said a voice. 'Easy, Miss Britton. You've almost made it.'

I looked up to see K, bracing himself with one arm and reaching out for me with the other.

'Once more,' he said. 'You will have to help me.'

With a last effort, he hauled me from the water and into

the boat. I lay on the boards, shivering; he took off his cloak and laid it over me.

'You told me,' I said, 'the last time I saw you. You told me we would meet once more. I took you up on the offer.'

'It was my pleasure, Miss Britton,' K replied. I sat up and began to dry my hair with his cloak. 'The cat gave me the message. A lovely animal, a frequent visitor to the Boar's Head, in fact. Charms the scraps from everyone's plates. She's beginning to put on weight. Might make it harder for her to squeeze through those narrow gaps.'

'K.'

'But then,' he patted his middle, 'none of us are as young as we were, time travel or no, eh?'

'K,' I repeated. He was, as he always had done, talking too much in order to avoid some other subject. 'I'm just glad you're here. The journey can't have been easy.'

K looked away. 'That it was not, Miss Britton. That it was not.' He took hold of the oars. 'Would you mind moving down the boat a little? It's only a little way across the Styx. North or south?'

I looked around. We were shrouded in a dense orange fog. The buildings and the bridge were dark, fuzzy shapes: all around I heard footsteps, the clatter of hooves, the roar of engines, and the rattle of trains. The interweaving sounds of all the city's history as time collapsed in on itself.

'South.'

K nodded and began to row. As he did so, I saw an immense plume of light explode from somewhere in the area of the Cut. The next moment, the surface of the river was pierced with a million points of white, shining brilliance, holes punched in the texture of reality to show the void beyond.

The fog and dust swirled thicker around us as we made our way from the river and towards the column of light. Progress was slow; the ground crumbled beneath our feet like sand. I turned to K.

'You need to leave me here,' I said.

'I will stay by your side, Miss Britton. To the very end.'

'You can't. You've done your duty, K. From now on, it's up to me.'

'I won't leave you.'

'You have to. There is no other way. If you try to help me, things may get worse. For me, for everyone.'

K smiled ruefully. In the fog, it looked as if he was already beginning to fade out of existence.

'I have a feeling that however this day ends, this is the last time you'll see me, Miss Britton.'

'Goodbye, K.' I held out my hand, and he kissed it.

'It is some small consolation,' he said, 'to know this may not be the last time *I* see *you*.'

He bowed, and the fog swallowed him up. I turned back towards the light, and began to run.

As I neared the source of the light, cracks began to appear in the earth. I could see four figures ahead: myself and the younger Doyle intertwined, frozen in time, and next to them the older Doyle struggling with Gabrielle. She was trying to pull the gauntlet from him: the crystal on the back pulsated with energy. He tugged away sharply, and delivered a sharp blow to her head. She crumpled at his feet, a shock of white hair spilling onto the ground. Doyle looked up as I approached.

'Always a little late, aren't you?'

I ran over to Gabrielle, and turned her over. Her eyes opened very slightly.

'I came back,' I whispered to her. 'I know how long you waited.'

'I tried to stop him. After he used the gauntlet . . .' She gestured vaguely in the direction Doyle was moving in. 'I tried to fool him. Lead him here and get him on his own. Stop. . .' Her eyes closed. I shook her. 'Too late,' she said, her eyes still shut. 'Too late. Let him win, Vee. Let him win.'

'An admirable sentiment,' said Doyle. I looked up. He was inspecting the frozen version of my younger self. 'Time is not your friend. Not anymore.'

He shifted the barrel of the gun my younger, frozen self held an inch to one side. 'That should be quite enough. You will still fire the gun, Veronica, and I will still be seriously wounded. Seriously, but not fatally. Badly enough for you to leave me for dead, anyway. A small alteration, Veronica, but one that makes all the difference. They were gathering for years, the Empire. A collection of dreamers and fools, looking for someone to lead them. Without me, they would have passed from history entirely unnoticed. Instead, the world is theirs.'

'No,' I said, 'I pulled the trigger. I checked you were dead. I killed you, Doyle!'

'Search your memory. Are you quite sure? Might you not have missed something in your haste to leave?' He stood back and looked at his handiwork. 'There. The time bubble will burst at any moment. And things will take a new direction.'

'Doyle,' I pleaded, 'your time is over. It should have ended here.'

He turned to face me. I was prepared for his appearance, but I still flinched. The particles of the cloud appeared to be eating away at his skin, so that he appeared wasted and withered, his hair sparse, his exposed hand like a claw, his teeth sharp and protruding from their sockets.

'Veronica Britton, the Angel of London. You are the one whose life should have ended here. Too big for your own good, that's your problem. Do you remember King Lud? He used to give out prophesies about you to anyone who would listen. And the Dead Letter. Your name was all over that, too. So many different times and places. More than there are stars in the sky. Even in dreams, I hear.'

He flexed the gauntlet. Its clockwork chattered as the hundreds of cogs and springs of which it was made tightened around his hand.

'Miss Pendleton struggled. I made the mistake of trusting to her better nature. I want you exactly where I can see you.'

Doyle approached me, the golden fingers of the gauntlet twitching. The crystal burned sapphire blue. I looked down at Gabrielle. I thought I saw her wink. She mouthed a single word.

'Switched.'

'I'm going to keep you in amber,' said Doyle. 'I've just adjusted the setting. I might keep you by my side for a long, long time. A sort of living statue.'

'Less talk,' I said, grabbing the gauntlet and pressing it against my chest. I could feel the power flowing through it. 'More action.'

Doyle's eyes widened. I twisted his wrist, activating the device. He swung his other hand across to try to turn it off. I pushed him away: Gabrielle reached out and pulled him to the ground. As he fell, the gauntlet let out a pulse of immense force that threw me backwards off my feet and onto the broken surface. I looked up to see Doyle frozen stiff. I helped Gabrielle to her feet.

'Vee,' cried Gabrielle. 'The gun!'

We ran over to the younger versions of Doyle and myself. I could see the tendons of my younger self's hand moving sluggishly back to life.

'I can't do it,' I said. 'I don't know why. I can't do it.'

'You don't have to, my dear,' she replied. She put her hand over the barrel. I laid my hand on hers, and slowly, painfully, we slid it back into position. The gun went off, and as it did so, the ground fell away beneath us. I felt my body beginning to dissolve.

'Don't let go of my hand, Vee,' I heard Gabrielle saying. 'Whatever happens, don't let go.'

ELEVEN

'Don't let go.'

'What?'

'Don't let go,' I repeated.

I opened my eyes. I was in a room stuffed with books and ornaments. A fire crackled in the grate. My own flat. I felt something stirring at my feet, and the sharp prick of claws through the blanket.

'Did it work?' I heard someone say.

I looked up. Over me stood a slim, tall figure, its face wrapped in bandages. It reached out and touched my forehead lightly with its thin, firm fingers. It turned to the person standing next to it — a young, beautiful woman — and nodded.

'Gabrielle?'

'Who else would it be?'

The Nameless bowed, picked up a doctor's bag, and moved away from the chaise longue on which I was lying. A few moments later, I heard the front door close.

'How much do you remember?' Gabrielle asked.

'I remember most of it. I remember you. What about everyone else?'

'Time-sensitives remember,' she replied. 'Some more than others. Quite a lot of people have been having very strange dreams recently. And I think Hodge here remembers every-thing.'

She smiled, leaned over, and kissed me.

'You can let go of my hand now,' I said.

'I don't want to,' she replied.

THE END

ACKNOWLEDGEMENTS

Many thanks to Steve Haynes at Proxima for all of his patience, hard work, and enthusiasm. Thanks also to Katy Darby and all at Liars' League for supporting my writing, and much fun over the years; to Tania Hershman, Jonathan Pinnock, Matt Judd, Liam Hogan, and Tim Stevens for reading and feedback; and to Kate Ames, Tim Young, Simon Guerrier, Debbie Challis, the James family (Maria, Pete, Sophie, and Pip), Rob Brierley, Bente Brattland, Janna Palmer, Lan-Lan Smith, and Richard and Topper Lane for friendship and gossip. Finally, thanks to my mother and father, who brought me up the best possible environment: a house full of books.